PRAISE FOR MEGAN CRANE'S NOVELS

Names My Sisters Call Me

"Funny, charming, and ultimately touching...An honest look at the way family, both fiercely loyal and deeply flawed, affects how we see ourselves and who we choose to love. Using humor, warmth, and a great eye for the intricacies of life, Crane draws you into this story of being lost in the midst of family confusions, then finding oneself."   —Heather Swain, author of *Luscious Lemon*

"Crane's newest book is just plain fun...a funny, smart rendering of the exquisite tenderness that sets in once the engagement is announced...For all of us looking back and for the legions of young women who've not yet had the pleasure of full-throttle wedding jitters."   —Sheila Curran, author of *Diana Lively Is Falling Down*

Frenemies

"Brilliant...hugely enjoyable...It's romantic, funny, intelligent, believable, and gripping."
      —Marian Keyes, bestselling author of *Angels*

"Megan Crane perfectly captures an underlying truth about the complexities of female relationships."
      —Diana Peterfreund, author of *Secret Society Girl*

"Keep your friends close, your enemies closer, and *Frenemies* right on your nightstand."   —Cara Lockwood, national bestselling author of *I Do, But I Don't*

"Addictive, compelling...I simply couldn't put *Frenemies* down."
      —Johanna Edwards, bestselling author of *The Next Big Thing*

"Four Stars! Jam-packed with hilarious one-liners and amusing scenarios...very satisfying."
      —*Romantic Times BOOKreviews Magazine*

"With a gift for creating characters with enough 'everywoman' qualities to make them realistic and enough quirkiness to keep them interesting, Crane reveals the sometimes tenuous, but more often ironclad, bonds of friendship through sharp dialogue."
      —*Today's Diet & Nutrition* magazine

more...

"Enjoyable and insightful."   —NightsAndWeekends.com

"RATING 5 out of 5! I loved *Frenemies*...Even minor characters are brilliantly realized and entertaining. And I haven't even mentioned the gorgeous Henry (swoon)."   —Trashionista.com

"A great beach read, or a great book to tuck into your briefcase."
                                                    —AllThingsGirl.com

"A fresh, upbeat read...with tart, snappy dialogue, a keen eye for detail, and mordant wit."
                —Martha O'Connor, author of *The Bitch Posse*

"An illuminating and extremely entertaining portrait of a woman who makes the leap from drama queen to mature adult."
                —Karin Gillespie, author of *Bet Your Bottom Dollar*

"[A] smooth, skillfully crafted tale...the ultimate girlfriend book."
                —Berta Platas, author of *Cinderella Lopez*

"A witty and engaging tale...will have you laughing out loud."
                —Stacey Ballis, author of *Room for Improvement*
                                              and *Inappropriate Men*

"A fun and frothy look at friendship, love, and growing up... insightful and often hilarious."   —Jen Coburn, author of
                The Queen Gene and *The Wife of Reilly*

Everyone Else's Girl

"Amusing, heartfelt, and emotionally sophisticated."
                                                    —*Kirkus Reviews*

"Megan Crane rules! You won't want to stop reading until you've devoured every delicious word."
                —Meg Cabot, author of the Princess Diary series

"A poignant, funny read that I just could not put down."
                                                    —*Rendezvous*

"Excellent...an entertaining read you will thoroughly enjoy."
                                                    —BestsellersWorld.com

"Laugh-out-loud...honest, romantic, and witty."
                                                    —RoundtableReviews.com

"Shines with reality and drama, all developed through detailed characters and situations...Provides both food for thought and head-nodding-agreement humor."　　　—BookLoons.com

"A snappy read...a funny, engaging novel."　　—FreshFiction.com

English as a Second Language

"[A] very funny, from-the-heart debut."
　　　—Melissa Senate, author of *The Solomon Sisters Wise Up*

"An engrossing, intelligent read never lacking in drama or humor, with a well-paced plot and enjoyable characters."　　—*Library Journal*

"A rollicking good time...Cheers to Megan Crane."
　　　—Jennifer O'Connell, author of *Bachelorette #1*

"Breezy...an accurate take on twenty-somethings who thought adult life began after college."　　　　—*Booklist*

"Entertaining."　　　　　　—ExclusiveMagazine.com

"Uproarious, fast-paced fun...While the plots and subplots are fantastic, the cast of characters is magnificent...Grab a pint, get comfortable, and prepare yourself for the time of your life! Crane is definitely an author to keep an eye on."　　　—MyShelf.com

"A tale that will ring true for anyone who's ever faced that scary task of deciding what on earth you want to do with your life."
　　　—King Features Weekly Service

"A lighthearted look at growing up and finding your place in the world...an enjoyable summer read!"　　　—BookLoons.com

"Will keep readers busily turning the pages...Anyone who's ever been through grad school, or their twenties, should recognize themselves here."　　　—TheRomanceReadersConnection.com

"A breathless, gossipy read that you'll giggle your way through. When it comes to love we're not so different, whichever side of the pond is your natural home!"　　—Carole Matthews, author of *Bare Necessity*

ALSO BY MEGAN CRANE

English as a Second Language
Everyone Else's Girl
Frenemies

names my sisters
call me

MEGAN CRANE

NEW YORK   BOSTON

Copyright © 2008 by Megan Crane

5 Spot
Hachette Book Group USA
237 Park Avenue
New York, NY 10017

Visit our Web site at www.5-spot.com.

5 Spot is an imprint of Grand Central Publishing.
The 5 Spot name and logo is a trademark of Hachette Book Group USA, Inc.

Book design and text composition by Stratford Publishing Services, a TexTech business

Printed in the United States of America

First Edition: April 2008
10 9 8 7 6 5 4 3 2 1

Library of Congress Cataloging-in-Publication Data

Crane, Megan.
    Names my sisters call me / Megan Crane. — 1st ed.
        p. cm.
    ISBN-13: 978-0-446-69856-6
    ISBN-10: 0-446-69856-3
    1. Sisters—Fiction.   2. Sibling rivalry—Fiction.   3. Philadelphia (Pa.)—Fiction.   4. Domestic fiction.   I. Title.
    PS3603.R385N36 2008
    813'.6—dc22
                                                        2007027129

This book is for your sister.
And for you.

acknowledgments

I am running out of superlatives for my wonderful agent, Julie Barer, who took an unwieldy draft of this novel and worked all kinds of magic on it. Which is just in a day's work for the greatest agent in the world!

I feel constantly and increasingly lucky to be part of such a fantastic team at Grand Central Publishing. I don't know what I'd do without Karen Kosztolnyik, who continues to edit my books into such terrific shape—and is so much fun to work with! Or Elly Weisenberg, who continues to promote them so beautifully. Thanks also to Caryn Karmatz-Rudy, Gina Di Meglio, Miriam Parker, Mari Okuda, the amazing art department, and Celia Johnson, not to mention everyone else at GCP, for working so hard to make the books so good. And even more thanks to Kim Dower of Kim-from-LA for working wonders with me!

Thanks especially to Liza Palmer for everything in general

and a certain critique in particular. And to Jane Porter for being one of the most generous people I've ever met.

Thanks to all my readers, for your e-mails and blog comments, or just for reading my books. I love you all!

Thanks again to Kim McCreight, Josie Torielli, and Louise Austin. And to my family, for their staunch support, sometimes involving the distribution of postcards.

And to Jeff Johnson, as ever. No story is worth telling unless I tell it to you first.

names my sisters
call me

If you cannot get rid of the family skeleton, you may as well make it dance.

—George Bernard Shaw

chapter one

When Lucas went down, right there on the sidewalk outside my sister's place in Chestnut Hill, my first thought was: ice.

It was February in Philadelphia. Ice was everywhere, along with slush, gray skies, the threat of more snow, and my personal and only slightly hysterical worry that *this* would be the year that winter refused to give way to spring, leaving us stuck in some Narnia-ish winter forevermore.

Lucas and I had skidded along down Germantown Avenue, from the train toward my sister's place, using our boot heels as impromptu ice skates. We'd attempted to avoid careening into the cute little shop windows, and I'd shared my fears of Narnia with Lucas, complete with my suspicion that the White Witch could be played to perfection by my sister Norah.

My boyfriend had just hit the concrete right in front of me, and this was what I thought about? Narnia and a mixture of frustration with my sister combined with guilt about my frustration? What if he required medical attention? I felt ashamed of myself.

"Oh my God," I said, throwing both hands out as if to catch him, though it was already too late. "Are you okay?"

Which was when I noticed that he was grinning up at me, which was a good indicator that hospitalization wasn't required after all.

And that he was actually on one knee.

"Oh my *God*," was my brilliant response.

"I love you, Courtney," Lucas said, as if I'd said something brilliant. Or even coherent. "I've loved you since the day you sat next to me in that café and made up better headlines for the Sunday *New York Times*."

"That was three months after we started dating," I pointed out, as I had many times before when he brought up that morning in Center City near my old apartment. And I continued with the usual script, despite the clearly unusual circumstances. It was habit. "What was I before that? Just a fling?"

It felt strange to stand there towering over him, when it was normally the other way around, so I knelt down to face him, expecting the cold and wet to seep through my jeans in seconds. The funny thing was, I didn't much care when it did.

"I suspected I loved you before," Lucas continued, only the slightest hint of longsufferingness in his voice—for effect. "But that was when I knew. Kind of like right now, when you're interrupting me in the middle of my romantic proposal. Moments like this one make me realize not just that I love you but that we must be perfect for each other, because first of all, I think it's cute, and more importantly, I knew you were going to say that."

"Yes," I whispered, reaching over to hold his face between my mittened hands. I thought about the years we'd been together, and how bright they seemed when compared to the years that came before. How bright everything seemed when he was near. "Yes, I will marry you."

"I haven't asked you to marry me," Lucas retorted. His gray eyes were calm and gleaming, all at once, and I wanted to look at nothing else, ever again.

"Well, hurry up then," I said. "Any minute now Norah's going to look out the window and assume we've finally gone crazy. Because most people don't propose on the street five seconds before an annoying family dinner, you know."

Lucas laughed and took my hands between his. He kissed each one and then let them go.

"I wanted to do this right smack in the middle of our life, because I love our life," he said. "I want our marriage to be a celebration of our life together, not something outside it."

He reached into his pocket and drew out a small box.

And that was when everything got *real* in a hurry. I was aware of a hundred things, all at once.

I couldn't believe this was actually happening. As in, to me, right then and there. I felt my heart thump against my ribs as I stared at the box in his hand, small and black and shaped to contain only one possible item.

I wasn't sure I was breathing.

In my fantasies, and I'd had a lot of them, this moment was usually accompanied by cinematic landscapes, orchestras, and possibly choirs of angels.

I'd seen so many films, and read so many books, that

I felt sort of flung out of my own body as I stared at the velvet box Lucas held out to me. As if I were sitting in a theater somewhere watching *this* version of The Proposal. Except the role normally played by the wispy Hollywood actress du jour was now being played by me. Instead of the romantic, gauzy sort of dress I'd imagined wearing while being knelt in front of, I was dressed to battle the Philly elements in jeans, boots, and a warm peacoat. To say nothing of my hat, scarf, and mittens. I'd imagined a rolling summer meadow with an orchestra of songbirds. Instead, there were minivans swishing along the suburban street, an obviously mentally challenged jogger in far too few clothes, and the general grim winter cacophony of the East Coast all around us. A cold street below and the threat of freezing rain from above. It was the last place in the world I would have expected a marriage proposal.

It was perfect.

"Courtney," Lucas said, never looking away from me. "Marry me."

I reached past the velvet box and the glorious, gleaming ring nestled inside it, and kissed him on his delicious, perfect mouth.

"I love you," I whispered.

"I know you do," Lucas replied in the same whisper. "But *now* is the time to say 'yes.' There's a whole set routine to these things, Court. You're messing up my flow."

I loved his teasing tone, and that tilt of his head. As if he was proud and serious and thrilled, all at once.

"How would you know?" I teased him right back. "You've never proposed to anyone else."

"I might have. I'm very mysterious. You don't know everything." He tugged my left hand mitten off. Then he slipped the ring from the jeweler's box and very carefully slid it onto my hand, where it fit perfectly and sparkled, brightening the dim afternoon all around us.

"It's perfect," I breathed, and then we were beaming at each other and kissing.

I eased back from a kiss and held him close in a hug that felt like it should go on forever. Like it could somehow encapsulate everything that had happened since that fateful night at a party I hadn't really wanted to go to in the outskirts of Philadelphia, and found him there, almost as if he'd been waiting for me. Like it could embrace all of our past and the future we'd already started knitting together between us.

It was a really good hug.

Which only ended when the door at the top of the steps opened and we both turned, still grinning foolishly at each other.

"Why are you causing a scene outside my house?" my sister Norah demanded, in the same slightly scandalized, authoritative tone I'd heard her use on her university students when they asked stupid questions. "Do you want someone to call the cops?"

"Oh," I said, gazing up at her, and then back down at the ring, cold and resplendent on my hand. "Um." It was like I looked at the ring and became hypnotized. I knew the appropriate words to use but couldn't seem to form them on my tongue. I looked at Lucas for help.

He seemed to glow as he helped me to my feet.

"Courtney and I are getting married," he told Norah, his voice sounding almost formal. I felt myself flush. *Married* was such an *adult* word. It carried so much *weight*.

"Well," Norah said, her voice much smoother. Maybe even pleased. "That's wonderful news." She smiled, and then looked at me. "And about time, if you ask me."

"No one did," I muttered, immediately reduced to behaving like a child. It took exactly one sentence from my bossy big sister. But Lucas squeezed my hand to keep me quiet, and we walked inside.

Norah led the way into her house, calling out the news like the town crier. And suddenly there was commotion, as my family crowded around us in the living room. I was still tugging my arms out of my coat sleeves as my mother rushed up to embrace me.

"I'm so happy!" she cried, and I breathed in deeply as her familiar scent enveloped me, a combination of shampoo and cold cream, and, sometimes, the faintest hint of perfume. "My baby's getting married!"

Across the room, I heard Lucas talking about his secret ring-buying excursions with Norah's husband, Phil.

"I actually cut the piece of string, and measured her rings," Lucas said, demonstrating with his hands and catching my eye as he said it. "Just like they tell you to do it in the magazines."

"So it's a surprise?" Phil asked, smiling in his affable way. "Norah and I picked hers out together."

"It's a complete surprise," I said, fanning out the fingers of my left hand.

Which wasn't entirely true. I would have had to have been asleep in my own relationship not to know how serious it had been for some time, and I hadn't been asleep. But I hadn't known Lucas was involved in clandestine ring measurements of my costume jewelry, either.

"The thing about Courtney is that she doesn't wear any particular jewelry all the time," Lucas said. "She has lots of rings she wears *sometimes*, but she likes her hands the way they are."

I had never paid much attention to my jewelry preferences, I realized then. But I made my living with my hands. I depended on them and enjoyed them. I wouldn't have known how to go out and choose something that would sit on them ever after. I was kind of amazed that Lucas had given the entire process so much thought.

Norah reached across my mother and picked up my left hand. She held it to the light, turning the whole hand this way and that as if examining it for flaws. It didn't seem to occur to her that it was still connected to my body.

"You'll really have to concentrate on your manicure," she told me in a low voice, as if she didn't wish to embarrass me in front of everyone else. "Your hands are going to be the focus of a lot of attention, and the last thing you need are scraggly, dirty nails."

I tugged my hand out of her grasp. My hands might not be confused for a hand model's, but I thought *scraggly* and *dirty* were taking it a step too far.

"Nobody cares about my nails, Norah," I told her, feeling defensive.

"You wouldn't believe the things people care about," she retorted. Because she, as ever, knew best. "I'm going to get the camera."

Norah was about control and had always been this way. When she was a kid, her control issues generally involved the sanctity of her bedroom and her refusal to lend out her toys and dolls. These days she thought a bit bigger.

She insisted that she was not in any way OCD, a laughable assertion, but one she felt comfortable making because, she would tell me, there was a right way and a wrong way to do things. She chose to do things the right way. End of discussion.

The right way meant that we had Family Dinner every weekend at her house, and she always used linen napkins. The right way meant that she and Phil refused to allow a television to pollute their home, preferring to read the newspapers from a selection of Eastern Seaboard cities, peruse the most esoteric literary fiction, and engage in stimulating intellectual debates concerning international politics and ethical dilemmas over fine wine. When Lucas and I expressed our preference for the Sci Fi Channel, anything on Adult Swim, and classic DVD marathons, they both pretended not to hear us. When it was pointed out to them that Eliot, their two-year-old son, might one day face ridicule in school for being completely out of the pop culture loop, Norah actually sneered.

She'd practically raised me, she would say. And last she'd checked, I was doing fine.

Someone had to step in and take charge after Daddy died, she would say with a sniff, *and I was the only one who could.*

Because she was the only one *capable*, was the subtext. Mom had been lost in a haze of grief. Our middle sister, Raine, had been acting out since she was a toddler. By the time I was ten, Raine had distinguished her sixteen-year-old self in our prudish Pennsylvania Main Line town by being wilder than all the other bad seeds put together, Mom had parlayed her grief into a continuing life choice rather than a debilitating incident, and Norah already had her first PhD. In bossiness. At eighteen.

"So," Norah said then, studying me across the roast chicken she was serving up onto her best china plates. "You're finally engaged!"

That *finally* was because Norah felt grown-ups shouldn't (a) date for longer than six months without Knowing Where the Relationship Was Headed, (b) live together under any circumstances before marriage because They Still Don't Buy the Milk No Matter How Feminist It Might Be to Give It Away for Free, and You Know How Liberal I Am, Courtney, and (c) continue to date after a year without being engaged, because You Either Know or You Don't. She and Phil got engaged on their first anniversary, married on their second anniversary, and that, as she'd told me many times, was the secret to their happiness. No "waffling," as she put it. The fact that Lucas and I had been together for three years without so much as a shared bank account confused and annoyed her.

I thought that the fact Lucas chose to attend these weekly dinners with me was proof of love far above and beyond the gorgeous ring he'd just put on my finger. The ring was the prettiest thing I'd ever seen, but Family Dinners were tests of strength and will. Norah maintained a constantly updated spreadsheet of checks and balances, slights and alliances, and was always waiting to pounce. I assumed this spreadsheet existed only in her mind, but sometimes I suspected the existence of a hard copy, too.

"I'm so happy for you," Mom was saying. "I remember what it was like to be young and in love." She beamed at me. "And what fun we'll have, with a wedding to plan!"

"Remember, Courtney," Norah chimed in, frowning at Mom. "Your wedding is about you. Not about some fantasy wedding Mom wished she had with Dad."

Twenty-eight years had passed since my father's death, and yet I winced a little bit at Norah's tone. Lucas reached over to grab hold of me, his hand warm and reassuring on my leg.

My mother didn't respond, a well honed battle tactic, though I could swear I saw her lips tighten.

"You'll have a summer wedding, of course," Norah said, wresting back control of the conversation as she served me a plate of drumsticks and stewed carrots, both of which I hated. But I didn't say anything. About the food, anyway.

"We haven't made any plans, Norah," I told her. "We got engaged fifteen minutes ago." Lucas squeezed my leg a little bit, and I felt a rush of giddiness. Engaged. We were *engaged*. To be *married*.

"It's never too early to start making plans," Norah said, frowning slightly.

When *she* got engaged, if I remembered correctly, she'd allowed seven point three minutes for weeping and excitement, and had then proceeded to book her venue, photographer, and caterer before the end of the day. Because Nora was nothing if not prepared.

"Eliot can be your flower boy," Norah continued, handing out plates to Mom and Phil. "Or your ring-bearer. It's up to you, of course."

I felt the strangest urge to apologize for the possibility that I might want control over my own wedding. But then, hers had turned out to be a disaster, despite the kind of planning that would have done Napoleon proud.

"Everyone will tell you that the process is scary, or stressful," Mom told me. "But I think you can decide how it will be. There's such a thing as too much planning, you know." It was a gentle dig, but Norah stiffened.

"Not everyone is satisfied with stopping by the courthouse on their way home from work," Norah sniped right back at our mother.

"Everyone is not you, Norah," Mom said in the even tone she used when she wanted to prevent an escalation.

"Mom, please," Norah said crossly. "Courtney doesn't want to elope!"

"I don't know what I want to do," I offered up into the tension. "I guess Lucas and I are going to have to think about it."

"But I'm betting you're not going to elope," Norah retorted—more to her plate than anything, and, obviously, to make sure she got the last word. We all knew better than to engage.

"While you're thinking about it, the first thing to plan is the engagement party," Mom said, using a getting-down-to-business tone. "Lucas, you'll have to invite your parents to come down." She made it sound as if the party was already planned, and happening the following week.

"I can't have any parties until the season's over," I told her, after sharing a dazed look with Lucas. *The season* in question was not winter, which was likely endless, but the more finite Philadelphia Second Symphony Orchestra concert season, which finished in late May.

"Then we'll do it this summer," Mom replied. "How about July?"

I couldn't answer her for a moment. An hour ago I'd been skating on Germantown Avenue with my boyfriend. Now I was discussing my engagement party and feelings on elopement. I wasn't sure I could keep up with the life shift.

"Wow," I said, feeling panicky. "I mean, this is really nice of you, but I'm not sure we..."

"I would be thrilled to throw it for you," Mom said, inclining her head at me as if that settled the matter.

"Um, great," I said. "Thanks." But something occurred to me. "Is the engagement party where we all sit around and play those weird games with the ribbons? Because I don't think I can handle that. With a straight face."

"That's the shower," Norah told me. "Like mine, which I didn't realize was so difficult for you."

Terrific. Another black mark next to my name in her mental *slights* column.

"An engagement party celebrates the engagement," Mom told me. "It can be a cocktail party, a lunch, whatever you like."

"We don't have to talk about it now," Lucas said smoothly,

with another squeeze to reassure me. Possibly he'd glimpsed the look on my face and feared, as I did, that I might succumb to dizziness in some eighteenth-century swoon. The thought was appealing.

"The sooner you get your plans set, the more you can enjoy the engagement year," Norah said, contradicting him. She was sliding into full-on lecturer mode. Sometimes I forgot she was only thirty-six, a mere eight years older than me, because she could sound as old as the hills.

"We're in no rush," Lucas told her, still smiling when she handed him a plate piled high with potatoes. Lucas hated potatoes.

"You'll be surprised how quickly the time goes," Norah assured us. "You have to get out in front of it, or the next thing you know, it's two weeks before your wedding and you have nothing."

"I'm sure Courtney will do just fine," Mom said then. Norah looked dubious.

"When has Courtney ever done something of this magnitude?" she asked. With unnecessary derision, I felt. "You don't have to listen to me, of course," she continued. "But I *am* the person at this table who was married the most recently."

"If by recently you mean six years ago," I pointed out.

"I know how long I've been married, Courtney."

"We all know how long you've been married, too," I retorted. "We were all there. I'm pretty sure we can all remember it as the last time anyone spoke to Raine."

Norah gaped at me.

"Are you saying you think we should have continued to speak to her?" she demanded.

"That's not what I—"

"Because I was sick and tired of rewarding her behavior, especially on the one day in my entire life that was supposed to be about me and not her!"

One of Norah's hands had crept over her heart, as if I had broken it with my careless words. Or stuck one of the serving knives into her.

Next to me, I could feel Lucas's interest flare. Having never met my colorful, estranged sister, he was intrigued by all the drama that was kicked up any time her name was mentioned. As was I, to be honest. Raine was nothing if not fascinating.

"I don't think we should go down this road," Phil piped up from his end of the table. Phil never said much, so we all stared at him and took in the uncharacteristic outburst. He was thoughtful and quiet, a professor of physics at Temple and some fifteen years Norah's senior. He was as likely to be considering the effects of gravity as he was to be thinking about whatever was going on in front of him, but even he had a strong opinion about Raine. Everybody did.

"Apparently," Norah snapped at him as if he needed a recap, "Courtney feels we were too hasty. The fact that *Lorraine*"—Norah deliberately used her full, hated name—"ruined our wedding reception is no big deal."

"That's not what I said," I told her more firmly. "I was just pointing out that we all remember your wedding vividly, *because* of Raine. And no one's saying what happened was no big deal. None of us have spoken to her since, have we?" I used my most placating voice, the one I'd learned growing up in this family but had honed to perfection in orchestra pits, dealing with overwrought conductors and prima donna first-chair cello players. Norah seemed to deflate. She cut a piece of chicken, and then toyed with it on her plate.

"I've spoken to her," Mom said.

Her voice was calm, but her words crashed down in the center of the table and rippled outward, almost as if she'd thrown a plate.

"What?" I stared at her. I heard Norah's fork clatter against the china plate, and knew she was staring as well.

"I speak to her once a week, usually," Mom continued, seeming completely oblivious to the tension all around her. She forked up some stewed carrots and chewed them with every appearance of calm.

"Mom, you have to be kidding me," Norah snapped. "How could you? All this time, I assumed none of us even knew where she was!"

And she, of course, had taken a certain satisfaction in that.

"She's my daughter, Norah, just as you are," Mom said, sounding completely unruffled. She didn't *quite* smile. "Of course I know where she is."

We left Norah's house shortly after that—because really, what could follow my mother's pronouncement? Certainly not dessert.

"That wasn't really how I saw this all happening," Lucas

confessed as we made our way down the dark street, easing carefully around the patches of ice. His words turned into puffs of smoke against the night air. "I thought there might be a toast or two."

"When Norah could make it all about her and her pain?" I scoffed in pretend astonishment. "Silly man."

"Next time we get engaged," Lucas said, reaching over for my left hand and fiddling with the ring through my mitten, "I'm rethinking the whole 'let's celebrate our actual life' part."

"I liked that part."

"Sure, but I could have done it *after* Family Dinner. We could have celebrated ourselves and then called everybody, like everyone else in the world. But no, I had to be different."

"I liked it," I told him, kissing him. "It was perfect. You're perfect."

"That's true," Lucas agreed, smiling at me and pulling me close. "I am. For you."

Later that night, Lucas was asleep in the big queen bed that took up most of the bedroom in our cozy two-bedroom apartment, and I got up to feed our obnoxious matching pair of tabby cats, Felix and Felicia.

Yes, despite Norah's warnings, Lucas and I had moved in together after dating for about a year and a half. And it had been another whole year and a half before he'd proposed. No wonder she'd been concerned. At this point in her relationship she'd already been married to Phil. For a year.

I shoved Norah and her pronouncements out of my mind as the cats rushed at me and twined themselves around my ankles. They were a brother and sister we'd happened upon at a curbside rescue right after we moved in together, and had been conned into taking when they were tiny four-month-old kittens. They were always up to something, and were often completely psychotic for no apparent reason. Which was to say, they were perfect little cats.

I laid out some wet food for them—after listening to them yowl and carry on as if the last time they'd been fed was months ago, instead of that morning—and then headed back toward the bedroom. Before I got there, though, my eye was caught by my cello and stand in the bay window of the living room. I flexed my left hand a little bit, and felt the familiar wash of guilt and panic. I should have spent the day practicing instead of celebrating. I knew my performance suffered if I didn't put in at least a few hours every single day, and I couldn't afford to let my performance suffer. Lucas, who worked at home, running his Internet security business, claimed he loved listening to me practice while he put out fires and slapped down hackers. Which was good, since I did so several hours a day. I would have to buckle down the next morning, which meant I should get to sleep.

But my mind was too riled up to rest.

I was engaged! After all those years of wondering if it would ever happen, it had. It had been a confusing night.

In the movies or on TV, engagement scenes were followed by musical montages and champagne toasts. Not tense family dinners and hours of telephone calls. Lucas had ended up calling every family member he had, and half of our friends. I'd been responsible for the other half. Once the ball started rolling, we'd had to keep going so no one would feel left out or slighted. It turned out that telling the same story over and over again was kind of exhausting.

But it also put the glaze and polish on the way we would tell the story. That was the strangest part. By the final couple of phone calls, we had it down to a few glossy sentences. I wondered if those sentences would be what survived the evening—like a photograph. A snapshot version of what had actually happened.

Maybe that meant I'd forget about the less pleasant parts, like Norah trying to micromanage my wedding within minutes of the proposal.

"She's overbearing," Lucas had agreed when we'd been peeling off our winter coats near our hall closet, "but she's only trying to help. I think this is her way of showing interest."

"She drives me insane," I'd retorted. "She's this almost impossible mixture of incredibly confrontational and completely oversensitive!"

"And that," he'd agreed.

After which, we'd had better things to do than psychoanalyze Norah.

I told myself to stop doing it now, in the dark, where it could easily be mistaken for brooding. Anyway, there were more pressing things to brood about.

The truth was, I was completely thrown by the fact Mom was in touch with Raine.

My sister Raine was almost as much of a myth to me as the father I'd never known. Even before she'd disappeared six years ago, she'd been larger-than-life. She'd been the fun one. That sounded like such a small thing, but it had been almost incomprehensibly huge when I was a kid. Our whole family life was arranged around one central, sad fact: my father's absence. We were all sad. Except for Raine.

While Norah stressed and fussed and bossed, Raine snuck out on the roof to smoke joints or danced by herself in her room with her eyes closed. Norah was the one who lectured me about my class schedule. Raine was the one who explained to me that boys who were really mean to you probably liked you, and it was okay to be mean right back. And then she'd showed me *how*.

The fact was, I'd always hero-worshipped Raine and only tolerated the more officious, busybody Norah.

They even looked like polar opposites. Raine was always dying her hair this color or that, wearing outrageous costumes, and engaging in performance art in the middle of family functions. Norah, on the other hand, had been preppy before she discovered business attire, and was a natural blond, which, she claimed, had forced her to be serious and combative from an early age.

Blonds are treated like idiots, she'd told me more than once. *You're lucky your hair is red.*

It's titian, *actually*, I'd replied, because I was all of eleven and was addicted to Nancy Drew.

I have to prove I'm smart the moment they see me, she'd said.

And she'd been doing it ever since. She wore black-rimmed glasses and kept her hair in a bun. She refused to suffer fools, preferring to gut them and hang them out to dry. She'd spent her thirty-six years being fierce and uncompromising. She'd be the first to tell you she was the brains in the family. She'd known from a very young age that she wanted to dedicate herself to academics, and so she had. She'd charged right through her undergraduate and graduate degrees without pausing for breath. She'd married Phil in the middle of her postdoctoral study, and hadn't let Eliot's birth get in the way of her work at several different universities in and around the greater Philadelphia area.

And yet, Norah was the one who took care of our cats when we went away. She cleaned out the litter box and never complained about it—which was more than I could say. She was the person to call if I had to go to the doctor or dentist and needed a ride home afterward. She would rearrange her schedule to take me to the airport, even if it was during rush hour. She must have driven down to Baltimore to pick me up or drop me off a million times when I was at the conservatory, and she never appeared without some form of a care package. She was dependable, available, and always conscientious. She was also the first to tell me so.

God, I loved her, but she was a pain in the ass.

Raine, meanwhile, had always seemed so *free*, so *alive*. She didn't claim to know anything—in fact, she'd spent her early twenties flitting from job to job, and city to city, without seeming to care much where she landed. She told epic stories about our lost father, and made him sound even more marvelous than Mom did. I held on to those stories, ashamed to remind them that I had no memories of him. Only tales they told.

I had adored her, and then I'd been so angry at her when she'd gone, and then, for much longer than that, I'd missed her.

And I knew that no matter what Raine had done at Norah's wedding, to all of us, it didn't matter.

I still wanted her at mine.

chapter two

My mother jumped on my engagement with all the forward momentum of a runaway train. I wasn't entirely sure what to make of her extreme interest in my engagement, or her insistence that she plan the engagement party herself. She picked me up from the train station on my next Monday off, and took me on the chauffeured tour of my hometown she'd started planning that day at Norah's.

I couldn't help feeling that this already seemed like a whole lot of *work*. My expectations of engagements—such as they were—mostly involved montage scenes and smiling people with impressive dental work. Nowhere in said montage scenes was there any hint of labor.

To be honest, I hadn't known until recently that there was such a thing as *the wedding industry*. Or that it was so...all-consuming. I found those sixteen-ton wedding magazines terrifying. And my single excursion to TheKnot.com had scarred me for life.

"We can't just have it at the house?" I asked Mom now, slumped in the passenger seat for all the world as if I were a disgruntled teen instead of a grown woman. I straightened my spine surreptitiously as my mother swept me a sideways glance.

"I thought we could take the opportunity to celebrate you and Lucas," she said in an even tone. The one, I knew very well, she used to avoid an escalation with Norah. "Set it apart from a typical family function. You don't agree?"

How was I supposed to respond to that? Especially when her tone indicated she was *handling* me? Nobody liked being handled—especially when, as now, I suspected I needed it.

"That sounds great," I said weakly.

Which was also what I said as we toured Mom's favorite restaurant, where the owner raced out from the kitchen and fawned all over her. Very much as if she were a local celebrity instead of . . . my mother.

"Anything for Bev Cassel's daughter!" the owner gushed at me, causing me to let loose an inane giggle that would have sounded grossly inappropriate coming from an overwrought thirteen-year-old girl. I didn't know why I'd returned to my teen years for today's visit to my hometown, but it was embarrassing.

"I didn't know you had a favorite restaurant," I admitted when Mom and I got back in the car. Though I realized it came out sounding more like a complaint. I also didn't know people called her *Bev* instead of the more formal *Beverly*. It made me feel almost as if my mother had a secret life—a concept so ridiculous it made me snicker to myself, again like a teen.

"I realize you girls believe that I spend my time sitting endless shiva in the privacy of my home," she replied, with an arch sort of look my way, "but every now and again I do like to get a bite to eat."

I blinked, my mind sort of reeling. Because she'd just called me out. I *did*, in fact, believe that she did nothing but work and mourn my father's death almost three decades before. But I thought that because that's what she'd always done.

The country club she drove us to next was all grass and flowers in the summer, but in the dead of winter it seemed impossible that either could grow in such a barren place. There was still old snow on the ground, and the trees stood stark and brown. The lake was covered in ice, the swimming floats marooned and forlorn on the empty beach. It was a far cry from the last time I'd seen it, in its full summer glory.

It had been six years ago, but I still felt the echoes of that summer evening as Mom and I climbed out of the car and made our way to what was called "the Clubhouse." Norah had had her infamous wedding reception here. This parking lot had its own set of upsetting memories from that evening. I tried to blink them away the same way I did the gust of winter wind that blew my hair in a tangle around my face.

Mom and I hurried through the doors, out of the February cold, and into the big dining room where Norah's reception had been.

"It feels so strange to be here," I murmured, my voice echoing a bit in the empty space. I looked around. The club served dinners in here during winter, but only on the weekends, so today there were empty chairs and tables laid out before us. The contrast between the dining room now and in my memories struck me as particularly severe.

Mom set off to find the manager while I stood in the middle of the darkest day in our family's history, and let it swirl around me. Norah in her white dress, her face red with the only tears I'd seen her shed in the past decade. Raine twirling herself dizzy on the dance floor, despite the fact no one else was dancing. Mom running back and forth between the two as if she could somehow broker a peace between them.

And me, of course. I remembered what I'd been doing, what I'd been feeling, at Norah's reception. And the secret I'd never told anyone in my family, not in six years.

"The manager will be out in a moment, but what do you think about something outside on the deck, overlooking the lake?" Mom called from across the room, near the entrance to the kitchen.

I plastered a smile on my face and walked over to where she stood by the glass doors. Outside, a wooden deck stretched along the side of the clubhouse. Everything outdoors looked cold and barren, but I knew that in the summer, when the lake gleamed in the sun and the lawn stretched down to the beach, it was gorgeous.

"It's pretty here," I said.

Though I had always thought so, I'd never spent much time here. Norah and Raine had spent their summers lounging around on the lakeside beach, taunting the life-guards (Raine) or competing in swim meets (Norah), but I'd always had something musical to do. Camps, or chamber music groups, or tutors to rehearse for. One of the best things about being a professional musician with an orchestra chair was that I finally got the summers off I'd never gotten as a kid.

"I'm thinking we'll have a lovely little cocktail party one evening in July," Mom said then, looking out at the empty deck as if she was envisioning it.

Maybe it was because she used the word *family*, but I found myself opening my mouth before I really meant to. Certainly before I thought it through.

"I think I want Raine to come," I heard myself blurt out. I felt my face redden, as if I expected the ghost of Norah's bridal self to appear in front of me, possibly still weeping. "I mean, I want to invite her to the engagement party."

Of course, it was more than that. It wasn't just the engagement party. It was an invitation back into the family. I knew that. Mom knew it, too. But then, she was the only one who hadn't banished Raine in the first place.

"If that's what you want," she said quietly. "I think that's a wonderful idea."

Norah was a different story.

"It's not my place to tell you what you should or shouldn't do with your own engagement party," she huffed a few weeks later, pretending to be so consumed with arranging bunches of flowers into various vases in her kitchen that she couldn't stop to look at me.

She bought herself big, colorful bouquets of flowers every Monday, not because she secretly wanted Phil to do it and was trying to shame him—as I had been known to do on occasion, because I could be breathtakingly passive-aggressive and childish—but because she genuinely liked to brighten up her home. Since we were currently endur- ing the *lion* portion of the month of March in Philadelphia, complete with howling winds and gunmetal gray skies, I thought she was onto something. Flowers felt like the spring I doubted we would ever see again.

"But I have to tell you," she continued, snipping at the stems with a pair of kitchen shears, all restrained violence and sharp edges, "I think that's crazy."

That, of course, being my desire to have my *entire* family at the events leading up to and including the wedding Lucas and I hadn't even started thinking about in any serious way. I played with the engagement ring on my left hand, worry- ing at the stone with my thumb. I still wasn't used to the weight of the band, the unexpected sparkle of the stone.

"I think weddings should be about family," I said then. Because deep down I wanted that to be true, despite all cultural and personal evidence to the contrary. Starting with *Sixteen Candles*. "Everyone acts like it's inevitable that they become these pageants of dysfunction, but I don't see why it has to be that way. We can *decide*, right?"

Not that my own family had ever done anything to lead me to believe such a thing, but hope sprang eternal.

"I can't imagine what Mom was thinking," Norah said ferociously. She gave no sign of having heard me, with her attention on the wet stems in front of her. "If she really thought it was okay to spend all this time talking to Raine, then why did she keep it a secret? I can't believe she lied about it!"

"She didn't actually *lie*," I felt compelled to point out. Not that our mother required a defense. As I had learned, she could be formidable when she felt like it. She'd already booked the club deck area for a Saturday night in July, and had left several ominous messages for me about invitations.

"By omission, of course she did." Norah made a noise in the back of her throat. "This is so typical. This is *vintage* Mom behavior. She can't be bothered to act like a parent in any traditional sense of the term, but when you least expect it, *boom!* She's *self-righteous* about staying in contact with Raine! I should have expected this."

I knew that Norah had a lot of anger toward our mother, but I never liked to see it spill over. But then, it was different for me. I'd had Mom and two older sisters to see to my formative years in their peculiar and separate ways. When one of my trinity couldn't do the job, another was there to pick up the slack. From all accounts, Mom had spent the first years after our father died consumed with grief and panic about providing for us. I reminded myself that Norah, who felt she'd had to raise herself and me, needed patience and understanding as much as anyone. Maybe more.

"But Mom's not the issue here," Norah continued, turning to look at me with her trademark frown settled between her brows, the kitchen shears clenched in one hand. "Your sudden interest in family time makes me wonder."

"Wonder what?"

"Well…" Norah looked lost for words, which was an alarming first. She shoved an escaped blond tendril back behind her ear. The fact that a tendril dared defy her bun was equally alarming, now that I thought about it. It suggested a level of internal disquiet that Norah usually quelled long before it became visible. "I'm wondering about *you*, to be honest."

"I don't know what you're talking about." But I'd expected something like this. It was why I'd come over for lunch, despite the fact I normally spent my Mondays off with Lucas. I settled further into my chair at Norah's kitchen table, and practiced scales and double stops under the table, where she couldn't see my left hand stretch out as if it were reaching for the lower register on the neck of my cello.

"I don't understand how you can pretend she didn't ruin my wedding," Norah said, glaring at me. "I mean, you were there. But if you go ahead and start inviting her to things, you're essentially saying that nothing happened. You're *rewarding* her for what she did!"

"I just want both my sisters at my wedding," I said, trying to sound soothing and nonthreatening. "This has nothing to do with you," I continued, exactly the way I'd practiced with Lucas the night before. Tone and expression. "I know it feels that way, but think about it from my perspective. Raine is my sister, too. And it *was* six years ago."

Unlike Lucas-as-Norah, who had been remarkably understanding and much funnier, the real Norah stiffened in outrage.

"You keep pointing that out," she snapped. "I wasn't aware there was a statute of limitations on how long I'm allowed to have hurt feelings. No one informed me that my time had run out."

"No one's saying that. I only want—"

"After everything I've done for you," Norah threw at me. "No matter what I do, you still like her better!"

I wasn't any good at confrontation, especially not with Norah. And especially not when there was a seed of truth to it. I felt guilt wash over me. Was she right? If the situations were reversed, would I be as adamant about tracking Norah down?

"That's not true—" I began.

"Of course it is," Norah snapped. "I lost this popularity contest years ago. Believe me, I'm perfectly well aware that the only reason you took my side back then is because she managed for once to hurt you too."

"What she did was awful," I said, trying again for the soothing tone. "My thinking so had nothing to do with..." I didn't quite know how to put it. "It had to do with her behavior, and nothing else."

"That is complete bullshit."

I hadn't heard Norah use a swear word since Eliot was born, so I could only stare at her, a little bit shocked.

"I can't believe you think I'm so gullible," Norah continued. She stopped pretending to arrange her bouquets into vases, and slapped the kitchen shears down on the counter. She threw her hands up and addressed thin air as if there were a studio audience hidden in the wallpaper. "Last time I checked, I had a master's and PhD from the University of Pennsylvania, which should be evidence enough that I'm not a moron. But apparently I must be, because my little sister is sitting at my kitchen table treating me like the village idiot."

I really hated the studio audience thing. That came from spending a lot of time pretending to be astounded by the stupidity of freshmen 101 classes, I knew. It was part of her teaching schtick. The fact that I was twenty-eight years old and not one of her students? Clearly irrelevant.

"Norah—"

"Lorraine, the sister you suddenly love so much, is a selfish drama queen who couldn't stand the fact that my wedding wasn't all about her," Norah interrupted me. At least she was looking at me, classroom histrionics set aside for the moment. "She hated the fact that there was a single day during which she had to step away from the spotlight. Do I need to remind you about the nasty, slurred speech she chose to make in front of all of my friends and relatives? The one about how I was so high-maintenance and had somehow bullied Phil into marrying me? Or how about when she tipped over the gift table?"

"She was out of control," I agreed quietly. A headache was unfurling in my left temple. "I'm not disputing the fact that she acted terribly."

"But you don't care about any of that, do you?" Norah demanded. "You would have forgiven her the next day, since she could never do any wrong as far as you're concerned. If only she hadn't involved Matt Cheney, right? *He's* the reason you care what she did."

"That's not true," I protested, but it was like the air had gone out of the room. Like his name was a spell. I didn't like hearing it. I didn't like remembering him at all, to be honest. I went out of my way to avoid it.

"You're just like her," Norah said, and I could see the

emotion in her face, and read how much of an insult that was supposed to be. "Does your fiancé know what this is really about, Courtney? Maybe someone should give him a little history lesson about Raine and the fact you had a crush on her repulsive best friend for most of your life. What do you think about that?"

Here's what I thought about that: not much.

Lucas knew about Matt Cheney. In fact, he knew the *truth* about Matt Cheney, which Norah did not. What did Norah think this was, a Lifetime movie with a plot that hinged entirely on one easily cleared-up misconception or half-truth? I wasn't one of those women who lied about her romantic history and then had to spend her entire relationship maintaining that lie. Who had that kind of energy? In any case, my wariness had been flashing above my head like a neon sign when we met, and Lucas, being the kind of man who didn't need to rush into anything, was perfectly content to wait. And what do you do while you're waiting? You tell stories. You get to know each other.

So *of course* Lucas knew that there hadn't really been anyone serious in my life, because I'd always had a crush on my older sister's best friend. Matt and Raine had met in kindergarten, and had been inseparable ever after. I thought he was a marvel. He made my breath hitch in my chest and he had dark green eyes, like the men in the paperback novels I had to hide in my cello case so Norah couldn't find them and lecture me about propriety and acceptable literature (i.e., anything boring that ended unhappily).

I'd been in love with him since I was a kid.

And then I turned twenty-two, and he finally noticed me.

He was my first love, and so I adored him heedlessly, impossibly, and to the exclusion of everything else. When he told me we had to keep our relationship a secret, it hadn't occurred to me to object. I didn't care if everyone knew or no one knew, I just cared that finally, we were together.

When he left with Raine in the wake of Norah's wedding it almost killed me.

It also made me the musician I became. Which was the point of the story of Matt Cheney, as far as I was concerned.

Thanks to heartbreak, I threw myself into the cello. For three years I did nothing but eat, sleep, and play. I won a chair on Philadelphia's Second Symphony Orchestra. It was a coveted position, though not on a Big Five orchestra like the city's more prestigious and famed Philadelphia Orchestra. Nonetheless, I was doing well, and could continue playing at just about the highest professional level as long as I maintained the same level of commitment and hours upon hours of practice.

Which was hard once I met Lucas, but I'd managed, for the most part, to keep music as my first priority.

How dare Norah threaten me with my own past? She'd never understood about Matt Cheney when he'd been around, much less six years after he'd abandoned me for California with Raine. He'd become nothing more than a footnote to a completely different story—one starring Lucas, thank you.

"I think I'm going to go," I told her, getting to my feet and not quite meeting her gaze. "I'm sorry you're upset."

"'Upset?'" she echoed, her voice sharp with temper. "As far as I'm concerned, you've basically just told me I don't matter."

"This is crazy." I shook my head, and found myself holding my hands out in a placating way. "You think I don't understand that she hurt you, but I do. I really do. I'm talking about reaching out to her, nothing more."

"You can do what you like," Norah retorted. "But you can't have it both ways, Courtney. You can have *her* or you can have me. Choose."

chapter three

I fumed the whole way back into Center City, barely noticing the usual irritants of Philadelphia public transportation because I was so annoyed with Norah. Sometimes I truly believed that she had no idea who I was.

How *dare* she throw Matt Cheney at me?

Especially when—and this galled me the most—she didn't know what she was talking about. She had no idea what had really happened when Matt and Raine disappeared that night, because she had no idea what had been going on that whole, long summer.

It had been awful when they'd left. Norah's wedding had been ruined, a fact she made sure to emphasize whenever possible, and I had felt frozen through to the bone. Frozen, and incapable of discussing it with anyone. Even my mother had wounded me to the core with a careless remark.

"Well," she'd said one morning shortly afterward, in the wake of one of Norah's rants about Raine and her follower Matt, "you always had stars in your eyes where Matt Cheney was concerned, didn't you?"

I loved him, I'd wanted to rage at her. *And he loved me, too.*

At least I thought he'd loved me. I'd wished it, wildly and often, though he had never actually *said* it. But it was the only thing that made sense of those few, desperate months we'd been together.

When I got back to our apartment west of Washington Square—in the Gayborhood, as it was affectionately known and handily marked with rainbow flags beneath the street names on all the street signs—I fired off an angry, venting e-mail to my best friend Verena, who spent her days working in marketing for a theater company and most of her evenings, when not involved in the company's shows, performing her stand-up routine in and around the city. This made her largely unavailable, but it was much better than the two years she'd spent singing on tour with yet another Broadway revival of *Oklahoma!* right after we'd graduated. It was difficult having a best friend who was so busy, but at least she was no longer the modern equivalent of a traveling minstrel.

Verena and Norah had maintained something of an armed truce ever since they'd met at the conservatory. Norah had not been impressed with Verena's goth attire or choice of introductory music (Trent Reznor). Verena thought Norah was controlling, which was true. Even so, they had often enjoyed each other's company over the years. But I was sure that wouldn't matter. Verena, I felt, could be trusted to express the appropriate level of outrage at Norah's behavior as soon as she checked her e-mail.

Lucas was out somewhere, so I fumed at the cats for

a while—a fruitless exercise, since they were cats and unconcerned with my emotions as they cleaned themselves and stretched—and then dealt with my anger the way I dealt with everything: by playing.

As I practiced my scales and arpeggios, I reminded myself that I was lucky, for so many reasons. I could even list them with each slide of my bow across my strings.

For Lucas, of course, who made everything worthwhile.

For my idiot cats, who lay stretched out in what little afternoon light poured in the bay window. They liked to bask in the music with me, purring along to the melody and pricking up their ears in protest when I played a sour note.

For my best friend, who always made time for me, no matter what drama might be going on in her own life.

For my cello, the one whose curves I knew so well that I could trace them with my hands in thin air. I loved the sweet magic I could produce with bow, fingers, and strings. I loved the sharp tang of the rosin I used on my bow and the glory of the music when those same strings sang.

And for Norah, too. She was a challenge, but she acted the way she did because she loved me. Her version of love involved holding on tight and squeezing for dear life. As if I were an instrument and she could coax the proper response from me if she simply practiced enough.

I could envision Norah in my head, bent over me as if I were the cello, her blond head against my copper one. Our identical brown eyes. Her fierce expression as she forced her bow across my strings, making melodies I didn't quite wish to play. It was a recurring image.

Sometimes I even dreamed it, and woke up in the night, gasping for air.

The phone rang, cutting that unpleasant image off, and I shook it out of my head as I crossed the room to snatch up the receiver, my bow hanging loose in my hand.

"You cannot be serious" was how Verena greeted me.

"That Norah said all that?" I asked. My outrage kicked in. "She has *no idea* what really happened, and she thinks—"

"I do know what really happened," Verena said, cutting me off. "And are you sure you know what you're doing? Why would you invite Raine back into your life? Hello—she ran off with your boyfriend!" Her voice was so incredulous, it nearly cracked.

"She didn't know he was my boyfriend," I retorted, on automatic pilot.

"*He* knew he was your boyfriend," Verena barked. "Those two are trouble, Courtney."

"I just want my family back together," I said, stung.

"Your family," Verena repeated, her voice making it very clear she didn't believe me. She sniffed. "Make sure that's what you're actually interested in having back together, that's all I'm saying."

Later, I poured it all out on Lucas the moment he walked in the door.

"Can you believe Norah?" I demanded. "It's not like I thought I'd *never* speak to Raine again—I just stopped for a while. She was always my favorite sister, you know."

"I think she's probably jealous," Lucas said, rummaging around in the fridge for a beer. He leaned back against the kitchen counter and twisted open the bottle cap.

"You should find your sister if that's what you want to do." He flipped the bottle cap into the sink. "It doesn't matter what anyone else thinks. It only matters what you think."

"It matters what *you* think," I told him. I considered for a moment, then dove in. "Apparently, Verena is under the impression that I'm secretly on a mission to find Matt Cheney. For suspicious purposes."

Lucas laughed, and I loved the way his eyes crinkled up at the corners. If he was threatened, he completely failed to show it.

"Good luck with that," he said. "Didn't she notice that didn't end too well the first time around?"

I decided in the middle of our final concert of the season at the end of May that I was going to California to find Raine.

We were playing an enormously complicated piece as part of our summer send-off—a selection of the Romantics, which meant a lot of interesting cello parts—and I should have been concentrating on the notes I was supposed to be producing.

Instead, I was having an epiphany.

Sitting in the cello section of a professional orchestra, engaged in a performance, was as good a moment to have an epiphany as any.

I was wearing my least favorite pair of black pants, the

pair that I felt made me look like a reject from the sort of eighties movie that might, independent of any plot, involve dance competitions and/or horrible hats to deflect attention from the shiny pants with their unfortunate cut and just-too-short legs. This was what happened when I forgot to pick up my dry cleaning.

The fact that Verena was right and I needed to pay more attention to fashion, if only to avoid another performance during which I was more concerned with how my butt looked than how my music sounded, was not the epiphany in question.

It had been two months since Norah's little outburst and Verena's phone call. Family Dinners had continued, and everything was perfectly pleasant. Mom and I debated invitations to the point of nausea (on my part anyway) and then sent them out for the party in July. Verena e-mailed me the most atrocious wedding gowns she could find online, complete with ostrich feather headdresses and whole trains made of sequins. I grew used to Lucas's ring, its weight and its place on my hand. I practiced, went to rehearsals, played concerts, and never mentioned Raine or Matt Cheney again.

But I thought of little else.

It was as if our engagement had lifted the lid off an entire aspect of my childhood that I'd been keeping shut up tight these past few years. After Norah's wedding, I had been so angry and hurt that I'd channeled it all into my cello and tried to block out the fact I'd been abandoned by both my first love and my hero, all in one fell swoop.

It was the hero part I kept going back to now. I missed Raine. That was the long and the short of it. I didn't want to get married without her. I didn't want to be without her any longer. I didn't know why six years had gone by without my feeling it, only to feel it now. I just knew I felt it.

So every day I sat down and started composing the perfect letter to send to her. It would patch up our differences, build a much-needed bridge, and do so without actually choosing any sides.

Except I wasn't a writer. At all.

Dear Raine, I wrote. *Wow, six years. That's a long time.*

Lame.

Dear Raine, I don't know if you've thought of me since the day you took off with Matt, but I—

Entirely too pathetic. And notably not about her.

Hi, Raine. This is your sister. Courtney.

As if Norah would write?

Dear Raine, Guess what? I'm engaged! His name is Lucas and I love him very much.

Yuck. It made me sound like a teenager, and made Lucas sound like a carnival prize.

I'd written so many versions of that letter I'd stopped counting them.

I was tired of writing that damned letter.

I was jolted back to earth—and the concert hall—when my stand partner kicked me in the foot. And since Marcello would have vaulted over my body if he thought it would get him closer to a seat as Principal Cello, it was a hard kick that would probably bruise.

And it was lucky he did, too, as I was about to miss our entrance.

I kept myself from yelping, and tried to put my family drama out of my mind for the rest of the performance, but a light had gone on in my brain.

Enough with the letter writing.

I was going to California.

chapter four

"I think that's a great idea," Lucas said. "I would have asked you to come with me before, but you said you wanted to spend the entire month of June reading books in bed."

I was all wound up from performance adrenaline and epiphanies. I was also limping slightly, thanks to Marcello and his fashionable shoes. I hobbled across our living room and sank down on the couch.

"I was too stressed to think about the fact you had business in *San Francisco*," I said, pulling off my boots and flinging them aside. "But I think it's high time I start acting like a business wife, and take your business trips with you."

I aimed a cheesy smile at him—my approximation of a Stepford Wife. He let out a laugh.

"I'll remind you of that the next time I have to go to Poughkeepsie," Lucas said dryly. "But San Francisco is beautiful. Streetcars and the Golden Gate Bridge. Your infamous sister...I have to do a lot of on-site client bullshit, but it's not like you won't have a million things to do to amuse yourself."

"Most people," I pointed out, "might urge caution here."

"Baby," Lucas said, handing me a glass of wine, "I keep trying to tell you I'm not most people."

I sipped at my wine and watched him move back toward the kitchen, dodging the cats as they rolled around each other in a sudden death match across the linoleum. Felicia squalled and dug her teeth into Felix. We ignored them both.

This man—*my fiancé*—delighted me. I liked the way he walked, all liquid and low, like he was prepared at any moment to fling himself in the path of danger. He had an abiding interest in various martial arts, was addicted to the Sci Fi Channel and select reality shows, and had studied philosophy at Penn. He had a great big family out in the far reaches of Vermont, all of whom were planning to trek down for the engagement party. He was easygoing and relaxed, in contrast to all the neurotic musicians and type-A academics I knew. He was the perfect man.

He was also great-looking. When he came to performances, the more amorous flutists always made approving noises and sighed over his smile. He was a good four inches taller than my five feet six, with those wonderfully calm, knowing eyes and a full head of chestnut hair threaded through with red. If modern day Vikings wore cargo pants and T-shirts, they'd look a lot like Lucas. The only downside to our relationship was that our babies would be redheaded through and through. I apologized to them whenever possible, in advance.

"What are you smiling about?" Lucas asked, settling next to me with a plate of cheese and bread he'd cut up.

Because he knew I liked to nibble after I played a concert. I rubbed at my aching foot, which I knew from past experience was likely to bruise.

"Our redheaded babies," I told him.

"Poor little bastards." He grinned. "At least they'll be smart and talented, right?"

"I guess that's something." I leaned into him and let out a contented sigh. "I'm so happy to be on vacation. I can't believe I don't have to go back to work for nine glorious weeks!"

Some people were unable to break the umbilical cord that kept them locked to their instruments, and maintained their punishing practice schedule all throughout our long summer break. Every year I vowed that I'd be one of them, because every year I took the break as an opportunity to pretend I had never heard of the cello and then proceeded to pay dearly for my relaxation come the fall.

Which I had no intention of worrying about tonight. No matter what, I was not going to play so much as a note of music for at least the first two weeks of my vacation. I made a vow right then and there.

Lucas gathered me next to him, and fed me a piece of sharp cheddar. I savored the way it popped on my tongue, and sighed in contentment.

"California, here we come," he said, waggling his brows at me.

"I think it's a stunningly bad idea," Verena said over paninis and coffee a few days later at the Village Coffee House.

We'd somehow managed to get one of the outdoor tables, a Philadelphia miracle, where we could enjoy the lovely May afternoon and watch the pretty boys stroll by.

I'd caught Verena before one of her open-mike "experiments," and I decided that maybe anxiety might be contributing to the frown she was aiming at me.

"I'll be honest," I said when she didn't elaborate. "That wasn't really the answer I was looking for."

"What do you think is waiting for you in San Francisco?" she asked, shaking her head at me.

"It's San Francisco!" I cried. "Free love! Janis Joplin! Flowers in hair!"

"That was in 1969," Verena said in repressive tones. "It's not magical today. It's a place. That's it."

"I thought I was going to get Old School Verena," I complained. "Remember? All you ever used to say to me was 'break out of your shell! Tell Norah to kiss your ass!' What happened to *that* Verena?"

Back in the day, Verena had been forever sleeping with cast members in rehearsals and then having to pretend to fall in love with them every night onstage for the duration of the show, having long since finished with them offstage. It was this sort of thinking that had prompted her to decide that despite her extensive training and experience in musical theater, she should become a stand-up comic instead, a field in which she had neither training nor experience. Her whole life had been a monument to the spontaneous decision.

Then she turned twenty-eight, and decided she had to Grow Up. She'd toasted her youth the night of her birthday several months ago, bid it farewell, and yes, it was exactly as melodramatic as it sounded. And here we were.

I blamed the media, and the endless "news" stories that claimed women would end up alone and it was all, somehow, their own fault. Because they were too fat, or too thin, or too needy, or too aloof, or too career-driven, or too relationship-obsessed. Though I knew better than to advance this theory to Verena when she wore that pissed-off little dent between her brows.

"What about Matt Cheney?" she asked. My appeal to her former self was, apparently, unheard. Or simply ignored.

"What about him?"

"What do you mean, 'what about him?'" Verena gaped at me. "You know exactly what about him. How are you going to handle seeing him again?"

"I don't know why you're assuming I will," I said with a sniff.

"Of course you will, and you know it," Verena said dismissively. "I don't like to bring it up, but you lost it when he bailed on you. You turned into an orchestra pod person."

"I focused on my career," I corrected her. Testily.

"You only *just* came out of that funk." Verena looked fierce. "And that's all thanks to Lucas. Your *fiancé*, Lucas. I don't understand why you would risk it. Does he know why you *really* want to go out there?"

"Is it really that hard to believe that I want to find my sister?" I asked, a little bit bewildered by the strength of her objection.

"Do you expect me to buy that?" she asked me right back.

"Since when do you and Norah see eye-to-eye on anything?" I demanded. She didn't like that—I could tell by the mutinous tilt of her chin. "And yes," I said, very distinctly, "I expect you to buy that I want to find Raine. Because it's true."

"I believe that you want to find Raine," Verena said, studying me from across the table. "I also believe that you want to find Matt Cheney. I believe they are inextricably linked."

She didn't say whether the *they* she referenced were Raine and Matt themselves, or her belief that I wanted to see Matt as well as Raine. I didn't ask her to illuminate me.

"This is not a stable, settled person we're talking about here, Verena," I pointed out. My voice was testy again. "This is Matt Freaking Cheney. He could have taken off for Tahiti years ago."

"When did Matt Cheney ever stray more than five feet from your sister's side?" She threw it out there. It was a deliberate hit. I winced at the truth in that question, but then, times changed, and so did truths. "You're going to see him, Courtney. You need to be ready."

"Six years is a long time." I rolled my eyes. "I think it's crazy to assume they're still living the way they did when they were teenagers, all in each other's pockets."

"Six years ago they were what? Almost thirty?" Verena sniffed. "I think the way they were living is just the way they live."

"They were twenty-eight, and this isn't about him," I insisted. "It's about Raine."

Verena remained silent. Pointedly silent.

Our panini cooled on the table between us, untouched.

"And who cares about him, anyway?" I was warming to the topic. "I'm not going out there to deal with Matt Cheney or any of his bullshit. I don't care where he is or what he's doing. This is a journey about *sisterhood.* This is about *family.*"

"You're engaged to Lucas now," Verena said. "Look at that beautiful ring on your finger. Why would you want to go digging around in the past when you have that?"

I looked at my ring, and then back up at Verena's face. She was watching me closely, almost as if she was looking for something in particular. Some sign, or clue.

"It's just something I have to do," I said, shrugging helplessly.

"I would do anything to have what you have," Verena said in the same sort of tone. "You should think about that."

"I just know that I want my family back together," I told her, willing her to understand. "Some girls spend their whole lives planning their wedding ceremonies down to the last detail. I never did that. But I know I want this. It doesn't make sense to me that Lucas doesn't know Raine at all. That he's never even met her."

Verena looked at me for a long moment, and then she sighed.

"I guess you have a point," she said. She reached over and cut off a piece of the panini. Cheese oozed slowly from the molten center toward the plate. "But I'm still suspicious about the Matt Cheney proximity."

"Duly noted," I assured her.

"You don't remember what you were like when you were all hung up on him," she continued darkly. "But I do."

"You're talking about someone who no longer exists," I told her breezily. Though she was wrong. I remembered, too. "I'm a grown-up. I know what I'm doing."

"Funny," Verena said, her brows arching. "That's what you said to me when you started dating him. *Secretly* dating him."

Something she was still pissed about, clearly.

"I'm beginning to think you're jealous that you're not coming with," I teased her. "I can't think of another reason why you'd be bringing up ancient history—unless, of course, you want to talk about *your* romantic decisions six years ago." I cocked a brow right back across the table and waited.

"Point taken," Verena said dryly, and shuddered. "Ew."

"I'm going to be fine," I told her after a moment. More softly.

Her eyes were still dark as they met mine.

"I hope so," she said. "I really do."

In the weeks that followed, Lucas and I bought plane tickets and spent hours poring over travel guides and itineraries. I dreamed about hills and fog, Victorian row houses, and the bright blue California sky.

June snuck into Philadelphia with chilly mornings that gradually heated into sweet, spring days. I wallowed in my vacation, demanded breakfast in bed daily, and received only laughter in reply—our summer tradition. I couldn't wait to feel even more relaxed out in sunny California.

"I want you to know that I am completely opposed to this trip of yours," Norah bit out at me as I was helping tidy up after a particularly delicious pot roast. It was the Sunday before our trip, and I was only surprised that she hadn't exploded at the dinner table.

"I figured you would be," I said mildly. I stacked the plates next to the sink. "I'm not trying to hurt anybody, you know. This is just something I have to do."

"Don't expect me to be here for you when she does something to rip your heart out," Norah said in a low voice. "Last time she ruined my wedding. If you think she'll stop there, you're kidding yourself."

Norah gave me a look that suggested she pitied me, and that I was incredibly naïve.

"She likes to top herself," Norah said, crossing her arms over her chest. "You're a fool if you let Lucas anywhere near her."

"I get it," I told her, holding my palm out in the *stop* position. "You don't have to keep throwing these things at me. I know how you feel about her."

"How *we* felt about her, until a few months ago!" Norah's lips pressed together and thinned. "You say this is about family, but you already have a family."

I searched her face, but she was like stone looking back at me. I didn't know how to make her see that I could love the both of them. I knew she didn't believe it.

"I want to see her, and see if there's anything to salvage." I shrugged. "That's all. It has nothing to do with you."

Norah made a small noise in the back of her throat.

"Of course it has to do with me," she whispered. "Don't kid yourself."

"I love both of you," I said, helplessly, but she had already turned her back to me and returned to her dishes.

chapter five

We took an early flight out of Philadelphia, switched planes in Dallas, and were in San Francisco by early afternoon.

It was amazing to me that a place like San Francisco could be so easy to reach, after a lifetime spent imagining those famous hills and the fantastic red bridge against the bright water below. It seemed as if fairy tale places should involve long and perilous quests, not a simple transfer in an unremarkable airport.

"I definitely don't miss carting the cello around," Lucas said as we lugged our two huge duffels out toward the taxi queue.

"I don't even have to lift weights," I bragged. I flexed one of my arms, as if there was anything to flex. "I'm so used to carrying it everywhere I go. Do you want me to help carry your bag for you? You look tired."

"You look like you're about to be single," Lucas replied. "Watch it."

"*You* better watch it," I retorted, because we were both twelve.

"Uh-huh." Lucas dropped his bag when we reached

the end of the taxi line and poked it with the toe of his sneaker. "Are you sure you didn't pack the cello in this body bag of yours? It's heavy enough."

"You can either carry heavy things or you can't," I drawled. "It's what separates the men from the boys, honey."

"The hotel reservations are in my name," he said, grinning. "One more slur against my manhood and you're on the street."

"But—"

"There's a time to push boundaries," Lucas told me, cutting me off. "This is not that time."

Clearly, I'd won. Triumph allowed me to be quiet until we were in the taxi and headed into the city.

I'd never been to California before, much less beautiful San Francisco. I shoved the ghosts of my sister and Matt from my head as I oohed and aahed over every glimpse of bay or curve of hill, and by the time we reached our hotel in the touristy, pretty Embarcadero district, I was in love.

"We have to move here right now," I told Lucas when we checked in. "You think I'm kidding but I'm not."

"I love this city," he agreed in the elevator. "Did you see all those people? On the bikes? All crunchy?"

"This is basically ground zero for hippies," I said expansively, feeling very knowledgeable because I'd watched *Charmed* for its entire run. More than once, if cable reruns counted. "If you feel the urge to grow out your hair and wear patchouli, holler. I'll wave your credit cards under your nose and bring you back to capitalist life."

"That's my girl," he said with a grin. "Always looking out for me."

Inside our room, we could see the city towering above us, waiting to be discovered.

"Grab your walking shoes," I told him, with the Rice-A-Roni jingle already polluting my brain. "We have serious ground to cover."

Later that night, we'd taken no less than one hundred and fifty-three pictures with Lucas's fancy digital camera, and I'd managed to exercise parts of my thighs I'd never known existed on San Francisco's famous—and freaking steep—hills. We'd eaten some of the best sushi I'd ever had and were a little bit giddy from too much sake when we fell into the California king bed I suspected was larger than the floor space in our living room back home.

"Have I mentioned that you're the love of my life and I adore you with every fiber of my being?" I asked as I stretched against the sheets.

Lucas smiled, and crawled across the bedspread so he could look down at me.

"I think it might have been implied once or twice," he said, and kissed me.

Outside our window, the skyscrapers gleamed in the dark, and the world felt alive all around me with possibilities.

It was already the best trip ever, and it had barely even begun.

In the morning, Lucas went into his client's offices even though it was a Saturday, and I took an extremely long bubble bath, because I wanted to feel decadent and pampered. And also because I wanted to think about my options. It had been fun to scamper around the city last night with Lucas, but it was morning now and I had to face the fact that I hadn't, actually, flown across the country to play Stepford fiancée.

I lay in the warm, slick water and thought about what would happen if I opened the door to my past. The fact was, I didn't know. But there was already so much else I didn't know. I didn't know why Raine had gone to California in the first place. Why Matt had left me. Why neither he nor Raine had ever gotten in touch with me after they'd taken off.

At first, when I realized they'd really gone to California together, I'd been devastated—but down beneath the frozen, horrified part of me there was a tiny kernel that had refused to accept it. That tiny part of me had whispered that Matt would call once he got there, that he couldn't have abandoned me so easily. The fact we'd been together had been a secret, that part of me had argued, so he couldn't have called me while he was on the road with Raine in that junky old Nissan Sentra of his. I'd made up complicated mathematical equations—this many days of driving plus this many days of sightseeing plus this many days of house-hunting or settling in. The trees were bare and the first snow was on the ground before I'd accepted the fact that he wasn't going to call me. And I had spent so long being brave, holding on to that little kernel inside, that when I gave in and finally called his cell phone, it made me cry with some toxic combination of shame, rage, and pain. But that was nothing next to the way I felt when the call couldn't be completed because his line had been disconnected.

He had disappeared. He had abandoned me.

As time passed, I assumed that my sister would call me sooner or later. She and I hadn't been in any battle that I knew of. While I couldn't bring myself to call her and possibly hear about Matt, there was no reason *she* shouldn't call her favorite sister. Norah thought the same, in those early days, and had often fired questions at me—as if hoping to catch me talking to Raine on the sly. But Raine never called. And the longer she maintained radio silence, the more it hurt my feelings. Why didn't she *want* to talk to me? What had I done that led family members and boyfriends to disappear? Knowing, now, that she'd stayed in touch with Mom made it worse. It had also spurred me into coming out here, if I was honest with myself.

I wasn't sure I wanted to go through with my grand plans. As I lay there in the hotel bath, I wasn't sure of anything. I felt small and a little bit scared. Maybe there was a very specific reason neither one of them had spoken to me since that day, and maybe they would be surprised that I didn't know what it was. *Courtney*, they would say with a shared laugh, *we thought you knew how much we needed to escape you—*

I was being ridiculous. And I hadn't come all this way to be a gigantic drama queen in a bubble bath. I sat up with a great sloshing of water and shook it off. I was still on East Coast time, which meant I had soaked myself into a pickle and it was still morning when I finally got out and got dressed.

I took special care with my appearance. It was important to strike the right note. I didn't want to look too severe; I wasn't Norah, who liked to bludgeon people with her intelligence and thus disguised her looks in strict buns, stern clothes, and her Very Serious glasses. Nor did I want to look like the fine arts college student I'd been when I last saw my sister, all rags and bad hair.

I wore my favorite pair of Levi's and a white T-shirt. Over that, I layered the black cashmere, zip-front hooded sweater Verena had given me for Christmas. She assured me that this single garment managed to be pulled-together, chilled-out, and cool all at once (thus making me appear to be the same), and I never argued with Verena about clothes. I pulled on my boots, fluffed up my hair, and added mascara to draw attention away from the freckles all over my nose and face. It was time to do what I'd come all this way to do.

Mom had said Raine worked nights in a bar to support her art, though she'd been fuzzy on the details of what Raine's art entailed these days. Knowing my sister, it could be anything from impromptu street performances to full-on metal sculpture pieces. Nothing would surprise me. What I was counting on was that people who worked nights tended to be home during the day, so I was likely to find her in, even on a Saturday when people might otherwise have daytime activities.

It occurred to me in the taxi across the hilly, windy city that I hadn't exactly planned what I wanted to say. I'd convinced myself that even though I couldn't manage to string sentences together to make a decent letter, I would be inspired when Raine swung open her door. Seeing her would cause the perfect words to appear on my tongue like magic. My belief that this was so had carried me across the country, and it completely deserted me as I sat, terrified, in the back of that taxi.

I was an idiot.

Norah was right—this was a stupid thing to do, and Verena was right, I was going to get hurt.

What could I possibly have been thinking?

But the car came to a stop, I handed the driver money, and then there I was out on the street. I blinked up at the numbers on the buildings.

According to Mom, this was it.

The street wasn't particularly picturesque, which was disappointing, since I believed that every square inch of San Francisco was supposed to be postcard-perfect. Even so, the cool air smelled of eucalyptus and cedar, and it made me want to fill my lungs completely.

I walked up to the door, taking care on a set of uneven steps, and rang the bell. The place appeared to be a town-house stuck up over a garage, which sounded far more aesthetically pleasing than it looked. I rang the bell again. I knew that if Raine didn't answer, it was entirely possible that I'd never gather the courage to return. I rang the bell a third time, and then stepped back.

This was a disaster. I should have written the damn letter or called her, like a normal person. Instead, I'd raced across the country like a lunatic. Maybe I was having some sort of breakdown. I'd heard people did that right around their thirtieth birthdays; maybe I was a little bit ahead of schedule.

I turned to go and heard the door creak open behind me.

I froze. I tried to imagine what she would look like now—the expression she'd wear when I turned around. Sleepy, no doubt, and surprised. I could handle that. It was the other possibilities I feared.

I took a breath and turned.

He seemed to fill up the doorway, all low-riding camouflage pants and the deep black dragon tattoo that stretched across his chest and dipped below his waistband into parts best ignored. His hair was dirty blond and stuck up in short spikes all over his head, as if he'd been running his hands through it. His eyes were still that dark green that should have been genetically impossible, and his wicked mouth kicked up a little bit as he took me in with one sweep from head to toe.

As usual, I felt as if he found me lacking. As usual, this made me wish I had actual breasts instead of a chest better suited to young girls in training bras. Or that I had Dove commercial skin instead of a mess of freckles that only Lucas found adorable.

What was new was the rush of anger that accompanied that feeling.

"Don't look at me like that," I snapped at him. "It's rude."

Of course, that only made him smile wider.

"Hey, Princess," Matt Cheney drawled, not sounding at all surprised to find me on his doorstep on a Saturday morning. "Long time no see."

chapter six

The last time I'd seen Matt Cheney, I had been twenty-two years old.

As if that wasn't bad enough, I had also been wearing a burgundy-colored, empire-waisted bridesmaid's dress with a matching flower tiara. The empire waist and burgundy shade would have looked fetching on a large-breasted woman with hair any color outside the wider red spectrum, which was unfortunate for small-chested, copper-headed me. The flower tiara was too awful to look good on anyone, and looked particularly ridiculous nestled against my hair, which was bone-straight, flat, and, at that time, a ragged length I'd produced with my own fingernail scissors.

If memory served, I had also been sobbing, an activity I knew made me look like a platypus. (Tiny eyes and elongated nose. I wasn't kidding.)

I had begged him not to go. He had ignored me and left.

Fast-forward six years, and it was still humiliating.

I couldn't even tell myself that it hadn't occurred to me that I might run into this particular problem. Verena had been quite vocal about the things I'd refused to consider. And in truth, I'd known it, too, I just hadn't *wanted* to imagine running into Matt. I'd ignored the possibility, even as I'd been secretly hoping it might happen, and so I was unprepared. I had no one to blame but myself. It was this exact attitude that had caused me to flub my first professional audition, a personal low that could also be laid at Matt Cheney's currently bare feet, since it had occurred mere weeks after his abandonment of me.

"What are you doing here?" Matt asked after a long moment, when it became clear to both of us, and no doubt the greater Bay Area arrayed around us, that I wasn't going to speak. I tried to tell myself that only I knew that I didn't have the slightest idea what to say, but that knowing look of his suggested otherwise.

"Oh, you know," I said after a particularly panicky moment during which I wasn't sure I *could* speak. I waved my arm in the direction I thought the cab might have come from. "I was in the neighborhood."

"Yeah?" He didn't buy it, if his smirk was any indication. "You hang out in San Francisco a lot?"

"As you can see."

What I was trying not to see was that tattoo, which was new. Or new to me, anyway. Who had larger-than-life dragons tattooed across their chests? How much must that have *hurt*? What was wrong with him? I refused to follow the sinuous tail to its inevitable end, though it was almost painful to force my attention away from that low waistband. He was still possessed of that same obscenely good body, which was all about genetics, since as far as I knew he did nothing to deserve it. On the one hand, that sucked—he should have been fat and balding as divine punishment. On the other hand, at least the ridiculously hot creature who stood in front of me was *worth* all those years of yearning.

"Does Raine know you're in town?" he asked.

"Is she here?" I asked, instead of answering him.

"She's sleeping," Matt replied.

Another long, awkward moment stretched between us, during which I entertained flashbacks of Norah's wedding. Matt in a tuxedo—good. Matt sneering at me and running after Raine—less so.

"Do you think she'll wake up sometime?" I asked. As if she was malingering in some coma, as opposed to simply sleeping late.

Of course, this was Raine. Anything was possible. Maybe Raine had interred herself somewhere as some kind of artistic statement, since she was exactly the sort of person who would find undergoing a voluntary medical coma an exciting creative challenge. I realized I sounded snarky inside my own head. Obviously, I had lost whatever tenuous grip on sanity I'd had before getting out of that cab.

"I'm not going to be the one who wakes her up before noon," Matt said with a short little laugh. He rubbed a hand on the back of his neck. "You can come in and catch up, if you want. I don't mind."

What a delightfully passive-aggressive invitation.

I could identify it as such, and yet, I still felt sucked right back into that familiar Matt Cheney vortex. It didn't matter that I might have valid reasons for harboring ill will toward this man. What mattered—though it galled me to admit it—was that *he* like *me*. Despite all of our history, I could feel that need burst to life inside me. Or possibly I was just nauseous.

If I'd had any spine at all, I would have used it to turn on my heel and walk away. It was what Matt himself would have done if our positions were reversed. I knew it without a shadow of a doubt.

Instead, I smiled brightly at him and his big black dragon, and followed him inside.

The house was old and weathered, which was apparent from the creak in the door and the give in the floorboards. Inside, it was chilly and dark, with unlit candles in dramatic sconces along the walls as well as electric lights overhead. Gloom collected in the corners, but even so, the place felt more like a college dorm than the sort of place two people in their thirties should live. But what did I know? This was San Francisco, where anything went. As public policy. I noticed that the walls had been decorated by hand—here a mural, there a tapestry—and incense spiced the air. It reminded me of Raine's room when she was in high school—exotic and mysterious, with undertones of sandalwood and jasmine. Matt disappeared down a long hallway, and I trudged after him, getting closer to Raine with every step.

At the other end was a living room packed cheek by jowl with a hazardous jumble of bookshelves and television equipment. It was like an entertainment cave. I tried to see signs of Raine in the furnishings or the posters tacked haphazardly to the wall, but nothing was familiar. Beyond the living room, two steps down and overlooking a patch of grass out back, was a large kitchen.

Matt walked directly to the refrigerator and rummaged around in its depths. I was about to attempt to make conversation with his naked back when I saw the woman lounging at the kitchen table. At first, I thought it was Raine and my stomach lurched in shock, but the woman who stared at me, cold and assessing, was a stranger.

I smiled politely, still reeling from the sudden terror that I might not recognize my own sister. Could she have changed that much?

Matt turned around, holding a Coke. He didn't offer me anything, which was the first comfortingly familiar sign so far. I had any number of memories of Matt in his teens and twenties, doing the exact same thing in my mother's kitchen.

"This is Raine's kid sister," he said, presumably addressing the woman.

Her expression changed slightly, while I attempted to digest that description. It was true. I was Raine's kid sister. And yet I hated the fact he called me that. *Really* hated it.

"You don't look a thing like her!" the woman cooed at me. She was wearing a blue bandanna over two thick braids, a flimsy little tank top, and yoga pants. The outfit called attention to her ample breasts and toned curves. She, too, was barefoot, and sporting a toe ring. No doubt to match the one she had through her eyebrow. She was more arresting than pretty, and I had no doubt whatsoever that she was sleeping with Matt.

"They have the same eyes," Matt contradicted his hippie chick. "They all do."

"Hmmm." She made a big production of frowning at me. "I don't see it."

"This is Bronwen," Matt told me. "She doesn't know Raine very well."

Or Matt, clearly, because she let him see her hurt at that remark, which even I could have told her from a six-year distance was the kiss of death. The more you clung, the more he enjoyed shaking you loose. Which, given the fact he'd had to remove himself to the other end of the country to get away from me, must have meant my own clinginess was epic. A thought that was not at all helpful, or conducive to a pleasant reunion.

"This is a nice place," I told Matt with an attempt at brightness, standing near the table and looking around as if I weren't in the least bit uncomfortable. I also tried to shut off my brain, with less success.

"It's big and it's cheap," he said, and shrugged as if he didn't care one way or the other. There was evidence of communal living everywhere, from the selection of mismatched mugs on the countertop to the notes in various hands left scattered across a dry-erase board on the wall. Two different bicycles hung from pegs near the back door.

"It's so funny," Bronwen drawled. "I can't imagine Raine as part of a regular family like anyone else. She's so..." She looked at Matt, and I suspected she chose a different word than the one she'd been thinking. "*Elemental*, you know?"

Bronwen stretched long and high, like a cat. Like she was something feral and unrestrained, and I felt very bourgeois, suddenly. Very suburban and foolish next to her unrestrained breasts and free-love hair. I suppressed the urge to fidget. Or apologize.

"Wow," she said when she was finished stretching. She leaned toward me. "Is that an engagement ring?"

I jolted a little bit, and could feel Matt's attention narrow in on me.

"Um, yeah," I said, fanning out the fingers on my left hand, as if I were still surprised to see the ring there. I straightened. "I mean, yes. I'm engaged. That's sort of why I'm here."

I thought I'd hit the appropriately adult tone there, though I was suddenly a little bit afraid to look over at Matt. I was taken aback by Bronwen's sudden laugh.

"I'm sorry, I just haven't seen one of those in a while," she murmured more to her ringless hands than to me. She looked up. "You know, for political reasons, some people won't wear diamonds. But yours is really, really pretty."

I hated her.

"Engaged, huh?"

I looked over at Matt and completely forgot about Bronwen.

"Engaged," I confirmed with a small shrug.

"Well," he said after a long moment. "Congratulations." It sounded very nearly like an insult when he said it that way. "Who's the lucky guy?"

"His name is Lucas." Like that mattered, or he cared.

We looked at each other again. I felt confused suddenly, as if I should apologize to Matt for the six years I'd had a life without him. The life he'd forced me to have by taking off, but somehow, that didn't seem to matter.

Bronwen had stopped smiling and was instead watching the back and forth between us with a calculating look. I was familiar with that look. I remembered wearing it myself whenever Matt's groupies ventured near him and I'd had to pretend I was nothing more to him than Raine's kid sister—which would then, inevitably, make me wonder whether or not that was true.

"Have you planned the wedding?" Bronwen asked, inserting herself into the conversation once more.

"Not yet." I could tell that I lost points for saying so, as if Lucas and I were on shaky ground because we hadn't booked a venue, caterer, and a band—things I only knew I needed because of my mother. I wanted to reach over and wipe that smirk from her face. "I wanted to sort out some family stuff first."

"How's Norah doing?" Matt asked in a deceptively bland tone. Deceptive because he wasn't as oblivious as he liked to pretend, and I knew it. He spent so much time with Raine he was like an honorary woman, and therefore fully aware of female politics. He knew that Bronwen was trying to alpha girl me.

"She's great," I answered him, looking away from stupid hippie Bronwen and her boneless insinuations. "She and Phil had a little boy a few years ago."

"Oh yeah?" Matt looked surprised. He laughed. "I can't really picture Norah pregnant. She must have hated it."

I had to laugh myself, even though it felt disloyal.

"Every minute," I confirmed. "I think Phil wants another one, but Norah says the only way that's happening is through adoption."

Bronwen made a sympathetic sort of noise.

"It's awful when people aren't in touch with their bodies," she murmured.

"Norah's in touch with her body," Matt said, still laughing a little bit. "She's in touch with the fact she wants it lean and mean."

"She lost her baby weight in about three weeks," I said, only slightly exaggerating. "We figure even her own body is afraid to defy her."

"I know I am," Matt agreed. It was a whole different thing to look at him and feel connected again. It was disconcerting. I looked away.

"She sounds uptight," Bronwen interjected, with an edge to her voice that I suspected meant she wasn't talking about Norah.

"You're talking about her sister, Bronwen," Matt said quietly. "Have a little respect."

Bronwen paled. She rose to her feet in a single, graceful move—I blamed the yoga she obviously practiced and immediately felt inadequate next to all that smooth muscle—and glared at him.

"I'll be upstairs," she announced, and swept from the room, making sure to throw a chilly look my way as she went.

Without her snide presence, the kitchen seemed a lot smaller.

I squared my shoulders and looked at Matt. There was no reason not to dive right in. While I had never been entirely immune to the force of the man's physical presence—and that had been predragon, for the love of God—the fact that he could be an incredible jackass usually tended to soften the impact.

"She seems nice," I said. Insincerely.

He shrugged. "She's not my girlfriend, she's just hanging out."

"I didn't ask." Though I took a dark delight in it.

"Well, in case you wondered, now you know."

I didn't have any idea what to say to that, and the fact was, I was still looming there near the table like a dolt. I shoved my fingers into the pockets of my jeans and rocked back a little bit on my heels. I'd spent my entire professional career learning about posture—because believe me, slouch too much and you'd pay the price, as I'd learned quickly—but it took all of twenty minutes in the presence of Matt Cheney for all of that to go straight to hell.

"So why are you here?" he asked. He leaned back against the counter and watched me, eyes hooded.

I shrugged. *I wanted to see if there was anything to salvage in my relationship with my sister*, I wanted to say. Among other things. But I couldn't seem to speak.

"Because Raine is more fragile than she looks," Matt continued when I didn't speak. "I don't want you upsetting her."

"*Me* upset *her*?" I could barely process that. "Don't you mean the other way around?"

"That's the attitude I'm talking about." Matt shook his head at me. "She doesn't need that judgmental shit."

"And she doesn't need you to run interference," I countered. "Last time I checked, she was all grown up and on her own."

"Look," Matt said. "I don't know if you genuinely just want to see Raine or if you're in the middle of some Twelve Step program and need to unload your personal crap on her. But be careful, Courtney. Some people don't want to look back."

I digested that for about three seconds.

"Be careful of what? That I might accidentally point out to my big sister that it sucked when she got wasted, ruined Norah's wedding, and took off with my boyfriend?" I sucked in a breath, and wished the words didn't have that particular bitter kick to them as they hung there in the middle of the cold kitchen like smoke.

"Yeah," he said. "That."

I shrugged as if I felt nonchalant, which, of course, I did not.

"Oops," I said.

Another quiet moment unfolded between us, and I found that I was aware of my own breathing, and the hum of the refrigerator.

The fact of the matter was, I didn't know what to say to him. I never had. My memories revolved around our silences. Me struggling for something to say. Matt seeming to imbue the air around him with signs and meanings, like some modern-day wizard, but never *saying* much. Me feeling the weight of all that meaning and squeaking out something—anything—to relieve the tension.

I will not talk just to break the silence. I will not talk just to break the silence. I will not talk just to break—

"You look good," Matt said. He waved, indicating my body or outfit, I wasn't sure which. "Classy." He managed to make the word sound vaguely uncool. And one of the many tragedies of being near Matt Cheney was that somehow I always wanted him to think I was cool.

Which, I'd faced years ago, I was not. By definition.

"Classical, maybe," I said, and laughed a little bit. Lucas would have thought that was funny, but Matt just watched me without moving. I stopped laughing. "I mean, I play in an orchestra. The Second Symphony. Classical music..."

"I thought you wanted to play in the New York Philharmonic," Matt said, as if maybe I'd forgotten the big dream of my college days.

"Everyone wants to play in the New York Philharmonic," I replied with something perilously close to a snort. "I'd also be thrilled to get a seat with the Philadelphia Orchestra, which is just as unlikely."

"At least you still play the cello," he said.

"Of course I still play the cello." I laughed. "It's my only skill. What else could I do? Become an accountant?"

"So you're basically still a band nerd," Matt said and grinned at me. "But as, like, a profession."

"Basically," I agreed cheerfully. "The upside is, I make a living playing music. What about you?"

He set his Coke can down by the sink, with his fingers that had once coaxed poetry from a beat-up acoustic guitar.

"This and that. I keep busy."

"Oh." The awkwardness rolled over me then, like a truck. "Sounds exciting."

"It can be." He pushed away from the sink. "It's nice to see you, Courtney. It's been a long time."

"It has." *Six years, you jerk.*

"I thought I was dreaming when I pushed open the door," he continued without looking away. "Because why would you show up on my doorstep after so many years?"

I didn't know what I might have said then to address that odd note in his voice that sounded a bit like yearning. It unsettled me too much.

In any case, I didn't have the chance to find out, because a figure appeared in the kitchen doorway the way actresses appeared onstage. With a sudden flourish, as if she expected the orchestra to cue her entrance. Both Matt and I turned to look at her.

"To see her big sister, of course," Raine said, answering Matt's question with a toss of her head. "Or was that rhetorical?"

chapter seven

Raine and I had the same eyes and the same chin. We shared both features with our father. Our eyes were brown and deep and tilted slightly in the corners. Our chins were a little too pointed, in my opinion, but noticeably the same.

That was where our similarities ended.

Raine was small and curvy. She had looked particularly good in the burgundy bridesmaid's gown, even drunk. Back then, she'd had hair of several different colors that, because she was Raine, had somehow worked with the flower tiara so that she looked almost okay in it. At the moment, she'd opted for very short and dark, to highlight her delicate bone structure. It gave her a kind of ethereal, almost elfin look. The Liv Tyler/Cate Blanchett sort of elf, obviously, not the Keebler kind.

Even her sleepy expression this morning and the raggedness of the sweats that clung low to her hips couldn't detract from how pretty she was. Nothing ever could. Norah was good-looking in a severe, sometimes cold sense. I was cute at best, with all the freckles and the red hair.

Raine, on the other hand, was so pretty it was almost like a handicap, or a weapon, depending on how she played it. Men stopped her in stores to tell her she was lovely, and waiters gushed about her smile. No one could believe that someone so pretty could be anything but sweetness and light to match.

She held her position in the doorway for an extended moment, and then she let out a little squeal and launched herself at me. All five feet two inches of her hurtled across the room and caught me hard in what was half a hug, half a tackle against the kitchen table.

"Little Courtney!" she cried. "I'm so glad you're here!"

She stood back and held both of my hands, and then *gazed* at me. I could feel a blush across my cheeks and suspected my grin was sort of goofy, but I couldn't quite contain it.

"Hi," I said, feeling foolish. And happy.

She sighed, delighted, and then dropped my hands. She pirouetted around and then made a beeline for the counter.

I had forgotten how small she was, and how gargantuan she made me feel in comparison, as if at any moment I might lumber into something perilous while she skipped along unscathed. She was a light, bright creature and I was content for the moment, savoring the fact we were in the same room.

"Don't tell me there's no coffee," she said to Matt, frowning at him, which did nothing to mar her pretty face. Quite the opposite, in fact.

"Don't look at me. I don't drink it."

"But your sweet little Bronwen does." Raine batted her lashes. "Whole pots of coffee."

"She's not *my* anything."

"No one cares about your private life, Cheney. Could you just make me some coffee?" She threw a wink over her shoulder at me, inviting me to join the interplay between them. I remembered how it felt to be their co-conspirator, and felt myself glow a little bit.

"Why do I have to make it?" Matt asked, grumpily. But he was already reaching for the pack of filters in the cabinet.

"You know you make it better. Mine's always weak and useless."

They shared a private look, while I stood there and watched how they interacted with each other. There was an unhurried intimacy in the way they spoke. They even moved together, anticipating one another's movements. Matt handed Raine a coffee mug just before she turned to reach for one. Raine did the same with the carafe.

I understood how Norah had refused to believe that this relationship had ever been platonic. It seemed too impossible. *Of course* they were sleeping together, or had slept together, or wanted to sleep together. They seemed so *connected*.

I had never believed it. Raine had told me that she and Matt *communicated on a spiritual level*, and I'd believed her.

It occurred to me that maybe I just *wanted* to believe her, but I quickly shoved that thought aside, and then spent a few seconds wondering what it said about me that *that* was what I was thinking about after six years.

Raine left the coffee-making in Matt's hands, and turned to look at me.

"You look wonderful," she told me. "You have so much more energy than you used to, Courtney. It lights you up."

"She's engaged," Matt contributed without turning around. "To be married." As if there were other forms of being engaged.

"Mom told me," Raine said. "She says he's wonderful." She didn't seem to care that Matt had turned and was glaring at her. She just waved him away. "Did you bring him?"

"Not to the house," I said, stating the obvious and feeling awkward. "But he's in town. He has business. So."

This conversation wasn't making sense to me, no matter how pleased I was to see her. It seemed to me that we ought to have been talking about the six-year gap, not Lucas, who was the good thing that came long after they'd disappeared without a word. It seemed as if explanations should have been the first order of business. Instead, Raine was acting as if she'd been hanging around waiting for me to visit, which was quite a different thing than her taking off and remaining incommunicado, I thought. But I tried to go with it. I had to blink a few times, and after a moment I produced a smile, but I still felt odd.

"You'll have to bring him by tonight," Raine said in her confiding, conversational tone.

"Tonight?" I sounded idiotic even to my own ears.

"The bar I work at? Very chilled out. I think you'll like it. Just tell the guy at the door you know me." She elbowed Matt and let out a peal of laughter. "Right?"

He sighed. "The guy at the door is me."

"You're a bouncer?" I was flabbergasted. What a waste of him. Of that smoky voice of his and his guitar.

"He's a bouncer and I'm a barmaid," Raine said wryly, flinging out a hand to sketch a dramatic bow. "We're very glamorous around here."

"Raine." I tried to sound very matter-of-fact. "I don't know about—"

"I want to hear everything," she interrupted me. "I want you to tell me *every single thing* that happened to you since I saw you last. I can't wait! But I can't do it right now." She turned to Matt. "See? I'm already getting emotional and we've barely said hello!"

"You're fine," he told her. It was sort of gratifying that she ignored him, too.

"I need to be completely emotionally centered to confront the past," Raine told me earnestly, lowering a hand to her belly as if to hold herself still. "And that's not something I can do when the past shows up in my kitchen without any advance warning on a Saturday morning. I have to get in the right headspace, okay?"

"I just wanted to talk to you." I felt very young suddenly.

"And we will."

She looked sincere, and yet I had the sudden, sinking feeling she had no intention of talking to me at all. Then I dismissed it, because why wouldn't she? I was being silly. And she was right. I'd appeared at her door without any advance warning. I'd had months to psyche myself up for this meeting. She'd woken up to discover me in her kitchen, and knew herself well enough to know she needed time to reflect. How could I not respect that?

"We'll just do it later, sweetie," she promised.

"It's okay," I assured her then. "I understand."

After Raine kissed me on the cheek and flitted off upstairs, Matt eventually following in her wake, I wandered out of the house. I had my cell phone already in hand and dialing, started walking, and now had absolutely no idea where I was. Every now and then I would catch glimpses of sparkling blue water beyond a hill or between pretty houses, but it didn't help me orient myself. Happily, I was too high after seeing my long-lost sister to care.

I left Verena a long, probably crazy and incoherent message, mostly centering on how great the whole thing had been, if also stilted and bizarre, and then I kept wandering.

I tucked my phone back in my bag and looked around, as if I were just coming awake. I'd been walking for a long time. It looked like I was nearly to the top of a hill, so I staggered onward, cursing the incline the entire way. Why would anyone live in such a hilly city? It was murder. The people streaming past me in cars, on bikes, in trolleys and buses had to be nuts.

Then I made it to the crest of the hill and realized why so many people overlooked the strain in the thighs. And created whole songs and counterculture movements to celebrate the place.

It was gorgeous.

An enchanted city straight out of some modern fairy tale. In front of me, trolley lines snaked down the hill I'd just climbed, headed for the sparkling water. The trees were green, the sun was bright up above, and there were islands in the blue bay. Granted, one of those islands was—I was almost positive—Alcatraz, but even so, there was no getting around the fact that I was standing in one of the most beautiful cities in the world.

I leaned my head back and let the light dance over my face. I breathed in the urban magic all around me and let myself relax. Then I breathed out the confusion and tension and let it dissipate in the early summer sunshine. I felt the city come alive around me, like it was welcoming me in with each swell of breeze and warmth.

It felt like music, and like music, washed the world away.

Lucas found me in the bathtub again, neck deep in bubbles.

"Don't tell me you spent all day in there," he said, coming inside and standing by the edge of the great big tub. His eyes danced when I wiggled my toes at him. "I can't let myself imagine what your skin looks like. It's too horrible. Let me see."

"I'm not pickled," I told him, lifting my face up into his kiss. He tasted like San Francisco sunshine. "I walked across the entire city. Possibly more than once, I'm not sure."

"Was it a fun, touristy walk or a terrible-mood-brought-on-by-family-trauma walk?" he asked.

"There was no trauma, exactly, but there was a whole lot of walking. I had no choice but to retreat back into the bath to make sense of it all." Not that I'd gotten too far on that front. Even after a whole day's reflection, I still felt that it had gone much better than I could have reasonably expected. Everyone had been polite enough. No one had yelled. Or cried. Or really even referred to actual past events.

All things considered, I'd decided, it was the best uncomfortable estranged family/ex-boyfriend reunion I'd ever heard of.

"You've convinced me," Lucas said.

I watched him as he shrugged out of his clothes, and then eased his way into the tub to face me. I let my eyes fall and play over him while he settled in the steaming water. I loved his body in an uncomplicated way I couldn't imagine loving my own. I had too many failed hopes and dashed expectations wrapped up in my own reflection. But Lucas I adored, and so I adored every inch of his skin as well. I lusted after his broad, sculpted shoulders, the sweep of his torso, his cute butt. I frowned over scratches and slapped his hands away from the blemishes he sometimes picked at. No matter how he saw himself—and generally speaking, he saw himself as someone who ought to hit the gym more often, which was as close as he got to body issues—I saw only love, safety, and the world's best hug when I looked at him.

"What are you looking at?" he asked, smiling.

"You." I smiled back. "It takes a man pretty secure in his manhood to sit in a foamy bubble bath."

"First of all," he said at once, "I'm sitting in a bubble bath *with* a girl. Hello. It's sexy in about ten different ways."

"Oh yeah?"

"And anyway, you have no proof this ever happened, or that I'm even here. My manhood is secure." He leaned back and sighed. I could almost see the tension ease from his bones.

"I could have a hidden camera," I pointed out. "Spies documenting your every move. You don't know."

"That would be unwise," Lucas said without opening his eyes. "Don't make me get all ninja on your ass, Courtney. I'd miss you if I had to kill you."

We entwined our legs around each other and soaked for a long moment.

"Do you want to talk about it?" he asked quietly. "Was it a mistake?"

I considered, playing with the washcloth.

"We could talk about it," I said slowly. "That's an option."

Lucas opened his eyes then and waited. I could feel that I was practically vibrating with excitement, and grinned at him.

"But Raine has invited us both to go and hang out at her place of business tonight, which is located in a neighborhood with the unlikely name of Cow Hollow." I swatted a mound of bubbles away from my chin. "It happens to be a bar. Matt Cheney is the bouncer at that bar. So option two is that instead of my sitting here and telling you, you can just see for yourself."

"What do you want to do?" he asked.

"It's entirely your decision," I said grandly. "I can go either way."

Lucas thought about it for a second or two.

"Okay," he said. "I pick Option Two. I say we hang out with the prodigal daughter. But you have to pick the dinner place, Court, and none of that 'I don't care what do *you* want' crap or we're having a fight."

"Oh," I said, pretending to glare at him, "we're having a fight all right. Consider it on."

"Bring it," Lucas said and splashed water directly into my face.

I screamed bloody murder. And then it was time to retaliate, which left no room to think about anything else.

"I don't know if you've noticed this, but Cow Hollow has a serious lack of cows," Lucas said when we stepped outside the cute little restaurant where we'd had dinner. There were adorable Victorians and sweet little shops and galleries, all threaded through with the famous San Francisco fog that had rolled in while we were eating, but no cows.

"In the absence of cows, I was hoping for a few fields," I said, tucking my arm into his. The night was chilly, and not at all the way I thought California—or summer, for that matter—ought to have been. "Maybe even a dairy."

"You heard the waiter." Lucas made a face at me. "There used to be dairy farms here, sometime in the 1800s. Hence the name. I thought he might actually lend us a history book so we could catch up."

"You know, I get that it's exciting to be a native Californian. Manifest Destiny, pioneers, whatever. But at one point I was pretty sure that he was claiming to have been here *himself* during the Gold Rush."

"That's when you choked on your fries!" Lucas laughed. "I knew it!"

We made our way down a sidewalk made dreamy in the drift of the fog. It breathed around us, muffling the sounds of the city and making the streetlights into halos. I supposed it was the perfect sort of night to introduce my new life to the one I'd left behind. Or, more accurately, the one that had left *me* behind.

According to Matt's terse directions, the bar he and Raine worked at was within walking distance—a claim I was beginning to understand San Francisco residents made about any address within the city limits. *It's a walking city!* our concierge had assured us in his aggressively cheerful manner, back when I'd still had the use of my thighs. The fact that one *could* walk, it seemed to me, wasn't necessarily reason enough to do so.

But a few blocks that weren't vertical seemed fine, and we marveled at the art galleries and the little stores tucked away beneath street level, always drawing closer to the bright neon that glowed high above a patch of light on the upcoming corner.

Lucas and I had dressed for the evening. I was in a shimmery sort of tank top over my favorite pair of black pants, the ones that made my butt look divine. Lucas was wearing his favorite button-down and khakis. I thought we looked especially good, though neither one of us had admitted we were making an extra effort to look fabulous.

I decided that the tension in my neck was a perfectly natural response to the unknown, and didn't mean that I was *particularly* worried about Lucas meeting Matt. I sort of wished there was a way for Lucas to meet him and thus be able to discuss him without *actually meeting him*, but I was at a loss on that one.

"I think that's it," I told Lucas, pointing at the bar on the corner.

"Should I get ready for some macho theatrics?" he asked, in a joking sort of voice completely belied by the arm he had around my shoulders, in support. "Because I'm ready."

"Oh yeah?"

"Absolutely." He pulled away and let his face go completely expressionless. He held it for a moment, and then jerked his chin once, while simultaneously flexing out his chest slightly. Then he dropped the pose and grinned. "See?"

"That was like a greeting wrapped up in a testosterone bow," I said dryly. "I had no idea you spoke *male animal* so fluently."

"Do we actually know each other at all?" He shook his head at me. "What, if a guy isn't obsessed with football, he's a punk? Is that what you're saying? Because, as I believe I proved in the bathtub earlier tonight, I can bring it."

"I'm sure you can," I soothed him, patting his arm.

"You watch," he suggested. "At the end of the night, I want a written apology and the offer of sexual favors. Which I'll be turning down, thank you, because you insulted my manhood."

"How much beer did you drink? Are you drunk?"

"Make that two written apologies, sexual favors, and an original musical composition by you, Courtney Cassel, called 'I Will Never Underestimate Lucas Again.' For cello and flute, please, with a hint of bassoon."

I was still laughing when Lucas wrenched open the door of the club to reveal Matt Cheney on a bar stool in the tiny foyer, as if he'd been waiting for us to appear.

For a moment, everyone froze. And then:

"It's the Ghost of Christmas Past," Matt drawled.

I was sure, in that moment, that my heart was beating so hard that it was actually visible.

"Hey," he said in a completely different voice, because he was addressing Lucas. "I'm Matt."

"Lucas." Lucas offered his hand. There was a perfectly nice shake, no chins or flexing, and he let the door fall shut behind him.

The two great loves of my life were shoved together in the same tiny space, sizing each other up, both with perfectly nice smiles on their faces. They launched into what sounded like a perfectly polite conversation, while my head began to spin.

Some people, like Verena, were all about incorporating former lovers into their lives. Some people *insisted* upon it, and tended to make speeches that included phrases like, *if I liked him enough to be with him, why would I suddenly hate him just because our relationship didn't work out?* Then all the like-minded people would throw back their heads and laugh their well-adjusted laughter, while those of us who were significantly less evolved hunkered nearby in silence and felt extremely petty.

But the fact was, I *was* petty. When I had been in love with Matt, I had expected to love him forever. I had *already* loved him forever. When he took off, it was like the girl I'd been when I was with him died. The life I'd expected to live with him disappeared.

Lucas was the only forever I knew.

So then, inevitably, I watched Matt and Lucas. My once-upon-a-time life versus my current life. I tried to see them the way a stranger might.

Matt had the better body. Lucas had the better smile. Matt was slightly fidgety and exuded edgy cool. Lucas stood still, calm with the barest suggestion of possible danger. Even now, Matt lounged against the wall as if he needed help to stand, his fingers tapping out lazy rhythms against the wood, while Lucas stood quietly on the balls of his feet, ready for anything. Matt was all about being spontaneous. Lucas preferred to prepare. I imagined that was why Matt was a bouncer and Lucas ran his own business.

It was like some kind of dream to see them standing together, laughing, giving every appearance of enjoying each other's company.

Not a dream I'd had, mind you.

Watching them together—Matt's smirk and Lucas's grin—I understood, far too late, that it was all a dreadful mistake.

I thought I might throw up.

As in, right then and there.

chapter eight

Blinded by panic, I yelped out some excuse, then forced my way across the bar and threw myself into the women's room, which was thankfully empty. Once inside, I hustled into the nearest stall and locked it behind me. Then I just sat for a moment, and breathed in to the wave of nausea.

I hadn't had a nervous stomach since back in high school. Back then, a change in barometric pressure was about all it took to have me racing for the nearest toilet. Any sort of tension and/or stress made my stomach heave, which was unfortunate if you happened to be a musician forever auditioning or playing concerts, with warring sisters and a grief-altered mother on top of it. By the time I set off for the conservatory in Baltimore, I was an old pro at worshipping the Porcelain Goddess.

But that had all been a long time ago. I'd thought it was just a teenage thing. Until tonight.

Trust Matt Cheney to bring out the worst in me.

Literally.

I concentrated on taking deep breaths for a while, and

eventually the fuzzy feeling in my head subsided, and my stomach settled. I let my spine relax slightly, and tried not to think about how ridiculous I probably looked—perched so primly on the edge of the toilet seat, fully clothed, working so hard just to breathe.

It could have been worse. I could have *actually* thrown up.

Which was when I remembered that it *was* worse: I'd left Lucas all alone with Matt Cheney. I all but swooned from the horror. No matter the state of my stomach, that was hideous. The things Matt could be *saying*...Private, awful things. Things that wouldn't match my personal version of my history at all.

I jumped to my feet, and let myself out of the stall. I managed to wash and dry my hands without once looking at myself in the mirror. I knew that if I opened that can of worms, there'd be no prying me away from my reflection. Because no matter what I'd decided to wear or what I'd attempted to do with mascara, the truth was, could *anyone* look good enough for a showdown with her past? I didn't think so.

I pushed the door open, prepared to take charge of the evening. I couldn't even begin to imagine what a conversation between Matt and Lucas might sound like. Or what subjects they might be covering.

Horrifying possibilities began to crop up in my head. I took a few steps, determined to put an end to the madness, and then stopped in my tracks.

Because this place wasn't just any old bar. It was...something else entirely.

The walls were painted deep black and covered with

what looked like art installations. Some were paintings, like the huge seascape dominating one side of the long room, done in reds and oranges. The wall nearest me held photographs, divided into groups by photographer, presumably. The focus of the large, loungelike room was a small raised stage at the far end, upon which two persons of indeterminate gender, clad in nude-colored body suits, appeared to be performing an interpretive dance. What they were interpreting remained a mystery to me. An alarmingly skinny-looking man sat to one side of the performers, playing on a ukulele while his long, stringy hair swung from side to side. It took me a few stunned moments to register the fact that the song he was playing was—more or less, emphasis on *less*—"Blinded by the Light."

Most of the patrons sat around the tables and/or lounged on the various couches, all watching raptly, applauding every now and again, or, in the case of a girl sitting cross-legged on the floor in front of the stage, weeping in apparent identification.

It was all so surreal that it seemed almost run-of-the-mill, almost normal, to look over into the corner near the bar and find my fiancé chatting animatedly with my ex-boyfriend beneath a representation of what I knew to be a Hindu god, made out of what appeared to be macaroni.

Lucas grinned at me from afar. Clear evidence that things were going as well with Matt Cheney as could be expected.

Whatever the hell *that* meant.

I had gathered myself to head in their direction and find out when a hand slipped around my elbow.

Since I knew exactly one other person in the city of San Francisco, I knew immediately who it was.

"Hey there," Raine said, smiling at me. Tonight, she looked more mysterious than she had in the harsh light of morning. She'd done up her eyes so they seemed endless and dark. Her hair was spiky, and she'd packed herself into what should have been a run-of-the-mill tank top and jeans, except on her, it was somehow captivating.

I felt myself fall as I looked at her, through the old looking glass and out the other side to my childhood, when I'd worshipped her completely. It was like Raine really was an elf, or some kind of siren. Somehow, one look at her was almost enough to make up for our time apart.

She slipped her arm around mine. "I'm so glad you came."

"Oh, hi," I said. I looked around. "You didn't mention that this place is so . . ."

"I know," Raine said, reverently. She pulled me close and squeezed my arm. "I didn't want you to prejudge your experience. I wanted it to be raw. After all, there's only one first time here at Space."

"What? Space?"

"Space is just that. *Space*. To *be*."

I wanted to ask, *To be what?* But I could tell from the practically devout way she drew out the word that it was supposed to resonate deep within me. I paused for a moment, in case something was resonating quietly or had possibly gotten swept up by the ukulele, but there was nothing. So instead, I looked toward the wall and the nearest cluster of photographs.

"Those are really cool photos," I said brightly.

"This is why I love you!" Raine declared. "You walk back into my life and *just like that*, you can somehow *sense* me. It's like it's in our *blood*."

I had no idea what she was talking about, so I just smiled gamely as she drew me closer to the photographs.

"I saw you standing over here, but I didn't realize you'd picked my photographs out," Raine continued happily. "How did you know? That they were mine, I mean?"

As I was not entirely dim, I realized she'd thought I'd recognized something about her in the photos, which were, evidently, her latest incarnation of artistic expression. Quickly, I scanned the first one. I wanted to say something meaningful about it, but the truth was, I couldn't make out what I was looking at. It seemed to be flesh. And some dark hair. And a sort of reddish bump. In fact, it sort of looked—

Oh, my sweet lord, no.

My mind balked.

Blinking, I looked at the second in the series. It was a different angle, and it confirmed my panicked fears. Just to be sure, I glanced at all the rest of them. I didn't want to look, and yet I couldn't look away.

My sister had taken photographs of her crotch. Ten separate, close-up photographs. As if that were not enough, she had then blown them up, mounted them, framed them, and displayed them on a wall—in a public forum, which also happened to be her place of employment.

"Well," I lied, hoping I didn't sound as hysterical as I felt, "I could just tell this was your work, somehow."

Raine sighed happily and gazed up at the wall.

"Family is so trippy," she said.

"Huh," I said, still trying to sound normal. "Are all of them, uh, of the same thing?"

"Oh, yes," Raine said, her tone serious. "This project was all about demystification and empowerment. About *displaying* and *naming*."

"What do you call the—ah—project?" I asked, for all the world as if I were talking about a nice garden statue. A garden gnome would be far preferable to this, that was for sure.

"It's called what it is," Raine said. She lowered her lashes at me almost demurely. "'My Vulva.'"

When I emerged from the state of hysteria that statement produced, along with the visual aids now seared forevermore into my retinas, Raine had herded me over to a table in the corner and sat me down.

"I promised you we'd talk," she said, folding her hands and resting her chin on top.

"Um, here?" I looked around at the people crowded in on all sides, some of them now dancing along to the ukulele. Though no one was actually waving a scarf in the air, I felt the manner of dancing referenced scarves somehow.

"Why not?" Raine was asking, a vague frown on her forehead.

How silly of me. Clearly, the woman who displayed her private parts on the walls of her place of employment would think nothing of discussing intimate family details in the same establishment.

It was hard to believe I actually felt a little stab of nostalgia for her solo interpretive dance period.

"No reason," I said, shaking all of that off. I squared my shoulders. "I thought maybe we should begin with Norah's wedding."

"Of *course* we should," Raine agreed immediately. "You know, I wanted to write you a letter and explain everything, but I just felt that putting it all into one document couldn't really do my feelings justice, and it took me a long time to *truly* access my feelings. My raw emotions, not my *interpretation* of them."

"Okay," I said, because what else was there to say?

"And the truth of it is that I allowed the alcohol to create a snapshot version of my feelings at Norah's wedding, when really, I should have just trusted myself enough to *express* those feelings." Raine sighed. "But as bad as that experience was, it was also an awakening." She shrugged. "I couldn't go back to sleep once I'd woken up to my reality, could I?"

That didn't seem to require an answer, but she was looking at me so expectantly, so I nodded.

"I've spent a long time learning how to trust myself, Courtney," she continued. "A long, long time. And it was a process I had to keep precious. I couldn't allow any toxicity or negativity or judgment in, because it would have stunted my growth."

She looked at me as if she had just explained it all. I nodded automatically, again, but was saved from having to respond further when a woman appeared at Raine's side.

"Raine," she said in an extremely urgent voice. *"Raine."*

My sister looked up and managed to look encouraging and regal all at once.

The other women inhaled in such a way that she used her entire body in a sinuous movement, flared her nostrils, and let her gaze go heavy-lidded. All this while clasping her hands directly beneath her impressive breasts, which appeared to know no bra of any kind.

"I am *awestruck* by your latest exhibit," the other woman eventually said, her voice thready with emotion. "What *bravery*! What a fearless slap in the very face of the patriarchy!"

"That was my hope," Raine said, inclining her head. Humbly. "I'm so glad it worked for you."

The other woman looked at me, still rapturous.

"This woman," she intoned, gesturing to Raine, "is genius. *Genius.*"

Raine demurred, the other woman insisted. I watched them go back and forth on this for several moments. Then:

"I have to study them further," the other woman finally said. "We'll have to talk about this more, Raine. I feel a poem coming together."

And then she swept away.

"That was Marisol," Raine told me. "She's a fabulous poet. This place is absolutely filled with the most amazing creative energy." She shook her head slightly as she gazed around the big room, as if savoring it. Then she looked at me. "But what were we talking about?"

"It sounded like you were saying that you think I'm

toxic, or negative." I tried to sound matter-of-fact, as if her saying so hadn't hurt my feelings.

"Sweetie, don't be angry," Raine said at once. She reached over and grabbed hold of one of my hands. "The fact is, Philadelphia is filled with so much negativity that I feel allergic when I'm there. *Sick*, Courtney. And don't even get me started on Norah's aura, which I've realized is black. *Jet* black, and I couldn't be around that any longer. I had to escape. I'm sorry I couldn't take you with me."

"Norah means well," I began, feeling defensive, and unsettled, too.

"Meaning well isn't the same as doing well," Raine replied gently. "I had to escape from the claustrophobic darkness, Courtney. Or *die*. It was that extreme."

"But..." I didn't know what to say. I couldn't argue about auras. I wasn't even sure I knew what an aura was. That wasn't true—I knew what auras were. What I didn't do was spend a lot of time worrying about their various hues.

"I wish things hadn't happened the way they did," Raine said softly, "but I'm not *sorry* they happened. I can't be. I would never have had the courage to pursue my art if I hadn't learned to express myself. And it all blew up at Norah's wedding. If she weren't so judgmental and small-minded, I would think she'd be happy for me."

I looked at her for a long moment. I still felt uneasy about the conversation I wasn't monitoring in the corner under the macaroni Shiva, but between vulvas, poets, and this interpretation of past events, I was starting to feel significantly confused by this one.

"I don't know what to say about all that," I managed to say after a while, when staring at her imploring expression became too much. "But that's only one part of what I think we should talk about. The more important thing is that you disappeared six years ago. *Six years*, Raine."

"Six crucial years in my development," Raine said, as if agreeing. "I don't mean only as an artist, I mean as a *person*, Courtney. A *woman*. From the things Mom's said, I don't get the impression Norah has really pursued her personal growth. If anything, it sounds like she's regressed, and you know what, that really supports my decision to get away."

"Okay, but I'm not talking about Norah." I sat a little bit straighter. "I'm talking about me. It's been six years since you talked to *me*."

My voice didn't crack when I said it, which made me unreasonably proud of myself.

Raine held my gaze for another long moment, and then sighed a little bit. But she didn't say anything.

"I always thought that what was between you and Norah didn't extend to you and me," I continued carefully, when moments passed and she still didn't speak. "I thought it was different with us."

"Oh, Courtney," she said. She looked away. "I couldn't."

"I don't understand." Because I didn't.

"Life in Philadelphia was so *small*," she said in a rush. She frowned, as if remembering. "I was boxed in. There were so many expectations and assumptions and I felt like I had to do my own thing. I had to be true to myself, and if that hurt you, all I can do is say that I'm sorry you took it personally."

It wasn't the same as actually apologizing, I couldn't help but notice.

She smiled then, announced her break was up but we would talk more later, and leaned over to give me a somewhat misty kiss on the cheek before heading across to the bar.

I watched her transmit her charm with every step: that saucy smile and the twitch of her hips. Men and women alike vied for her attention, and not only because they wanted drinks. She drew every eye in the place. Because she was so cute, yes. But also because she radiated something like heat. Everyone wanted to be close to it.

I didn't know how to process what she'd told me. Beneath all the self-help-y talk about finding herself and being true to herself, it seemed to me that the bottom line was, she hadn't thought enough of me to stay in touch with me. Whatever had boxed her in, I'd been a part of it. Enough so that she'd completely cut herself off from me.

There had been a time when I'd shared everything with Raine. I'd valued her opinion above all others. I might not understand exactly what she got out of photographing parts of her body I, for one, preferred to keep private, but it was hard to ignore everything that had gone before.

She thought my life was tiny, constrained. She hadn't said so directly, but it had been implied. After all, the life she'd felt she had to escape had been the one with me in it.

And what if she was right?

chapter nine

But I had to shake that off, immediately. I was being ridiculous.

Raine hadn't said that—and even if she had, she was talking about six years ago. When I'd been all of twenty-two. She wasn't talking about the present—because she didn't know anything about it. She hadn't even met Lucas yet. She had no idea what my life was like now—big, small, or anything in between.

Which was what reminded me that whatever my life was, it was very likely to be over—given the fact that I was sitting, staring off into space at a table while *who knew* what was happening beneath the macaroni god.

I got up and tripped over no less than five hippies in my haste to get to Lucas.

Who, when I arrived at his side, only smiled at me as if he spent all of his time hanging out with my ex and they were old buddies.

"Feeling better?" he asked, wrapping his arm around my shoulders and giving me a squeeze.

"I'm fine," I said. There seemed to be very little reason

to panic, if I were to judge the situation by his body language.

I looked from Lucas to Matt, who was watching the two of us closely. The whole thing felt hideously uncomfortable to *me*, but neither of them seemed to be the least bit bothered.

"You always did have that tricky stomach," Matt drawled in a tone I might have considered affectionate if I hadn't been looking at him. He looked at Lucas. "There was this one time when she was supposed to try out for some really fancy cello tutor, and she lost it all over the kitchen floor at her Mom's place."

"Oh, no," Lucas said, laughing, for which I would have to kill him later. "That's terrible!"

I tried to understand how this was happening. What had I done, in a karmic sense, that had made this moment inevitable, possibly before I had even been born? Who had I wronged? How could I be standing quietly by while my ex-boyfriend regaled my fiancé with tales of me puking up my guts on the kitchen floor?

"That's nothing," Matt was saying. Because, apparently, he wasn't finished. "She had to audition for the conservatory in Baltimore, too, and let me tell you—"

"Enough," I interrupted. Because my standing there staring at him in horror wasn't working. "You're making my life sound like an episode of *Jackass*, and by the way? This topic of conversation is disgusting."

"I think I'm glad I met you after that whole phase ended," Lucas said. It was clear the phase he was referring to encompassed Matt.

"But has it ended?" Matt asked in his laziest voice. "What about tonight?" His implication was also clear.

"Maybe it's not a tricky stomach after all," I suggested, baring my teeth at him in a very broad interpretation of a smile. "Maybe it's just you."

"Who needs a drink?" Lucas asked then, as if unaware that there was tension between Matt and me. Or, possibly, he was negotiating the peace.

"This round's on me," Matt said at once. When Lucas started to counter, he just held up a hand. "I insist. You two are guests in my city."

"Thanks," Lucas said cheerfully.

I sensed there was some complicated male oneupman-ship going on with that, but I was happy to let it fly under my radar, especially since Lucas didn't seem to mind. I watched Matt move through the crowd toward the bar, and then duck behind it to help himself.

"Are you okay?" Lucas asked, pulling me closer. "Matt told me that was your sister you were talking to over there."

"I don't actually know if I'm okay," I confessed. "I don't really know where to start." I looked at him, and pretended to think for a moment. Then pretended to remember. "Oh, yes: Raine has taken photographs of her genitals and dis-played them on that wall over there. Be very careful if you use the bathroom, or you might end up with an eyeful. That's all I'm saying."

Pure delight bloomed across Lucas's face.

"I don't know if I want to run over there and look right now, or run out the door," he told me, putting a hand over his heart as if overstimulated. "That's simultaneously the best *and* worst thing you've ever told me."

"I can't speak of it, ever again."

"I understand you completely." He gazed across the room in the direction of the photographs. "I thought the dude with the ukulele was going to be the headline story from this place. I had a whole impression planned. But this?" He sighed blissfully. "This blows a paltry ukulele and hippie dance right out of the water."

"I'm sorry I left you with Matt for so long." I tilted my head up to search his face. "Was it awful?"

"Did you expect it to be?" he asked, his tone mild but his expression quizzical.

"I don't know. Yes." I sighed. "He always seems to push *my* buttons."

"I noticed." He shifted his weight. "You're kind of twitchy."

"He's just..." I looked over toward the bar, where Matt was engaged in an obviously flirtatious conversation with a pretty brunette. He treated her to that slow, sexy smile of his. She responded the way all the girls responded, by practically drooling on the bar. I looked back at Lucas. "I was kind of worried that he wouldn't be particularly nice to you."

Lucas let out a bark of laughter.

"What?" I was confused.

"That's not how guys work," he told me with another laugh. "It's not like that movie you keep trying to convince me to watch."

"*Mean Girls*?"

"Exactly." He was still smiling. "He's kind of what I expected."

"I'm not sure I want to know what you expected," I muttered.

"I do," Matt said, appearing at my elbow, sans drooling girl. He was bearing drinks and looked delighted to discover he was the topic of conversation. He grinned at Lucas as he handed him a beer. "What were you expecting?"

"You've got the whole bad boy thing working for you," Lucas said, grinning right back and leaning lazily against the wall. He waved his beer in Matt's direction, summing him up. "All brooding and tortured and tattooed. Apparently girls go wild for that shit. And why not? You seem like a nice enough guy." He raised the beer in a toast and took a pull.

I wondered if Lucas knew how much Matt would hate to be described that way. A glance at the amused expression on his face assured me he did. Matt had always presented himself as someone who *simply was*—and therefore couldn't possibly be deliberately *working the whole bad boy thing*. Not to mention, the Matt I had known would have died rather than be known as something so insipid as *nice*.

Nicely played on Lucas's part.

"Glad I lived up to expectations," Matt said in a tone of voice I interpreted as *pissed*. He smirked a little bit as he handed me a large, fruity-looking pink drink.

"What is this?" I asked. Although I knew perfectly well what it was, being female and alive and thus having watched no less than five complete seasons of *Sex and the City*.

"Your favorite drink," Matt told me, still smirking.

"Apparently," I narrated for Lucas, "in addition to being a bad boy who's good with the ladies, Matt is stuck in a time warp."

"All I know is, you and that freaky best friend of yours demanded Cosmopolitans." Matt shrugged at Lucas. "Nightly."

I loved how he did that—made it sound as if I spent all of my nights with him. Exactly what any fiancé yearned to hear.

"Verena—who is not freaky—had a very serious *Sex and the City* obsession," I confided to Lucas. "The only thing that could break it was total immersion in *Veronica Mars*, and time."

"You must mean a long time. Like six years," Matt replied at once, crooking his eyebrow at me. "Because it was really more of an addiction than an obsession."

Except it didn't sound like he was talking about Verena.

"Something like that," I agreed. I raised my eyebrows right back at him. "Either way, it's gone now."

We shared a look that didn't quite tip over into a smirk, but skirted the edges, and then Lucas put his beer down on the shelf behind me and announced he was going to the bathroom.

"And maybe I'll check out the art," he said.

"It is definitely unmissable," I said, shooting for a dry tone that was neither insulting nor encouraging, in case Matt's support of Raine included approval of those photographs.

Matt watched the interplay between us and then, as Lucas headed across the bar, watched me. I flicked a look at him, but was more interested in Lucas's progress across the room.

First Lucas had to dodge the five angry hippies I'd tripped over earlier, who had by now gathered together into some kind of healing circle involving knitting and, in one case, a unicycle. Then he stopped for a moment to fully appreciate the ukulele. I watched him stifle laughter, and then turn toward the back of the room and the bathrooms.

"He's not what I expected," Matt said after a long pause. I saw that he, too, had turned to watch Lucas make his way across the room. "I guess when you said you were engaged I pictured someone..." He shook his head. "Different."

"Different, how?" I asked, as he no doubt intended. I immediately wished I hadn't, as I imagined that qualified as another door best left shut.

"He's just not what I expected," Matt repeated. This was clearly supposed to render me insecure and anxious.

I sipped at my drink, which was so sweet I thought the enamel on my teeth might dissolve in protest. I set it down on the shelf next to Lucas's beer and helped myself to the beer instead. I looked back at Matt.

"I find it hard to believe you had any expectations one way or the other," I said, emboldened by the pure absurdity of the situation.

Matt held my gaze for a long moment.

"I don't think I get why you're so angry," he said.

"You don't?" I was flabbergasted. "Are you kidding?"

I wanted to scream at him. I could feel the urge thrum in the soles of my feet and through my blood. But we weren't alone. Raine was here, and as far as I knew, she didn't know that there had ever been anything between us besides my endless adolescent crush. Lucas was here, too, and I didn't want him to see me lose my cool with Matt.

"It doesn't matter," I said when I was sure I could speak without giving in to the urge to yell. I was proud of how even my voice was, how calm I sounded. Verging on the dismissive. "It was all a long time ago."

I didn't look at him. Instead, I looked across the bar to where Lucas was. And saw that Raine had intercepted him and was giving him a guided tour of her photographs.

Inappropriate hardly seemed to cover it.

"I have to go," I muttered in Matt's direction.

"I'm sure he's fine." Now it was his turn to sound dismissive. "Raine doesn't bite."

"I kind of wanted to introduce him to Raine myself." I chose my next words carefully. "I'm not sure her pictures are the best way to start off their relationship."

Matt's green eyes lit with glee.

"It's kind of like diving in the deep end," he agreed. "Sink or swim."

"It is."

I didn't like the way he watched me then, or how unsettled I felt.

"He seems nice," Matt said eventually. Softly, but distinctly. And I knew he meant it exactly the same way Lucas had.

I ignored him, and then tried to shove him out of my mind as I hurried across the room.

". . . which, obviously, completely flies in the face of

feminist thought," Raine was saying when I walked up to them.

"Obviously," Lucas agreed very soberly, as Raine carried on talking. He shot me a bland look over the top of her head, and I struggled to keep a straight face.

Raine had her arm linked through Lucas's, and was gesturing emphatically. She stopped talking when she saw me and broke into a huge grin.

"Courtney!" she cried. "Your fiancé is *wonderful!*"

"Thanks," I said. Lucas nodded slightly when I looked at him, and kept smiling his high-wattage smile at my sister, who seemed to bloom in response.

And then, oddly enough, I thought of Norah, and the warning she'd leveled at me right before we'd left. *She likes to top herself,* she'd said. *You're a fool if you let Lucas anywhere near her.*

It was as if Norah could see all the way across the country from the middle of her Philadelphia night and see that I was still reacting to Matt Cheney. And I felt exactly as guilty as if she had done so. Which didn't make any sense, since it had been Verena who had been so worried about Matt...

"What's wrong?" Raine asked.

I snapped out of my head. Neither Norah nor Verena were here, I reminded myself. They had been talking about phantoms. Ghosts. I was the one who was standing in front of the real Raine, with the real Matt across the room surrounded by his usual selection of devoted groupies. They were both exactly who I thought they would be, in a place that suited them. It didn't matter that I thought the place was nutty. What mattered was that they loved it.

"Nothing's wrong," I assured Raine. I felt benevolent, and also proud of myself for coming all this way to build bridges. "It's just really good to see you, and Matt. It's good to see you're okay."

Raine searched my face for a moment.

"Of course we're okay," she said. "Maybe I shouldn't tell you this," Raine said then, giggling and leaning toward Lucas. "But Courtney used to have the *biggest* crush on Matt. The poor thing would turn bright red every time he entered a room."

Lucas shot a scandalized sort of look my way. Which he was faking. He was enjoying himself.

"I am shocked," he lied. "Courtney, you never told me this."

"Oh, shut up," I said, whether to him or Raine I wasn't sure. "This is the most humiliating night of my life. First Matt decides to give Lucas a little tour through some of my 'tricky stomach' moments—"

"Ouch," Raine said, but she was laughing. Because it was hilarious, as long as you weren't me.

"—and now this. Turning red in front of Matt when I was like *thirteen*. Thanks for that, Raine. Really."

"It was more like eighteen, maybe even twenty," Raine told Lucas. She sobered when I glared at her. "What? It's my job as your big sister to publicly embarrass you."

I couldn't deny the warm feeling that produced inside. She was, after all was said and done, six years or no six

years, still my big sister. It wasn't the same as her saying
that she'd missed me, but that was how I took it.

"I guess you're right." I suspected that the smile I aimed
at her was goofy, but I didn't care. "I would never want to
keep you from doing your job."

She smiled back at me, and then winced.

"Speaking of which, I should get back behind the bar if
I want to keep my other one." She waved a hand in the air
as she turned to go. "Come get drinks! Hang out, make
friends!"

Lucas and I stood and watched her go for a moment,
then turned to look at each other. The carnival atmosphere
of Space swelled all around us. Two skinny white guys
with dreads were engaged in some kind of tribal dance in
front of the bathrooms. Or maybe that was a Hacky Sack
they were kicking about.

"So," I said, turning to Lucas. "You finally met Raine."

"She's something," he said. He reached over and put his
hands on my shoulders, his thumbs brushing against my
collarbone. "Is everything still okay? Because we can go
any time you start to feel weird."

"I feel okay." I shook my head. "I mean, I feel better than
okay—I think this is good. I'm glad we came."

"And just think," Lucas said. "None of this could have
happened in a better environment. We have a ukulele,
and weeping poets. We have a *lot* of patchouli. And best
of all," he said solemnly, holding my shoulders in his big
hands and then turning me ever-so-slowly so I could face
the wall of photographs before me, "I got to meet not only
your sister, but her va—"

"Do not say that word," I ordered him.

"It's important to *name*, Courtney. We're *naming* and *displaying* here."

"Don't make me hurt you."

"Go get me another beer," Lucas said, kissing me on the forehead. "I have to go snicker like a twelve-year-old boy in the bathroom." He walked off, presumably to do just that.

But I stood still for a moment before I went anywhere. I didn't focus on the photographs—which were, in any case, burned forever into my brain—but on the fact that twenty-four hours ago, I hadn't seen or spoken to Raine or Matt in six years. And now here I was.

I might feel a little more turmoil about Matt than I'd like, but that wasn't the end of the world. It was just tension—a reasonable response, I thought. And I might not have been as persuaded by Raine's current art as I had been years ago, but that was okay, too. None of that mattered. We were all different people now.

The important thing was that I was here. I was banishing old ghosts just by reaching out.

If that wasn't worth celebrating, I didn't know what was.

chapter ten

I woke on Sunday morning to the sound of my cell phone blaring.

Lucas groaned as if I were the one making the noise directly into his ear.

"Please do something about that god-awful sound," he demanded. Or that's what I thought he demanded—his head was buried in the pillows and he didn't seem to be able to move it in order to speak.

He had a lot of nerve, complaining about the ring. He was the one who thought it was so funny to load my cell phone with ring tones from the likes of the Black Eyed Peas, Britney Spears, and the current selection: Justin Timberlake. All of which went over well with the rest of the orchestra when he called me during our breaks, of course.

I heaved myself out from under his arm, then out of the bed. I had to upend my bag on the bed to find the obnoxious cell phone, still bleating out the notes to "SexyBack."

I glared balefully at Lucas's prone form as I snapped the phone open and barked out a greeting.

"Uh-oh," Raine singsonged. "Someone sounds tense!"

I was given to understand from her tone that "tension" was to San Franciscans what sloth was to East Coast types (i.e., anathema).

"I'm not tense," I said at once.

"If you say so, I believe you," Raine said.

"I was asleep."

"Well, it's time to rise and shine, sweetie," Raine said smoothly. "I had the most wonderful idea! I think it came to me in a dream."

Which was how I found myself dragging my ass—and that of my yawning, bleary-eyed fiancé—onto San Francisco's BART train for the forty-five-minute trip across the bay to Berkeley.

And it was BART, not *the* BART, according to the huffy pedestrian we'd accosted for directions to the correct stop. Apparently, San Franciscans were as pissy about their articles of speech as they were about their politics. The highway was a freeway and it was called 101, not *the* 101, and should you forget this, you were likely to be reminded. Sharply.

Raine's great idea was that I should attend her yoga class. Once we saluted the sun and assumed the dog position—and I was just making that up, because I'd done a yoga tape exactly once in the comfort of my living room, and not well—she thought we would bond. More than we had while she was working, or so she hoped.

Lucas had no interest in bonding over chakras, aligned or otherwise. But he was game for a trip out to Berkeley, where he figured he would find a coffee shop and the paper, so he rode over with me.

Once off BART, Berkeley shone before us in the Sunday morning light. Lucas slouched behind his sunglasses. I inhaled. Deeply. The air smelled like pine, sea, and incense. Sleepy-looking students in dark blue Cal sweatshirts shuffled along the streets, next to political protestors reeking of marijuana and total commitment. Ragged-looking street people with dogs and guitars gathered on the sidewalks of Telegraph, while drums tapped out a rhythm somewhere in the hills above us.

It looked exactly the way it was supposed to look.

I was filled with the urge to foment worker rebellion, convert to vegan activism, and overthrow the current administration. All at once.

Instead, I deposited Lucas at a coffee shop near the university and found my way to Raine's yoga studio, tucked away in a little California Craftsman bungalow.

Raine was waiting for me just inside the door, a vision of bright eyes and flushed cheeks. I didn't understand how she could look so healthy and well rested when she'd been up working half the night. I had seen what I looked like, and I'd supposedly been relaxing.

"I'm so excited about this!" she cried when she saw me. "I can't think of a better way to share our true selves after all this time than yoga, can you?" She didn't wait for me to answer, suggesting she knew me better than her question indicated. "You can tell a lot about a person by their yoga, you know."

"I think you might be able to tell that I'm not very flexible," I told her. "More than that, I don't know."

"Flexibility is sixty-percent in your mind," Raine said

with a laugh, and then motioned for me to follow her into the large open room that served as the actual yoga space. There were wind chimes in the front windows, and everything was very white and soothing. I immediately felt more highly evolved.

"This is a women's class," Raine told me in a whisper. "Some of us like to experience only feminine energy while we practice. I think you'll like it."

And for a few moments, I agreed with her. I spread a mat on the floor and sat down on it cross-legged, trying to imitate Raine's casual swami position without seeming to do so. Other women filed into the room and smiled at one another, and I felt delighted that I could raise my consciousness simply by sharing in all this wonderful female energy—

—until Bronwen walked in.

Or, to be more precise, *slithered* into the room, a fresh pair of yoga pants riding low on her toned hips, her only other garment a torso-baring halter top. Her hair was piled on the back of her head in some bohemian updo involving a collection of braids, and her piercings glowed in the morning sunshine.

I immediately felt all my insecurity about my appearance—which I had been pretending not to feel because of Raine's equally cute attire—collapse on top of me. I was wearing track pants and an oversize T-shirt. This was the closest thing I had to yoga clothes, and I hadn't planned to mention the fact that the only reason I even had the outfit at all was I'd been sleeping in it.

Trust Raine, in her matching yellow yoga pants and

fluttery T-shirt, and stupid hippie Bronwen to be contenders in a yoga fashion show. I felt like a flat-chested, dorky troll. Which did not, I was aware, bode well for my attempt at relaxation. Or spiritual enlightenment.

Bronwen looked at Raine and nodded. Raine nodded back serenely. Then Bronwen turned to me, and looked at me for a while. It was a long, cool stare. She didn't bother to crack a smile, which I decided meant I wasn't obliged to throw one out there either.

Which was just as well, seeing as I was obsessed with the grungy inappropriateness of my clothing. You would have thought that it might have occurred to my sister to mention the fact that she liked to attend yoga classes where the main requirement—apparently—was to *already* possess abs of steel and an exhibitionist streak. It was higher consciousness for the already highly health-conscious. Mine was the only covered midsection in the room.

A quick survey confirmed that mine was also the only midsection that *needed* covering. Joy.

"Good morning," Bronwen said in a voice that carried to the far corners of the room. I jerked my attention to her, horror dawning as everyone else smiled expectantly at her. "Let's get started."

Because, of course, Matt Cheney's latest bedmate wasn't just a self-righteous anti-engagement-ring activist. She wasn't just lithe and muscled and happy to flaunt her toned abdomen. Oh, no. She was also a yoga *instructor*.

I wanted to kill myself.

And then, shortly thereafter, wanted to die and who cared how, because when Raine had told me that her Sunday morning yoga class was *a lovely exercise that really gets you in tune with your body*, what she'd apparently meant by that was that it would get me in tune with *her* body. And *her* body was, apparently, made of rubber and perfectly content to be twisted into shapes that would make a pretzel cry.

My body, needless to say, was not.

My body did not know how to perform the fluid stretch-up-then-fall-to-the-floor-then-perform-a-push-up thingie that every woman around me seemed to flow through, happily and without effort. My body, in fact, got caught on the stretching-up part.

My body—which I had never taken the time to catalogue in quite so comprehensive a fashion before—decided after about five minutes of Bronwen's yoga death march that it would prefer staging a civil war to any further yoga attempts. It decided this on its own, right about the time I attempted to perform a headstand.

A *headstand*.

The last headstand I had attempted to perform had been an abject failure in my sixth-grade gymnasium. It was not coincidental that I'd become a cellist. When I said I had no other skills, I meant *no* other skills, including those most children seemed to possess naturally. Headstands, somersaults—I even tripped when skipping rope.

Not that my lack of physical coordination in gymnastics concerned me much in the orchestra pit.

Bronwen, naturally, flipped her legs over her head and just sort of *extended* herself, as if she were a marionette and someone was plucking her string and lifting her, feet first, toward the ceiling. So unaffected was she by this pose that she continued to talk to the class as she performed it, never pausing for breath or even sounding the slightest bit muffled.

Raine, seemingly oblivious to my horror, easily slid into the same position without appearing to try very hard. Or even appearing to concentrate terribly hard, for that matter. Headstands were *second nature* for Raine.

And for the rest of the class.

I, meanwhile, rocked and kicked and toppled over to one side, red-faced and furious.

"Don't worry," Bronwen purred at me, triumph glowing across her face as she lowered her hips and returned to sitting position in one easy motion. "It can be a very difficult pose."

My face reddened even further as the entire class turned to look at the loser. Since I was, obviously, the only person in the room (and, possibly, in all of Berkeley) to find it difficult at all.

Next to me, Raine held her headstand just the showiest bit too long, as if in emphasis.

I had the urge to shout out that there were things I could do that I'd bet they couldn't, like play Prokofiev's Symphony-Concerto, op. 125. Maybe not *well*, precisely, since it was renowned to be perhaps the most difficult cello piece around, but I could play it—hard articulations, difficult transitions, and all—so maybe they should stick *that* on top of their smug headstands—

But I restrained myself. I had learned long ago that if you felt pressed to declare your achievements in an aggrieved and dramatic tone, that was probably a sign that you should do nothing of the kind.

So I stayed quiet, and spent the rest of the class failing, moment by moment, to achieve all but two of the ridiculous poses all the other women in the class struck and held for ages. When it came time to relax against my mat and meditate, I found my mind was empty of just about everything except a burning need to leap up and start kicking people with my shaking, aching muscles. Or regale them with my professional achievements. Both very mature impulses.

Oh, and vivid images of Bronwen's body—which I had now seen in almost every conceivable position (and some previously inconceivable ones)—intertwined with Matt Cheney's. The dark ink of his dragon tattoo figured prominently.

When Bronwen announced that the meditation period had ended, and said something that sounded vaguely Eastern, I opened my eyes and glared at the ceiling. I felt as if I'd actually walked in on her and Matt, thanks to my treacherous imagination and the fact I'd seen her legs bent behind her head more than once in the past hour.

Raine alit from her meditation looking truly refreshed, even renewed. She arched her back and smiled at me.

I had to actually bite my tongue to keep from growling.

"Well done, Bronwen," Raine called toward the front of the room.

Bronwen bowed her head slightly, and shot me an arch look from beneath her lashes.

I am better than you, her smile said. Loudly, I thought.

"Great class," I managed, with an insincere smile of my own.

The only time in my life I had ever felt more like a sulky thirteen-year-old, I reflected in that moment, was when I actually *was* a sulky thirteen-year-old.

Raine and Bronwen exchanged a series of deeply unconvincing *namastes*, which I thought made it perfectly clear that they loathed each other, and then Raine tucked her hand in mine and tugged me away.

"I love that class," Raine told me as we emerged into the cleansing Berkeley sunshine. She cast out a hand, as if she might at any moment begin singing. "It makes me feel so *alive* and *connected*."

I slid my sunglasses onto my face.

"It was fun," I lied.

"I get the sense you're not really into yoga," Raine said as if I hadn't even attempted to be polite. "I have to tell you, I can't imagine being creative without it. It's how I refill the well."

I blinked. I had never really considered the inspirational properties of yoga. I'd simply lusted after certain superstars and the bodies they swore came from yoga practice with little dietary restriction, a claim I'd long found suspicious. I worried this shallowness was evidence that Raine was right and I lived a tiny, tiny life.

"I don't have much time for yoga." I found this a lame excuse at best. So I tried to make it all about work. "Between rehearsals and practice."

"You poor thing." Raine tucked her arm through mine. "It must be terrible, all that pressure. I remember what a wreck you were about the whole orchestra thing. I'm a little bit surprised you decided to go that route. It's not what I expected from you, after all the things you said about it that summer."

By *that summer*, of course, she meant the summer I was so in love with Matt that had he announced he wanted to spend the rest of his life creating music with found objects on the beach, I would have packed my bathing suit without comment, headed for the Atlantic, and set up shop on the Jersey Shore. But I didn't know how much she knew about that summer. I assumed that *of course* Matt must have told Raine. Except what if he hadn't? I had no way of knowing without directly asking, and somehow I couldn't bring myself to do it.

"It was a rough summer," I said noncommittally.

"I remember how angry you were that you'd spent all that time preparing to do one thing," Raine said, musing. "You could only do the one thing, and what if they wouldn't let you do it?"

It was also the summer directly after my years at the conservatory, and after four years of auditions and orchestras, I'd been feeling a little rebellious. I'd complained about the tyranny of it all. A lot.

"Lucky for me, they let me," I said, grinning.

"Do you feel lucky?" she asked, tilting her head to the side and studying me.

With that, I felt last night's strange insecurity about my life creep back in. Even though, again, she hadn't said anything directly to make me paranoid. Had she?

"You're not suggesting that I shouldn't have tried out for

an orchestra chair, are you?" I asked with a little laugh. "Mom must have mentioned that I've been playing in the Second Symphony. You know, professionally."

Raine looked at me. Her gaze was almost sympathetic. It swept from my (undoubtedly lank) hair to the soles of my feet, taking in my grubby T-shirt and baggy track pants. Instantly, I felt the way I had when I was thirteen. I'd been such a painful dork, all braces and red hair I didn't know what to do with. And Raine had been nearly twenty, and so impossibly, easily gorgeous. I remembered her as a ray of light. Next to her I'd felt *too much*. Too tall, too klutzy, too silly, too ugly. And if I'd needed that point underlined, there was always Matt Cheney right there with her. Back then, he'd been practically feral. And Raine's shadow. I'd dreamed of possessing even a scrap of the grace they'd both worn like skins.

Standing on a sidewalk in Berkeley, I found myself feeling exactly the same way I'd felt then. And it was just as awful. Maybe there were downsides to spending more time with big sisters. Age thirteen seemed to factor a little too prominently.

I looked past her and saw Lucas sitting on the patio of the coffeehouse. He had his paper spread out before him and was propping his chin up with his fists. He looked scruffy and delicious, and I felt a rush of longing for the simple pleasure of touching him, feeling his skin beneath my hands. Falling into him and becoming my real self again. My adult self. As if he was my reward for *not* being thirteen anymore.

Then I noticed that Raine had followed my gaze, and

that she'd turned that odd look of hers on Lucas. She turned back to face me and reached out to squeeze my arm.

Lucas looked up and saw us. A smile crept across his mouth, and I smiled back. Then I turned to find my sister watching me.

"I don't know how to answer you," she said softly, letting her shoulders rise and fall. Her eyes were big and, worse, sincere. "I just had bigger dreams for you, Courtney. I hope that's not out of line to say."

chapter eleven

Lucas got up early on Monday morning, and prepared for a day in the office doing his business mogul thing. I woke up enough to give him a kiss and a sleepy promise to be safe, and then fell back against the pillows. I slept for a few more hours, and only woke up when I accidentally rolled over and found myself squinting in the sunshine pouring in through the big window at the foot of the bed.

I ran a bath and soaked myself for a good hour before I accepted the fact that I was in a bit of a mood, and likely to remain that way. I decided it was because it was my last full day in San Francisco and I had no plans. Raine had been very noncommittal about her schedule, which stung, but was understandable since she hadn't been expecting me. It also meant I was on my own. I climbed out of the tub, wiped off the bubbles, and got dressed. I had no idea what to do with myself, so I figured I might as well enjoy the fact that I was in the best walking city in the nation, according to everybody I met. Why not...walk?

Cargo pants, a tank top, a sweatshirt, and I was ready to go. I grabbed my iPod and set out.

I wandered down to the water and headed aimlessly along the piers. I could see a big bridge stretching across the bay. As it was not red, I felt very knowledgeable and identified it as *the other* bridge.

My head was spinning a little bit. Make that a lot. I decided my choice of music wasn't helping, and spun my iPod dial away from Neko Case singing about floods and toward my go-to Mood Enhancer: Vivaldi. Specifically, Vivaldi as interpreted by Yo-Yo Ma and his gorgeous baroque cello. I hit play, and let the smooth beauty of his mastery of our common instrument sweep me into its lush embrace.

Eventually, I turned right into the downtown part of the city on Market, and followed along that road for ages. I walked and walked. There were tall buildings and busy shops. People, cars, the rush and clatter of the city all around me, and Vivaldi in my ears. After a long while, I saw the rainbow flags flying and figured I was in the Castro. Not long after that, I began to wind my way up into the hills, the cello urging me along, forcing my steps, around and around, until I found myself at the pinnacle.

It had taken me almost four hours, but I had walked across the city. I was on Twin Peaks, and could look back at Market Street, which I'd followed almost the whole way in from the waterfront. My feet ached, but I felt a sort of exhilaration, too. I switched off my iPod and looked at the city spread out at my feet. To my right, the way I'd come. To my left, Alcatraz glittered in the bright water near the famous dark red bridge.

Finally, I let myself wonder again if my sister was right. If my life was supposed to be bigger. Better.

Because I knew where she was coming from, after all. That was what made her words echo so loudly in my head. Six years ago, I'd been sick unto death of classical music. Not the music itself—which would, I imagined, thrill me deep in my soul for the rest of my life, that was just how I was wired—but everything that went along with wanting a career in classical music. The neuroses, the fighting for position, the pettiness, the uncertainty.

Matt Cheney had been like the antidote to all that. He alone could ward off all the boys I'd known, and the dreams they had, of seats on Big Five Orchestras, solo careers, recording contracts, and so on. Everyone I knew had the same fantasies. Matt alone could propose I do something completely different and, with a crook of his mouth, make the unknown seem so appealing.

Six years ago, Matt Cheney had left for an entirely different world, and I'd been too afraid to go with him.

I'd wanted to. That whole, hot summer I'd dreamed of the places we'd go, the music we'd make. Matt with his guitar and me with my cello. But when he'd announced that he and Raine were leaving, I'd balked.

California, he'd said, as if we were already in the middle of a fight, while I was still caught up on the "leaving" part. *Tonight.*

What? I'd dreamed about how we would dance at Norah's wedding. The band had been playing a slow number inside at the reception, and I'd never danced with someone I loved before. I wanted, finally, for everyone to realize what was going on between us. That I didn't have some schoolgirl's crush on him. That this was real.

But Matt hadn't wanted to dance. He'd wanted to go to California.

You heard me. He hadn't looked at me; he'd looked across the grass of the country club lawn toward the trees that surrounded the lake. *I've had enough of this place. I hate this town, and everything in it.*

I'd wanted to remind him that I was in this town, but I was terrified he'd already taken that into account. It had been as if I'd forgotten how to breathe.

I don't know what to say, I'd said instead.

He'd looked up then, and had scarred me with that fierce glare of his.

You said plenty right there, he'd retorted.

And I'd never discovered what he meant by that, because I'd never had a chance to ask him. Because inside, the band stopped playing, and Raine's slurred, drunken voice commanded the mike. We'd heard it even through the glass doors, shut tight to keep in the air-conditioning.

Oh, no, I'd whispered, far more worried about Norah's reaction in that moment than about Matt or what he'd said.

I could talk to him later, I remembered telling myself.

But there never was any *later,* I thought now, taking a deep breath and staring out at the city that could have been mine, if I'd been brave enough six years ago. Raine had staggered from her drunk, insulting speech to the gift table and after she'd splintered it, Matt had taken her home. He and I had exchanged only a few more sentences out in the parking lot, and by morning, the two of them were gone. I wouldn't see them again until I rang their doorbell six years later.

Who would I have been if I'd come with them? I wondered, letting the breeze caress my face, staring out across the sweep of hill and valley to the bay encircling the city like a hug. What would my life have turned out to be if I'd escaped the East Coast and come out here?

I couldn't imagine that other, lost life. The one in which Matt and I stayed together, and I'd thrown my loyalty in with Raine instead of Norah. Other questions followed: What if I'd never known my nephew? What if I'd stayed out of touch all this time? What if everything I'd ever known was inverted?

Would I have stayed in love with Matt? If I had, I didn't think I would have thrown myself into my playing the way I had when he left. And so I wasn't sure I would have bumped up my skills the way I had, which meant I wouldn't have found my seat on the Second Symphony.

Which meant I wouldn't have met Dennis, the violinist, who'd invited me to his sister's party that night. The party where I'd looked up from stuffing my face with cheese to find a gray-eyed, latter-day Viking laughing at me from across the table. He'd offered me a cracker and changed everything.

What would my life be like if I'd never met Lucas?

If I hadn't let Matt become the One Who Got Away?

As if I expected the city to answer, I waited there at the summit of Twin Peaks for a long time.

San Francisco was like a song to me. I felt its melody humming in my veins, coursing through my blood, getting stuck in my brain. I wanted nothing more than to keep on singing it, until I *became* it somehow, or it became me.

I felt as if I should have started singing it six years ago.

*   *   *

Heading back down was harder, for some reason, and not only because I'd stiffened up a little bit. I put on some Hem and let the folksy/country blend of their melodies transport me. I realized I was starving, so at the bottom of the hill I wandered until I found a coffeehouse in the Castro and snacked on a pastry and some strong, bitter coffee. Then I hailed a cab and collapsed in the backseat.

I checked my voicemail on the ride back across the city. Three calls from Verena with demands for information. She hadn't liked my cryptic text message: Yoga class w/ Raine and evil contortionist Bronwen. One call from Lucas at around noon, wondering what I'd decided to do with myself all day and telling me he was stuck with work people for dinner.

I was feeling a little bit blue by the time the taxi pulled up in front of my hotel. I handed the driver some cash and then staggered toward the entrance, my legs protesting every step.

I wasn't prepared for the burst of activity when I stepped up to the door. A scrum of businessmen in severe suits burst through the glass doors, congratulating one another at top volume, so I had to either dive to the side or stand and be mowed down. I chose the former. This sort of thing happened, I knew, when I'd been lost in my own iPod bubble too long. The real world tended to feel like an implosion once I could hear it again. I was never prepared for how intrusive it felt with my earbuds out.

I avoided tripping into a plant, skirted a selection of

valets, and was preparing to make another run at the door when I stopped dead.

Because Matt Cheney was standing on the other side of the pack of businessmen, those absurd eyes fixed on me, waiting for me to notice him.

It turned out I wasn't prepared for him, either.

I swallowed, and it seemed as if doing so was more difficult than it should have been.

"What are you doing here?" I demanded, walking over to where he lounged against a pillar, no doubt giving the nearby attendants respiratory distress. "Where's Raine?"

"Sometimes," he drawled, "I even go out on my own."

Since this was exactly what he'd said to me—in response to the same series of questions—on that May night when he'd appeared at my mother's house to see me, thus starting off the entire heartbreaking chain of events six years ago, I'd be lying if I said my heart didn't clutch a little bit in my chest.

I remembered that other night with perfect clarity. I remembered that Raine had been away somewhere, and I'd been cranky about that because it meant Matt wouldn't come by as often. It had been raining that night, but still hot, a harbinger of the sweaty summer to come. I'd been wearing cutoff shorts and a green T-shirt. I remembered the exact shade of the T-shirt since I'd bought it precisely because its color reminded me of the way Matt's eyes gleamed when he laughed. I remembered how the bricks in my mother's front hall felt cool beneath my bare feet. I remembered that I'd been stringing my bow and so held it in my right hand, like a weapon.

But more than that, I remembered Matt.

I remembered how the water clung to him, coursing over his T-shirt and jeans. His hair stuck to his head, somehow making him brighter by contrast. It was as if he brought the night with him when I opened the door, the rain dancing against the hot street beyond, the crackle of thunder in the distance. He'd grinned at me, and it had made my spine tingle all along its length, from neck to rear.

Want to take a walk? he'd dared me then.

And look what had happened.

I snapped back into the here and now.

"Thanks for the flashback," I said stiffly. "Is that why you came?"

"Is that why *you* came?" he threw right back at me.

"What are you talking about?"

"You left the bar the other night without even saying good-bye. Raine says you're going back home tomorrow." He raised his hands and then let them drop. "So that's it? You wanted to rub your life in my face? You wanted to make sure I was still hurting?"

I felt the scream I'd suppressed in the bar surge back toward my throat, and clamped it down with every bit of strength I possessed.

"You were the one who left," I hissed at him. "Remember?"

"What I remember is how hard you didn't try to find me," Matt said bitterly. "You didn't even call. Your appearance on my doorstep was great, Courtney, but it would have been a little bit more meaningful six years ago."

"I don't understand this conversation." I was completely confused, in fact. Was he trying to tell me I should have chased after him? Was that what he'd wanted? I sucked in a breath. "If you'd wanted me to follow you, you could have called me. I didn't go anywhere. I was in the exact same place you left me. All you had to do was dial a number."

"And have your fiancé answer?" Matt's mouth twisted. "No thanks."

"I grieved for you for *years*," I threw at him. I felt as if I were yelling, but it came out a whisper. "How dare you stand here acting like it wasn't *enough* somehow!"

"Well, you seem to have gotten over me quickly enough," Matt pointed to the ring on my finger. "It looks like everything turned out really well for you. Maybe you should thank me."

I willed myself not to cry. I'd cried over him for years. I never wanted to cry over him again.

"I loved you more than I've ever loved anyone else in my life," he told me then. My resolve not to shed any tears took another serious hit.

"What am I supposed to say to that?" I asked him. "And what does it matter now?" The worst part was, I wasn't even sure if I believed him.

No, that wasn't the worst part. The worst part was, I *wanted* to believe him.

"It matters, Courtney."

His attitude was beginning to make me mad. The casual observer might have missed the fact that he was the one who'd done the leaving, not me.

"The only thing that has ever mattered to you is Raine,"

I pointed out. "You chose her. So don't tell me how much you loved me."

Matt made an angry sort of noise.

"It's not like that with Raine, and you know it. She's my family."

"She's *my* family," I reminded him. "And you took her away from me."

"I didn't take anything," he retorted. "Raine made her own choices, just like you did."

He held my gaze for a timeless, angry breath, and then he broke away as if he couldn't stand to be near me for one more moment. He walked off into the mist, like this were a movie and he was the hero.

I stared after him for much longer than I should have.

chapter twelve

The next morning, Lucas and I jolted awake to the alarm and began the unpleasant process of packing to go home. I attempted to shove our clothes into bags that seemed to have shrunk over the long weekend, while Lucas tried to convince his clients that they didn't need him to come in again before we headed back east.

We were both unsuccessful.

Lucas left for the office, and I continued packing. By the time I'd dragged our bags downstairs to the front desk and checked us out, I was feeling somewhat aggrieved. I shoved the claim ticket for our luggage into the pocket of my jeans and set out to find Raine for our final meeting.

She'd told me to meet her by the fountain at Justin Herman Plaza, which had worried me slightly. What if I couldn't find the correct fountain? What if I missed my last chance to really talk with my sister? What if that horrible yoga class was the sum total of our time together?

I walked across the concrete plaza, making my way through the groups of people already clustered there. I looked around for a fountain, expecting something glorious and inspiring like the fountains along the steps of the Philadelphia Museum of Art. All I saw was a huge structure that looked like cement tinker toys thrown haphazardly together. I'd walked by it before and assumed it was just more San Francisco public art.

Of which there was plenty, in both human and other forms.

Today, I noticed that there was also water in the gigantic structure, some of it cascading from a height. This, I would bet, probably qualified it as a fountain.

I ventured closer, taking in the extreme urban look of the sculpture. If by *urban* I meant *ugly*. It looked like a jumble of upended pieces of other broken things, and made me think about earthquakes. In California, home of the earthquake. It would not have been my choice for the centerpiece of a high tourist area.

I went over and sat on one of the wide concrete sides, near the water. I soaked in the cool breeze and the sun, and thought about sticking my feet in the water. I refrained, but only because I didn't feel like wrestling my boots off my feet.

I wasn't sure I was ready to go home. I believed that this city was magical. That it sang to me. And it seemed to me that once you happened upon magical places you should stay there, happily ever after. I wasn't sure why characters in the fantasy novels I read were forever battling to return to what they knew. They already knew it—what mystery could it hold? Maybe, if I stayed in San Francisco, I would discover who I was really meant to be.

"There you are!" Raine sounded exasperated, as if I'd

been hiding, right there in plain view of everyone who entered the plaza. I looked up at her.

"Hi," I said. I blinked. "Uh...were you painting something?"

My sister was wearing paint-splattered white overalls and a bandana on her head. This outfit only made her look adorable, like she was some kind of house-painting mascot. She wrinkled her nose at me.

"I'm experimenting with watercolor," she said. "You can't imagine how frustrating it can be to switch media. It can be super rewarding, obviously, but there's such a learning curve. I'm really having to trust the Universe."

"Yeah," I said, trying hard to sound like I, too, routinely put my trust in *the Universe*.

"Come on," she said, holding out her hand as if I were still small. "Let's get some coffee."

"It's too bad Lucas had to work again," Raine said as we sat on a bench outside the Ferry Building with our drinks. "I feel like I barely got to talk to him."

"This was a business trip for him." I defended him automatically, and then wondered why I felt I needed to defend him at all. "I'm sure he wished he was on vacation, too." I smiled at her. "We'll have to come back when we can both spend more time out here."

Raine rolled her white cardboard cup between her palms. I watched her for a long moment, mesmerized, which felt comfortable. It was so familiar.

"Our engagement party is next month," I continued,

looking away from her hands. "I was kind of hoping you'd come home for it." My ring seemed to catch in the California sun then. I couldn't tear myself away from it. "I know it's a long way to come for a party but, I don't know, I thought maybe we could look at it as a dress rehearsal."

"A dress rehearsal?" Raine sounded amused.

"I'd rather not have a repeat of Norah's wedding, if I can help it." I felt myself flush a little bit. "Not that I'm saying it would happen that way, or anything."

"Norah and I have a lot of bad blood between us," Raine said, as if mulling it over. "She has a *jet black aura*, Courtney. I'm not making that up."

"I really want to bury the hatchet," I said. "No one's saying we have to be the Partridge family. But I thought maybe you could do it for me. As, you know, a gift or something."

Raine was quiet for a long moment, long enough that I began to feel embarrassed that I'd asked her in the first place. I concentrated on the blue of the sky and told myself only good things could happen beneath it.

"What does Norah think about my prodigal return?" she asked eventually.

"I haven't exactly asked her."

"Like that would stop her from sharing her opinion."

"I don't think she's delighted by the prospect, if you want to know the truth." I shrugged. "But why does it matter?"

"I'm not sure it does," Raine said noncommittally.

There was another long silence. I wouldn't have minded so much, I told myself, except time was slipping away and I had to catch a plane.

"I'm glad I got to see you again," I said then. I snuck a glance sideways. "I missed you, you know." I could hear the uncertainty in my voice, and hated it.

"I'm glad I got to see you, too," Raine said. She flicked me an arch sort of look. "Maybe next time you come to San Francisco it will actually be to see me. And not..." She shrugged as if enjoying a joke. "Other people."

"I didn't come to see Matt!" I was appalled. "How can you think that? I didn't!"

"Of course you didn't," she soothed me. "Don't worry, Courtney. I don't blame you. He's Matt Cheney. These things happen."

To her, I was still the kid with the crush. It was so infuriating, I nearly screamed.

"I wanted to see *you*," I told her, my voice as even as I could make it. "I had no idea he'd be here. You're my *sister*." I waved a hand in front of us, taking in the beautiful morning and the bridge in the distance. "And I really wanted to see San Francisco. It's so beautiful here."

"It is," Raine said, but she sounded almost sad. She shrugged and looked around before looking back at me. "But it's just a city, Courtney. Prettier than some, sure." She wrinkled her nose a little bit as the breeze picked up. "Six years is a long time no matter where you are."

"Let's make sure it's not another six years before we see each other again," I suggested, trying to lighten the mood. I looked at my watch and swore. "I have to go," I said helplessly. "I have to get to the airport."

Raine looked at me for a long moment. I thought she

might say something—about the years we'd been apart, or about the future, but she didn't.

Instead, she leaned over and kissed me soundly on the cheek, like she was dispensing her blessing.

"Oh, Courtney," she said in her sweetest voice. "I missed you, too."

And then it was as if everything went into hyperdrive.

I got to my feet. We hugged good-bye. I took one last look at my sister's face. Then I was racing back to the hotel, where Lucas was already waiting in the lobby.

"Cutting it a little close, don't you think?" he asked. In a tone that might have started a fight, but we didn't have any time for that.

"Let's just get on the road," I said.

"Wait a minute. Are you all right? You look…"

"I'm just tired," I said, warding him away with my hand. "I'm fine. Are you ready?"

"Let's go," he said.

Soon enough, we were in a taxi and on our way to the airport, where everything was *rush* and then wait, *rush* and then wait, until we found ourselves wedged into our economy seats at the back of the plane.

I took the window seat. Lucas took the middle, because, he said, he viewed air travel as an opportunity to catch up on his sleep. Since I was incapable of sleeping in any form of moving vehicle, be it on land, air, or sea, I needed something to amuse myself with. Even a view.

I felt as if I should protest when the plane pulled back from the gate. Stage a riot, start screaming; anything to get off the plane and back into San Francisco. But causing a scene was likely to get me thrown in jail, not delivered to my hotel room. I stayed quiet.

Lucas put his hand on my leg as the plane began to taxi down the runway. He tilted his head back. Within seconds, he was fast asleep and could, I knew, remain so for the duration of our trip across the country. It was already evening in Philadelphia. It would be the middle of the night when we arrived.

I kept a vigil as the plane took off. I thought I owed the life I might have led at least that much attention.

San Francisco disappeared, and then California, and the expanse of the country opened up before me, dragging me further and further into the dark.

chapter thirteen

We staggered into our stuffy apartment well after midnight, laden down with our bags and that stale airline smell, and collapsed across our bed without bothering to unpack a thing. The kittens celebrated our return by pouncing on our feet, swiping at us with their sharp claws, and then purring with their whole bodies and nuzzling into our necks when we lay down. Norah had obviously kept them well fed and in good spirits in our absence. Just one more task she completed to perfection, about which I was destined to feel guilty. She was good like that.

It was hard to maintain the level of gloominess I'd picked up during our flight home with two acrobatic and vocal furry animals leaping around the apartment. I was giggling without meaning to, as the kittens broke off from expressing their displeasure with us only to attack each other ferociously.

"Home sweet home," Lucas said, nudging the ball of angry kittens aside with his foot. They squalled in protest and pounced on the offending foot—in tandem.

I don't think I moved again until the next morning,

when I woke up just long enough to watch Lucas swing out of bed and head for his office. Groaning, I pulled the covers over my head and went back to sleep.

Much later, I stretched languidly and reminded myself that I was still on vacation. Though our trip to San Francisco had seemed to take whole years, it had actually been only a few days.

A few strange days I was having trouble assimilating.

I crawled out of bed and shuffled down the hall. I could hear Lucas hard at work behind his office door, so I just went into the kitchen and made myself some coffee. I padded out through the living room and over to my music stand and cello case. Putting my mug down on the nearby table, I bent to open the case and run my palm across the gleaming wood of my cello. Something eased inside my chest, the way it always did when I touched my instrument, even just to say hello. I closed the case, grabbed my coffee, and made my way through the swishing kitten tails to the small desk where I kept my laptop.

I settled down at my computer and checked my e-mail. Sure enough, there were no less than ten e-mails from Verena, each more over-the-top than the last. She was outraged that I'd left her hanging. I had better hurry up and tell her what had happened in San Francisco or she refused to be held accountable for her actions. Though, she warned me, they would be *drastic indeed.*

Of course, she used far more exclamation points and deeply unsuitable language.

I wasn't sure exactly why I hadn't called her or anyone else while away. I thought it had something to do with wanting to surround myself with San Francisco and keep myself safe inside that little bubble for as long as I could, so I could entertain all those *what if* notions. No wonder I'd been a little mournful to leave and get back to real life. Who liked leaving the safety of a bubble, particularly when it featured as many glorious views as San Francisco? I was just getting ready to call Verena and give her the full, pierced-bubble update when the house phone rang.

Norah.

I sat there for a long moment, staring at her name and number as it flashed on the caller ID. I could imagine how this conversation would go. And the truth was, I wasn't at all sure I was ready to hear her comments about Raine, which she had no doubt been preparing the whole time we were gone. I knew with perfect clarity that if I picked up the phone, Norah would upset me.

But the guilt was too strong. And after all, she was the reason we'd come home to find the house clean rather than overtaken by cats. And our cats were known to protest-poop in the middle of the bathroom floor when they didn't like our absence, so who knew what she'd had to deal with?

More to the point, I worried there was something wrong with me for feeling this mix of guilt and foreboding every time her name came up on caller ID, *especially* after all the things she did for me. What kind of sister was I?

I snatched up the receiver on the eighth and final ring before the answering machine picked up.

"Hi!" I cried with far more enthusiasm than I felt. "How are you? Thank you so much for taking care of the cats. We had *such* a great time in California!"

I didn't wait for Norah to respond; I launched into an animated description of the wonders of San Francisco. I talked about the hills, and my thighs, which would never be the same. I raved about the sun and the fog in equal measure. I went on and on, and it was easy to do because I meant every word I said. What I did not do was mention our prodigal sister or my encounters with Matt Cheney.

"I'm glad you had fun," Norah said when I'd wound to a close, having outdone myself with a lurid description of sourdough bread with fresh butter.

"What a great city!" I cried, no doubt exhausting us both with the force of my enthusiasm.

"Yes, well, I'm actually on campus now, between meetings. I just wanted to see if you were still interested in Family Dinner tomorrow," Norah said. There was a definite stiffness in her tone.

"What do you mean?"

"Exactly what I asked," Norah said tartly.

"Um..." I rubbed at my face. "I've never not been interested in Family Dinner before."

This was, strictly speaking, untrue. But my not being necessarily interested in Family Dinners had never prevented me from attending them. Even when Norah got tricky and moved them to Friday night for no apparent reason.

Again, I felt a twinge. Maybe when Raine had said she had bigger dreams for me, she'd meant than *this*. Surely, extraordinary people didn't suffer through Family Dinners every week, fuming and seething but still going back for more. Surely they were too busy being extraordinary.

On the other hand, maybe it was only the extraordinary people who could deal with the trauma of it all.

"Who knows what might have changed while you were gone," Norah was saying in her tartest voice.

"Nothing's changed as far as I know." It was the right answer as far as Norah was concerned. I wished I knew if it was actually true, in a global sense. It would take a lot more thinking.

"Well, fine," she retorted.

"Fine," I said.

"*Fine*," she said, her voice hurt, and she slammed down her phone.

And when I hung up a moment later, awash in guilt and formless anger, I realized that I was destined to feel about thirteen years old no matter which side of the country I was on.

Apparently, all it required was a conversation with one of my sisters.

The tension around Norah's dinner table the following evening reminded me of many similar dinners we'd all shared when I really was a teenager. Even Lucas's hand, protectively placed in its usual position on my thigh, failed to make me feel better. Mom was making the sort of light, interesting conversation that floated around the table and didn't require any response. It was a kind of classy chatter I'd seen her wield at any number of charity events when talking to strangers. But it didn't in any way divert attention from the focus of everyone's attention.

Norah was in a rage.

I could tell from the faint pink along the edge of her ears and the tight way she held her lips together when she wasn't speaking.

There were other tells.

The fact that her hair was in a messy sort of ponytail instead of its usual, scrupulous bun. The fact that her eyeglasses were slightly askew on her face. The fact that her eyes literally burned with temper. She'd been terrifyingly quiet ever since we'd entered her house.

With Norah's disapproval hovering over the family like a rainstorm about to drench the room, we were all forced to make insipid conversation while we waited for the inevitable.

"This humidity..." Mom breathed then, as if the weight of the air outside made it too difficult to complete her sentence, all of a sudden. Or, possibly, she didn't want to incur Norah's wrath. No one did, except Raine of course, and she was only at the table in spirit—in the form of Norah's tangible fury. "Summer seems to get worse every year."

"I don't mind it," Phil chimed in, looking up from whatever arcane problem he'd been worrying over in his head. "I grew up in the South. You want to talk *humid*, you should spend some time in a Tennessee July."

"No, thank you," Lucas said with a laugh. "I can barely handle Philadelphia humidity. I think Tennessee would kill me."

I was far more concerned with the possibility that Norah might kill us all, possibly with the force of her glare, though I was afraid to voice that fear. Without looking at her directly, I forked in a mouthful of the chef's salad she'd prepared, and wondered how everyone else could even pretend to care about the humidity with Norah bubbling just beneath the surface.

About five minutes later, she broke.

"I can't believe no one's going to bring up the elephant in the room!" she cried, dropping her fork and letting it clank against the china plate.

"I don't think there's any elephant in the room," Mom said. She said it so dryly that I found myself studying her face for a moment, seized with the sudden radical notion that she was actually teasing Norah.

"Don't be ridiculous, Mom," Norah snapped at her, entirely missing the dry tone. "We're all dancing around the fact that Courtney went to California to see Raine."

Had Mom said something like, "I don't patronize bunny rabbits," like the befuddled father in *Heathers*, I would have known she was having some fun at Norah's huffy expense, but her face remained smooth. I found myself entertaining the idea that there were whole secret worlds behind her smooth exterior. It was unsettling, to say the least.

"Well?"

I was studying Mom, so it took me a moment to realize that Norah had turned her attention to me. I jerked a little bit in my seat when I felt her angry gaze on me.

"Tell us everything," Norah demanded bitterly. "Go ahead."

I opened my mouth and then closed it.

"I was happy to see her," I said finally. I met Norah's

stare, feeling mutinous. Mostly because I felt guilty, which in turn made me mad. Why *shouldn't* I see Raine if I wanted to? "I'm sorry if that upsets you."

"I can't believe you actually did this," she said, and her voice was trembling. I couldn't tell if it was from rage or pain, or both. "But I was the one picking up cat shit in your apartment while you were doing it, so maybe the real problem here is me."

"All I did was visit her," I said with a calm I didn't feel. "Talk to her."

"And what did she say? Oh wait, let me guess. It had something to do with Raine, Raine, and more Raine." She pursed her lips with distaste. "And oh yes, I'm the villain, somehow, who *drove* her to ruin my wedding. Right?"

I didn't like the fact that she was on target with that. I wanted her to be wrong about Raine. Which I thought she was, it was just that the surface looked a whole lot like what she'd described.

"What does it matter?" I asked, avoiding the question. "The fact is, she's doing well. And so are we. Can't we be happy about that?"

"I'm thrilled." The acid in Norah's voice could have peeled paint.

"We just talked," I said with a sigh, wishing she would see it as an olive branch. "That's all it was."

"That is *not* all it was!" Norah cried out, and what hurt me was the genuine pain I could hear in her voice.

Lucas's hand was back in place on my leg, emanating heat and quiet support. I took a deep breath, steadying myself for whatever she was going to throw at me.

So I was surprised when my mother's voice cut in instead.

"Norah," she said, her voice unfamiliar in its sudden crispness. "Let's not ruin a lovely meal."

A gunshot across the dining room table couldn't have produced more shock or awe. Mom usually suffered through Norah's attacks, big or small, with resignation. The way she had the night Lucas and I had gotten engaged. This was...*not the same*, that was for sure.

I stared at my mother. A quick look around confirmed that everyone else was staring at her, too. Norah, in particular, was fighting off shock.

Mom, for her part, looked unperturbed. She was the only person at the table who continued to eat as if nothing had happened.

"Mom," Norah said after a few moments had passed. "What are you—"

"This is neither the time nor the place," my mother said, again in that crisp tone, which brooked no disapproval and which I didn't think I'd ever heard before. Not directed at Norah, certainly.

"But—"

"Lucas," my mother interrupted her, ruthlessly. She gazed across the table, as if at a gentle afternoon tea. "What business did you have in San Francisco? Had you been there before?"

I felt Lucas tense slightly beside me, but he gave no other outward sign. Dutifully, he began talking about his business, for all the world as if he thought his Internet security work was a rational segue.

At the head of the table, Norah sat still, frozen into place. When it became clear that Mom wasn't kidding, and that the conversation had continued on despite her obvious fury, Norah quite evidently didn't know what to do. I watched out of the corner of my eye as she swallowed a few times, then carefully placed her napkin next to her plate. Her fingers were trembling. I didn't know why that made me want to hug her, especially when I knew that she was so prickly that if I tried, she'd take my head off. Or maybe take a swing at me the way she had once or twice when we were kids.

"Excuse me," she said in a small voice that tried hard to be dignified, and then she rose from the table and disappeared into the kitchen. Moments later, Phil excused himself and went after her.

Lucas and I exchanged a quick glance, and I braced myself for the sound of crockery hitting the wall—but there was nothing.

And I could swear my mother looked triumphant, somewhere in there, beneath that same smooth surface.

chapter fourteen

"What the hell just happened?" I demanded of Lucas when we were finally on our way home. I swung my arms as we walked down Germantown Avenue, in a vain attempt to generate a breeze. "I can't believe I witnessed that!"

"I have to say, I didn't think your mother had it in her," Lucas agreed. He laughed. "I've waited a long time to watch somebody put Norah in her place."

"That's not fair," I said quickly, thinking of the way Norah's fingers had shook as she'd excused herself from the table. And also about her *jet black aura*, which I hadn't seen but had started to imagine hovering around her when I thought of her. Which made me feel like a horrible person. Which did nothing to dispel the image.

"It is fair," Lucas said at once, snapping me out of imagining Norah's aura, whatever color it might be. "I think everyone's perfectly clear on how she feels about Raine. It's unfair of *her* to keep throwing fits. You have just as much right to like Raine as Norah does to dislike her."

"I hate when she's sad," I muttered, shoving my hands in the back pockets of my jeans. The ones I very much wished

I hadn't worn, since the late afternoon was unpleasantly warm, and no one needed to be quite so *aware* of the circumference of her thighs. "Particularly when I know perfectly well I'm the reason she's sad. I just want to fix it."

"It's not up to you to fix everyone," he said.

"I guess." I felt that even if it weren't up to me, I should make more of an attempt. What I couldn't figure out was how to do what I wanted while also trying to keep from hurting other people's feelings. Why did every choice that involved my family seem to pit those things against each other?

I asked Lucas.

"Because it's family," he replied with a snort of laughter. "That's what families do."

I didn't feel that answer was at all sufficient.

"I don't know," I said noncommittally, because I didn't have an argument against the answer, either.

"I do know," Lucas said. "I don't like to mention it, you know, because it's up to you to handle your family however you see fit, but you put up with a lot of shit from these people. You know that, right?"

"Norah has this thing—this justifiable thing—about Raine, and my wanting to see Raine clearly exacerbated it." I waved my hand in the air in a sort of loopy gesture, as if that could explain my sisters.

"Norah has a thing about Raine, Raine has a thing about Norah..." Lucas shrugged. "Where are you?"

"You can see how different they are," I said, not answering his question. "Norah gives lectures on the Industrial Revolution and Raine exhibits pictures of her vagina on the walls of a bar. Of course they don't get along. I love both of them," I said, to stave off another visual of those pictures, for the love of God. "I'm not an idiot. I know they're both..." I searched for the right word. "Challenging. They both have very strong, very different personalities, and they always have. I guess I'm more like my mother, because I kind of let them have their strong personalities while I did my own thing."

"Except maybe your mother could have put a stop to all this a long time ago, by *not* doing her own thing so much and being a little more involved while you were all fighting this out," Lucas said not unkindly, but firmly. "I'm just saying. Norah thinks she runs things because your mom let her run things for years. It was weird to see her step up and be the mom today. *My* mom lets everyone in a seventy-mile radius know that she's in charge, all the time, and she always has." He made a rueful noise. "Which is one reason why I live outside that radius."

One of the joys of locating a life partner: if you wanted him to be involved in your life, he got to comment on it, too. Even if it was an incisive, unpleasant truth about your family. No one ever mentioned *that* side effect of love and intimacy in the movies.

"Do you want me to say I'm mad at all of them?" I asked him. "Is that what this is about?"

"Hey. I'm on your side here."

"I don't have a side," I told him, trying and failing to keep the cranky out of my voice. "But I am having a wedding. And when I thought about my wedding as a little girl, it didn't include a blood feud between my sisters. I'm having some trouble adjusting."

"You've been back from San Francisco all of two days," Lucas pointed out after a moment. Maybe to let his own crankiness subside, if the snap in his eyes was any clue. "I don't think you're required to have figured out how you feel about stuff just yet."

"What stuff?" I could hear that my voice sounded far sharper than it should have.

Which was when I remembered that in all the hustle and bustle of packing, seeing Raine one last time, and flying back East, I'd somehow forgotten to tell Lucas about Matt's appearance outside our hotel.

I'd meant to. But there'd been so much rushing around and now here we were. I should tell him right now, except how could I bring it up? I'd just denied I had *stuff* to think about, so I could hardly admit there was more stuff than he knew.

Lucas stopped walking and looked at me more closely. The late afternoon sun cast long shadows along the pretty row of houses, and I felt as if he could see inside me to all the dark, ugly places I preferred to hide.

Places shot through with golden threads, one of which was the fact that Matt had said he'd loved me. Even all these years later and long after it mattered, I found I clung to that. How could I possibly tell Lucas that?

"I mean, what stuff are you talking about?" I asked after clearing my throat a little bit. "Specifically."

"I mean, the stuff that has you acting a little bit strangely," Lucas said. "Like now. Specifically."

"I'm not acting strangely," I protested, but sighed when he just looked at me. "I mean, not on purpose."

"And yet." He raised his eyebrows and waited.

"I want to reassure Norah," I said, when that wasn't what I should have said. It happened to also be true, so I ran with it. "But she wants to hear that I hate Raine and want nothing to do with her, and I can't tell her that. What am I supposed to do?"

"I think you should consider giving yourself a break," Lucas said. He put his hands on my shoulders and looked down at me, his face serious. His hands were hot against my skin. "You saw your sister for the first time in six years, which is bound to stir things up. You also saw your ex-boyfriend. Your only other boyfriend, really. I think you'd have to be superhuman or something not to be a little thrown."

I could see that he was deliberately opening up this conversation—giving me a way to talk about Matt without me having to bring him up myself. But I felt that admitting exactly how thrown I was by Matt would somehow be a betrayal, so I looked down at the ground. I knew that this was the perfect moment to tell Lucas what had happened—what Matt had said and how shocked I'd been to discover that I still cared so much about the past.

But I didn't see how I could explain all this to Lucas without also explaining how my traitorous heart had thrilled to the things Matt had said. How those words had been circulating in my head ever since.

I was still trying out possible ways to broach the subject in my head when Lucas leaned forward and kissed me on the forehead.

"Give yourself a break," he advised me. "You don't have to solve your entire family history in one week."

And I knew, right then and there, that I was drawing a line in the sand. I was allowing something new, and potentially dark, into our lives—separating us into a *before* and *after*. It was a wedge between us, and it widened with every second I stayed silent. Maybe it had already happened, back in San Francisco, when he'd gotten back from work so late and I hadn't turned on the light and told him immediately about Matt's appearance and my confusion. But this moment, right here in the sweaty heat of a Chestnut Hill summer afternoon—this was putting the polish on it. This was deliberately not telling him, and I wasn't just letting it happen. I was doing it.

I realized all of this. I knew it. But I said nothing about it to Lucas, and let him lead me home.

Verena, on the other hand, would not be satisfied with anything less than a word-by-word reenactment. And unlike Lucas, she didn't trust me where issues of the Matt Cheney variety were concerned, and would, I knew, keep asking trying questions until I provided her with every last detail. So the following Monday I left Lucas hard at work in front of his computer monitors and set out on the longish walk to her theater. Of course, after my marathon walk in San Francisco, a mere mile or so walk across Philly was nothing.

I arrived at the theater and called Verena to let her know I was downstairs. Then I waited for her around the back, near the stage door. She came bursting through it moments later, laden down with shopping bags and with murder in her eyes.

"I cannot *believe* you didn't call me back, or e-mail me, or acknowledge my existence in any way," Verena threw at me, in lieu of a simple "hello." "What happened to you out there? Did you get sucked into the black hole that is Matt Cheney?"

"Do you want me to tell you what happened?" I asked. "Or do you want to talk about your pain? And not everything is about Matt Cheney, you know."

"Something I've been telling you for the past ten years," she snapped at me. But she visibly shook off her annoyance as I glared at her. She raised her hand in the air, shut her eyes, and straightened her shoulders. Then opened her eyes to look at me. "Go on. Tell me. Really, I want to know."

And so I did. I ignored the fact that she was annoyed. I also ignored the June heat that was sapping the will to live from my bones, and I told her every word that had been said. Everything I'd felt while talking to Matt, and Raine, and even that awful Bronwen. Everything, up to and including Mom's intervention into Norah's tantrum and the fact that I'd elected not to share any of my feelings on most of these subjects with Lucas the night before. No detail was too small, especially when it involved ukuleles or macaroni Hindu gods.

It took a long time. While I talked, Verena led me on a tour of some of her favorite Center City shopping spots, where she proceeded to return the contents of her shopping bags while greeting the employees by name. Verena felt that denying herself the pleasure of shopping constituted cruel and unusual punishment, so she bought anything and everything that caught her fancy. However, she lived on a paltry theater company salary these days, so she rarely kept her purchases. Half the fun, she'd told me once, was returning everything because it was like Christmas twice: once when you bought pretty things, and then when you maintained your pretty credit history.

When I was finished with my story, my throat was a little bit dry, but I felt somewhat better. No wonder Catholics claimed confession was good for the soul. Maybe they were onto something—not that I planned to find out, as I was fairly certain it would make my Jewish ancestors spin in their graves if I so much as considered entering an actual confessional. Verena would have to do.

By this point, we had exhausted most of Verena's admittedly generous lunch hour-and-forty-five-minutes, and were standing in a sluggish Starbucks line.

"Well," Verena said after she'd taken a moment to digest the whole story, "we'll just have to jump over the photo display of Raine's, uh—"

"Vulva," I took pleasure in saying, loud enough to appall the preppy businesswoman in front of us in line, who actually flinched away from us. "The photographs were of her *vulva*."

"—because it turns out I'm not mature enough to discuss it."

"I wasn't mature enough to see it in the first place!" I protested. "I know that I'm supposed to be all down with feminism in all its forms—"

"Oh, spare me," Verena interrupted. "Despite what you might have heard in San Francisco, you can still be a feminist even if you think you could have lived without having your sister's crotch up in your face. I mean, *come on*."

"I think a proper feminist would have thought it was all an act of courage, like that poet woman," I hedged. Not because I suddenly believed in those photos, but because I wanted to believe that Raine had taken them for a reason. A reason beyond the need to shock, as I'd done with the preppy woman. Who was now treating me to a filthy look from behind her not-dark-enough-to-conceal-her-eyes sunglasses.

"I define acts of courage as things that I, a big coward, can't do," Verena said. "And since I *could* take embarrassing pictures and hang them on a wall, though I *would* rather die first, I think it's excluded."

"I don't know," I said, musing more than disagreeing with her. "I mean, there's something to be said for living your life outside the lines, don't you think?"

Verena stared at me for a long moment.

"Is this a joke?" Verena asked finally. "Are you defending those ridiculous pictures?"

"I'm defending Raine's *intention*," I said after thinking about it for a moment.

"Uh-huh." Verena pursed her lips. "Did she change radically? Because that didn't come through while you were talking. It *sounded* like Raine was still the same old attention whore she used to be."

"I think *attention whore* might be a bit too—"

"We're talking about *Raine*, Courtney," Verena said in a withering tone. "Do you remember the first time I met her? I sure do. We were in your house for some weekend away from school and she pranced into your room wearing go-go boots, tap shorts, and no top."

I'd blocked that out, but the image came back to me as Verena spoke.

"I think that was a Halloween costume."

"Does it matter?" Verena shook her head at me. "Most people say hello, but not Raine. Why? Because she feeds off of attention. Always has, always will. Why she didn't take her drama to the stage, where it belongs, the world will never know."

We had made it to the head of the line, saving me from having to reply. We placed our orders with the barista, a young girl with a Technicolor dreamcoat of hair cascading from her scalp like she was some kind of anime heroine. It was so awe-inspiring that I was almost unable to complete my order. Verena and I exchanged looks.

"That takes a level of commitment I just don't have," Verena said, sadly I thought, when we had to search for a table and thus had to stop staring. "I mean, there are at least seven different blonds in there, Courtney. And the entire purple and blue spectrum!"

We found a tiny round table for two up near the windows, so we could gaze out at Walnut Street.

"And aside from everything with Raine, I don't have the slightest idea how to feel about the whole Matt thing," I said after a moment, playing with the oversize straw in my mocha Frappuccino.

Verena snorted. Loudly.

"What?" I asked.

"Here we go," Verena said. "Didn't I tell you this would happen? Didn't I predict it?"

"You were right."

That took the wind out of her sails.

"You were right," I said again with a small shrug, when she only looked at me. "You told me to prepare and I didn't. And it was really, really hard to see him." I shook my head. "Talking to him made me feel like I was crazy. Like he thought I was so young and naïve that I should have magically forgiven him for taking off on me. How could he have believed I was ever that young?"

"You're not crazy," Verena assured me, reaching over to give my hand a squeeze, because she was my best friend even when she wasn't happy with me. "Please. But when he knew you, you were twenty-two. And you know I love you, but you were kind of a young twenty-two."

"I was not *that* naïve." And it was annoying that she insisted otherwise. "No one alive, ever, could be as naïve as you think I was."

"I'm sorry, Court, but you were," Verena said. "And it's not like Matt didn't know that then. Or now, obviously. I hate that he tried to retroactively make you the bad guy." She took a sip of her drink. "Though I'm not exactly *surprised*."

"What do you mean?"

"And you claim you're not naïve." Verena squared her shoulders, and leveled a stern sort of look at me. "Courtney, hello. This is what he does. And this is also what you do—you sit around and agonize over everything he says or does, trying desperately to make it all *mean* something."

"I think it does mean something," I argued.

"I'll tell you what it means," Verena snapped. "It means he's a dick."

I didn't like that at all. I especially didn't like the unpleasant echoes from years before.

"Are you really going to pretend that it's completely abnormal to want to talk about the interaction I had with my first love?" I demanded. "Because I was under the impression that it was pretty much the cornerstone of friendships to talk about upsetting encounters."

"Wanting to talk about the interaction is fine," she replied, throwing me a bone. I felt patronized. "But you're worrying at it like a cat with a chew toy, and that's not leading anywhere good. What did Lucas think about all of this? How did he handle the Matt Cheney Experience?"

"He was fine." I could see that she didn't believe me. "Really, he was. He thought Matt was kind of funny. He wasn't threatened or anything, if that's what you're looking for."

"What I'm looking for is a scenario in which Lucas exterminates Matt Cheney once and for all," Verena said dreamily.

"I always forget how much you hate Matt," I said softly.

"I always forget how much you don't," she shot right back.

We were both quiet for a moment. I clutched my cold Frappuccino in my hand and let the sounds of coffeehouse traffic soothe me. But it wasn't much like music. No sea or pine or California sun. It was just loud Motown music on the speakers, the hum of other conversations, and the loud whir of the espresso machine. And all the things I didn't want to talk about, like static in between.

"You don't have time to worry about this," Verena said after a while, sucking the last of her drink through her straw, noisily. "You have an engagement party to plan, not to mention a wedding. I've allowed you to laze around for months now, but I have every intention of making sure your bridal gown is *stellar*. So prepare yourself."

"How do you even start to find a dress?" I asked. It was a largely rhetorical question, which did not prevent Verena from answering.

"We go to a store and you try on everything in your size while I take illegal pictures with my cell phone on the sly," she said, very matter-of-factly. "I've been practicing."

"I can't deal with a wedding dress." I rubbed at my temples. "I can't deal with a *wedding*. Dealing with this engagement party practically makes me want to break out in hives."

"Those are not the words of a blushing bride-to-be," Verena pointed out as we stood to go. "Is this Raine's influence?"

"I'm not influenced by every stray breeze, Verena," I snapped at her, finally losing my cool. And my volume control. "For God's sake!"

She held up her hands in surrender. Her cheeks flushed to a dull red, like she was forcing herself to remain in control. So who knew what she *wanted* to say.

"I'm sorry" was what she said at last. She cocked her head to the side, and considered me for a second. "But we always go on and on about how controlling Norah is.

When the truth is, I think Raine is equally controlling. She just has a different approach."

That was the part that I kept returning to as I walked toward home.

I had never thought of Raine in that way. It was hard to do so now, but there was something in me that thought Verena was right. I kept going over my time in San Francisco, looking for clues. Raine had, after all, decided where and when we would talk. She'd run that conversation, and when it got uncomfortable she'd ended it. She'd also minimized our contact. Made me take a yoga class, insisted we meet where she wanted to meet. The only difference between Raine and Norah was that I'd *wanted* to do what Raine wanted me to do, for the most part. Was it *controlling* then? Or something else?

Not that it mattered. What mattered was that I was so incredibly naïve and controllable, according to Verena, that everyone took advantage of me. Raine, Matt, Norah. I couldn't help thinking that if I wasn't so malleable, none of these things would be happening.

I didn't think of myself as naïve. But who did? Maybe naïve was like crazy in that way—those who were never thought they were. Unfortunately, that left me with few options for ceasing to be naïve. It was like the wedding stuff—I didn't know where to start. As far as I knew, I couldn't pop into Target to pick up some healthy cynicism and a clue. Of course, I didn't know where to start shopping for my wedding, either, so *as far as I knew* wasn't all that far.

My phone buzzed in my pocket then, a happy diversion. I looked at the display to read BLOCKED ID. This usually meant Verena was calling from her work phone.

"I thought you had to get to work," I said without saying hello, assuming she was calling to apologize for being harsh, as she had been known to do on occasion. Or to discuss the latest photos posted on Go Fug Yourself, which she did far more often.

"Hi, Courtney," Raine sang at me. "Oops, did you think I was someone else?"

"Oh," I said, thrown. Did that sound naïve? I tried to sound stern and tough. "No. I mean, yes, obviously." So much for that. "How are you?"

"You know what?" She laughed a little bit. "I'm good. But I think I owe you an apology."

"You do?" I wished that hadn't come out like a question. It felt like I was proving Verena's point.

"Well," Raine said, "I don't think I showed you how delighted I was to see you again. I'm sorry about that. I guess I was more thrown by your sudden reentry into my life than I wanted to admit."

That had not been what I was expecting. In my memory, Raine had never apologized. She was Raine. She didn't have to. It occurred to me to wonder why that was so, when I'd always felt compelled to apologize for everything, but I brushed it aside.

"I did just show up on your doorstep," I reminded her.

"But it's all fine," she said quickly, her voice kindling with that delight that made me want to listen to her talk forever. "I can make it up to you."

"You can?" I shook my head as if to clear it. What was wrong with me? This was my sister. I was behaving like a kid with a crush—a feeling I remembered vividly and had no need to revisit. "I mean, of course, that you don't have to do anything—"

"I've been meditating on this since you left," Raine interrupted me, gently. And insistently. "And my life coach thinks that I was subconsciously striking out at you because I have so many unresolved issues about home and Norah and Mom and whatever else."

"Huh," I said, hoping that hit the appropriate note of interest or concern, whichever was required. How would I know? *Meditating* and *life coaches* weren't topics that seemed to crop up much in my Philadelphia life.

"So she thinks that the best thing *in the world* I could do is come to your engagement party. And finally confront all my demons!" Raine's voice rang through the phone.

I thought about that for a moment.

"Except maybe my engagement party isn't the best place in the world for you to confront your demons?" Again, I felt that might have sounded more impressive had it emerged from my mouth as a statement.

"Oh, of course not," Raine said, as if that was the silliest thing she'd ever heard. "That's why I'm taking the whole month off!"

"The whole month?" I wanted to be excited, but all I could think was that I'd have to explain this to Norah.

And that if I thought Norah was *already* pissed, this was going to send her through the roof. I didn't want that.

"All of July," Raine confirmed happily. "Isn't that terrific?"

On the other hand, this was what I'd wanted, wasn't it? Both my sisters in attendance at my engagement party as a sort of rehearsal so everyone could get their bad behavior out of the way before the wedding.

Norah would deal, I assured myself. She might even find that this was a good thing. A step she wouldn't take on her own, but the right step to take even so. Because I had to believe that gathering the family together was better than letting it lie splintered. It had to be.

"Yes," I declared, trying it on for size. "It's terrific. I'm really glad you're coming, Raine."

I thought there should have been a soundtrack playing down Locust Street, to underscore the importance of the moment. But there was only the dirt and congestion of the city in the sweltering heat.

"Me, too!" Raine squealed. And then her voice cooled a little bit. "Oh yes," she said, "and one more thing. I'm bringing Matt."

chapter fifteen

I couldn't say that I was *surprised* by Raine's little bomb. I hadn't sat around thinking about whether or not she would come with Matt, if she chose to come at all, but that was probably because I hadn't had time to do so since returning home.

I was forced to admit to myself that on some level, I'd wanted her to bring him. That I'd suspected she would, and had hoped she would—because of those secret, golden threads and because I wasn't ready to let go of them. Of him.

Which made me feel that wedge between me and Lucas widen.

None of which made me happy with myself.

And in case the fact that I wasn't a good person needed underlining, there was my mother's obsession with my wedding to contend with. You know, the wedding that I hadn't planned at all, and here I was almost six months' engaged. It wasn't lost on me that as the bride, I should have been exhibiting an interest in my nuptials *at least* equal to the interest being shown by my mother.

After Mom left me no less than seven voicemails in a three-day period, all with *ideas* for me (translation: action items), I decided that instead of passively lolling around in the air-conditioning in our living room, listening to Lucas work his ass off in his home office, I could be proactive for a change. It had dawned on me in the time since we'd returned from San Francisco that *proactive* was something I didn't do very often, unless it had something to do with my cello. And that perhaps this had something to do with the apparently widespread notion that I was a naïve pushover.

The very least I could do, I figured, was show *someone* that I wasn't that controlled, manipulated child. Why not my mother? Her last voicemail message had dipped a bit too far toward the sarcastic for my liking. *Please call me back if you're interested*, she'd said in that dry tone. She hadn't said, *if you're interested in your own wedding*, because she didn't have to. She was now all about the implication.

Deciding it was time for action, I headed to 30th Street Station the next morning. I got myself a huge coffee at Dunkin' Donuts, fries from McDonald's and only then—properly fortified—was I able to face the newsstand and its wedding magazine section. I didn't comparison shop, I just pulled out one of each. Four magazines in total, weighing in somewhere above twenty-seven pounds. Each.

Sitting on the train on the thirty-minute ride out to my hometown, I flipped through the glossy pages and read up on what a failure of a bride-to-be I was. I should have registered for gifts already. I should have notified my wedding party (possibly via a mock proposal, flower delivery, or tasteful dinner party), begun dress shopping (after identifying which silhouette I felt best flattered my figure and then deciding what the dress of my dreams said about what kind of bride I was), and begun the comparison hunt for a wedding reception site (country club, art gallery, or secluded beach—what your dream venue says about your love). It was clear that I was expected to have thoughts about our wedding ceremony. Religious or secular? Inside or outside? Write our own vows or repeat old ones? Then there were all the things I was supposed to have done/be doing for our engagement, starting with a punishing fitness and beauty regime, neither of which involved the consumption of Dunkin' Donuts or McDonald's. Each magazine featured anemic-looking models striking bizarrely stiff poses, with atrocious hair, so they looked more like grotesquely large insects than glowing brides. This was supposed to inspire me to purchase one of the highly unattractive dresses, many of them festooned with feathers, sequins, or in one case, what looked like an *actual* mermaid tail, complete with scales. Each magazine also presented me with a handy pull-out checklist, thoughtfully broken down by months, as to what I ought to be doing at any given moment. None of which I'd so much as thought about, much less done.

Thinking about it now filled me with panic.

Were these other women aliens? These women who wrote in and described planning processes that read as more complicated and involved than the invasion of Normandy? Did their engagement rings somehow send off some kind of homing beacon that awakened the party-planning Über Bride within? Because if so, my ring clearly wasn't working.

I tried to shake it off, but couldn't. I didn't understand what my problem was. I'd entertained fantasies about getting engaged my whole life. They hadn't been concrete fantasies, but I'd had them. I'd wondered who my husband would be. Every time I'd been to a wedding, I'd wondered what mine would be like. So why wasn't I jumping in, feet first, now that it was finally my turn?

I couldn't answer that question.

I climbed off the train and set off on the five-minute walk to Mom's office, tucked away in the upstairs of one of the pretty buildings on the main street of town. I loved everything about the quiet Main Line town I'd grown up in. I loved the manicured lawns and old Colonial houses, the sound of lawn sprinklers and cicadas in the afternoon air, the solid feel of hundreds of years of history in the ground and Revolutionary War memorials scattered here and there about the town.

And next to that, the more fragile and tempestuous feeling of the Cassel family history, which I also felt settle around me as I walked.

Across town, where the roads started to slope upward into gentle hills that bore no resemblance at all to the hills of San Francisco, was the house where we'd all grown up. It was brick and stucco, cool in the summer and freezing in the winter, and a permanent shrine to my father.

As I walked, I thought about the photographs of my father that covered the surface of every table in the small room we called my mother's sitting room, steps off the

living room. On the wall, a huge abstract painting dominated the room that was filled with his laughing brown
eyes. It was one of my father's three finished paintings.
The other two hung in Raine's old room.

The facts of my father's life were these: he and my
mother eloped when they were both very young and fresh
out of Temple University. They bought a house in a town
near the one where my mother grew up, had a couple of
kids, and lived what seemed to be a perfectly unexcep-
tional life, until my father announced that he needed to
"find himself" and, like so many before him, headed west,
as Raine would do—no doubt in homage—many years
later. Coincidentally, he discovered this need right about
the time my mother announced that she was pregnant
with me.

Dad had headed to Los Angeles with plans to wander up to San Francisco. He'd never gone north, and he'd
never come home. Eight months after he'd gone, when,
according to one of my mouthier aunts, Mom had been
just about ready to consider a divorce to go along with her
impending labor contractions, my mother received word
that he'd died of a heart attack in his friend's small apartment near the Sunset Strip. I was born several weeks after
his funeral.

Those were the facts. Around these facts, my family had
created any number of epic stories. My mother had never
gotten over his death, and had raised us to remain ever-
reverent of him. Raine worshipped him, and had decided
to follow in his footsteps. Norah, on the other hand, was
far more critical of his decisions. But we all loved his pic-

tures. We would often debate which ones we liked best: Raine liked one of the Polaroids he'd sent home from L.A., a grinning man with big sunglasses to match his mut-tonchop sideburns and the Hollywood sign in the back-ground. Norah loved the one of him holding her as a baby, gazing down into her face as he held her in his lap.

My favorite was a candid someone had taken while my father was still in college. He was looking through a record bin in some old record shop, and he was unaware that the camera was on him. I thought I recognized his intense focus. I loved his slight frown, and the determined set to his jaw. He looked so at ease in himself, in his T-shirt and jeans, and also so purposeful. When I'd been starting out on the cello, I would think of that picture of him and imagine myself making the same face as I concentrated.

Because the truth was, my father was just a myth to me. I had no memories of him that weren't stories told by someone else or pictures interpreted by someone else. Unlike my sisters, I didn't have even the smallest, foggi-est memory of his voice or his face to cling to through the years. It had always made me feel guilty somehow. And more alone.

I wasn't sure what had brought on all those thoughts of my father. It was funny, what losing a parent before you were born could do. Having never known what it was like to have a father, I couldn't say I missed it, necessarily, and sometimes I felt that way—that it was no big deal. Other times, I worried it was a visible wound.

As these were not thoughts that were likely to impress Mom with my new interest in wedding planning, I ruthlessly

shoved them aside as I pulled open the glass door to her
office building and climbed the stairs to the second-floor
suite. I had done the same so many times that even the
smell of the carpet felt like memory lane. Sometimes, after
a late practice when I was still in high school, I would
meet Mom here and we'd have dinner, just the two of us.
I'd spent many an afternoon on these steps, waiting for her
to lock up.

Today, however, I was planning to surprise her. I knew
she usually had her lunch at her desk, while the two part-
ners wined and dined clients or made absurd requests she
was a master at denying. I pushed open the outer office
door, expecting to see her in her usual place at the reception area facing the entryway. But the outer office was
empty. I heaved my heavy armload of glossy wedding
magazines onto the surface of Mom's desk. I was about
to sit down in the waiting area when I heard the sound of
her voice from down the hall. Her real voice, some part of
my brain noted, not the smooth one she usually put on in
professional settings.

Thinking I could really surprise her at this point, I
crept down the hall. I knew the file room was straight
ahead, having spent some school vacations helping Mom
out. I knew which office belonged to Stan, the passive-
aggressive one who still wanted Mom to pick up his dry
cleaning because his trophy wife was too busy Botox-
ing, and which belonged to Leonard, who Mom generally
found exasperating every third day. She was in Leonard's
office. I poked my head around the open door, started to
speak, and then stopped dead.

Mom and Leonard were sitting on the leather sofa together, the remains of their lunch on the coffee table before them. Which was unremarkable. What was remarkable was that Mom's feet were up in Leonard's lap, and he was massaging them, since he clearly knew—as I did— that her arches ached when she wore the shoes she loved.

Their casual, and thus evidently long-term intimacy hung around them like a sepia tint.

I may have been naïve, but even I could see the freaking obvious. Which was that Leonard and my Mom were...what? Dating? My mind skittered away from that word.

I could feel that my mouth had dropped open.

"Hello, Courtney," Mom said. She made no attempt to leap away from Leonard or move her feet from his grasp, though I could swear his fingers tightened. "This is a surprise."

And suddenly, an old memory came rushing back to me. I must have been all of ten years old, and Mom had started having late dinners out with one of the lawyers at her firm. In retrospect, it must have been Leonard, though I had no particular memories of him.

My mother had been sad and solitary my whole life. Then, suddenly, she was all about warm hugs and smiles. I'd loved the change in her. But my sisters acted as if they'd caught Mom cheating on Dad. They behaved as if he'd still been alive, and they'd discovered her in the act of cheating on him.

Raine had been furious with me for acting unconcerned with the intruder in our lives. She gathered all of the photographs from the sitting room into her arms, lay down, and cried with them in the front hall as Mom came home one night. As dramatic displays went, that one was a show-stopper.

Norah, meanwhile, had been furious with me for defending Mom, who, even then, she thought was a failure of a parent who relied entirely on Norah's ability to actually get things done. Even at eighteen, she saw herself as the beleaguered martyr.

It was one of the few times in my life I could remember the two of them agreeing on anything. They had stood shoulder to shoulder and railed at Mom. Norah had demanded to know *what was next*, and had shaken one of Dad's framed pictures in the air over her head one night instead of sitting and eating her supper. Raine had sobbed. For weeks. It had so impressed Mom that she'd stopped the dinners altogether, and soon after, stopped the smiles and the hugs as well. We had all retreated back into our various places of comfort, or familiarity. I think it was soon after that I found the cello thanks to a music program at school, and I hadn't thought of my mother's near-miss in dating since.

"I can't believe this," I said now, as the implications set in. I wasn't angry. Stunned was more like it. "You never stopped seeing each other. And you've kept it a secret all these years?"

"Not quite *all* these years," Leonard said in that gruff voice I knew so well. How many times had he called the house to speak to Mom? How many times had she taken the phone into her bedroom to speak privately? How stupid was I?

Mom moved now, swinging her legs off of Leonard's

lap, slipping on her shoes, and rising to her feet. She and Leonard looked at each other for a long moment, and the fact that they quite obviously communicated a great deal was clear to me. It wasn't that I was opposed to the idea of Mom having a boyfriend, I told myself. It was just taking me a moment or two to adjust to the fact that she'd *been having* a boyfriend, for quite some time.

Leonard also stood, aimed a polite sort of smile at me, and then looked back at my mother.

"I'll be in the conference room, Bev," he said quietly, and then eased past me.

"Come on in," Mom said to me, looking almost rueful. "Sit down. What are you doing here?"

I couldn't bear to think about those glossy, irrelevant magazines and the Bridal Borg Brain to which everyone was connected except me.

"I thought I'd show you that I was, actually, interested in wedding planning." I walked over and sank into the couch, and watched as she settled next to me. "But now it turns out I'm much more interested in your secret life!"

"'Secret life' is taking it a little far," Mom demurred.

"A secret boyfriend is a secret life, Mom." I couldn't decide if I was scandalized or intrigued. Maybe both. "When people say 'secret life,' a secret boyfriend is the first thing that comes to mind." I considered. "Or a bank account, I guess. Or even serial killing. But a secret boyfriend is up there."

"The first thing you should know is that I never meant to have a secret life," Mom told me. "It just ended up that way."

Mom really had broken things off with Leonard back when I was ten. She'd been terrified that her dating would somehow damage Norah and Raine, and she'd worried they were already damaged enough. They'd lost their father, and had spent the long years of their adolescence trying to kill each other. What if the addition of Leonard was too much?

"You," she told me with a faint smile, "I didn't worry about. You started the cello soon after, and in any event, you'd seemed so happy about my relationship with Leonard."

Because I didn't have a father's memory to cling to, I thought with the usual flash of frustration and guilt, but I motioned for her to continue.

She and Leonard had a certain chemistry. After some time passed, things happened. She didn't elaborate and I didn't ask—because, ew, this was my mother, not Verena. What they'd originally decided to keep secret only until Raine was out of the house, grew. Leonard had his own children who he saw over the holidays. Years passed. Once I left for the conservatory, they only kept their relationship secret when we returned home. Finally, they agreed that it was time to break the silence—at Norah's wedding. Where better to announce their happiness than such a happy occasion?

"Oh no," I breathed, covering my mouth with my hands.

"After the scene Raine made, and how upset Norah was, the occasion wasn't so happy." Mom looked down. "Leonard thought we should announce ourselves anyway. I disagreed."

"Oh, Mom," I murmured. "I'm so sorry."

Mom lifted her shoulders, and then dropped them. "Everything was a mess. Leonard and I separated for a while, in fact."

I wondered how we'd all managed to avoid noticing that all three of us had been reeling and wounded in the aftermath of that wedding. That it hadn't been only Norah's pain. But Mom was still talking.

When they'd gotten back together, they'd promised each other that there would be no secrets. They wouldn't lie again. As soon as their relationship was noticed and commented upon, they would admit to it.

But neither Norah nor I noticed.

Not when Mom brought Leonard to holiday parties, I thought now, as it all unrolled before me like a film. Not when she'd announced, repeatedly, that they were going away together. If I'd thought about it at all, I'd thought it was a business thing, or that Mom felt sorry for Leonard because he was so alone after his divorce.

"You must be so proud of your keenly observant daughters," I said dryly.

"More than you know," she replied in much the same tone. "Leonard's children didn't know for many years either, to be fair." She looked at me. "Of course, they live in Arizona and Washington State."

I sat with it for a moment. Talk about dropping a bomb. The fact that Raine was bringing Matt home with her seemed mild in comparison.

"I would prefer you not tell Norah at the moment," Mom said then. "She's having a rough time already."

"Don't you think you should just make an announcement

or something?" I asked. "You've been keeping it secret for way too long."

"Norah likes to think of herself as tough," Mom said, "but she's really quite fragile. And she's so upset about Raine, and you..." She shook her head. "I'm not sure she could handle it."

I didn't want to think about that. I definitely didn't want to explore what sounded like a rebuke in her tone, either.

"I think it's a good thing," I said then. I meant it, too. I smiled at her. "I'm glad that you haven't spent all this time mourning."

"No," she said, looking down as she smoothed her skirt. "I haven't been mourning. I've been living my life."

I would have to think about it more, of course. There was a whole, my-mother-as-sexual-creature thing I would have to deal with, or repress. But it was better than mother-as-walking-shroud. Definitely.

"So," she said briskly, changing the subject. "Did you say something about wedding plans?"

After my mother's secret life was exposed—if only to me— it was like June picked up speed. Lucas was slammed with work, and took three separate business trips, to Worcester, Buffalo, and Pittsburgh. I didn't accompany him, which made him tease me about my fair weather interest in being a business wife. In the increasingly hotter weeks that he trekked around the country, I had a lot of time to think about the ramifications of my mother's having had a boyfriend for the past fifteen years or so. Norah and Phil went on a two-week vacation to Phil's parents' place in Rehoboth, so it was just Mom and me and the countdown to Raine's arrival. It felt a lot like it had when Norah and Raine were out of the house, I was in middle school and then high school, and Mom and I had fended for ourselves in the big empty spaces my sisters left behind them.

Unlike women my age, Mom didn't talk much about her relationship with Leonard. Maybe she'd never gotten in the habit, having hidden it so long, or maybe mothers who dated didn't talk about it to their daughters. I didn't know what the protocol was. At any rate, she was far more interested in talking about the wedding I had pretended to want to jump into, and the two of us embarked on a reception site scavenger hunt all over the greater Phila-delphia/New Jersey area. We spent hours comparing ball-rooms and suggested menus, until I felt I had seen all the potential rubber chicken and every possible banquet hall there was to see between Philly and New York City.

None of this comparison shopping made me feel more bridal, though I was now conversant about things like mandatory minimums and Chivari chairs.

I found that it felt kind of liberating to know the truth about Mom. It made me feel closer to her, bonded. It also made me feel a bit better about myself, because I'd sus-pected there was more to her than met the eye, and I'd been right. If some fifteen years late. This alternated with my feeling terrible that my sisters and I were such tyrants that my mother had felt compelled to keep her life such a big secret in the first place.

In my more optimistic moments, I thought it was lucky

we were all getting together again this summer. Lucky because who knew? Maybe we could all get to know one another again.

And then before I was ready, it was July and Mom insisted on a Welcome Home dinner for Raine, and, by extension, Matt, both of whom would be staying with her. She was taking the Prodigal Daughter thing to its pre-ordained conclusion, fatted calf—or, anyway, barbecued hamburgers—and all.

Mom called to announce that she would pick Raine up from the airport, and that Lucas and I didn't need to bring anything except ourselves to the dinner, as Norah was taking care of the salad.

"Norah's coming?" I asked, not believing it. She'd returned from vacation and I sort of expected that she would launch a boycott of Raine and, by extension, the rest of us. Possibly, I thought, Norah would choose to disappear for the next six years. After that it would be my turn, and by then, who knew, I might be gagging to escape these people.

"Of course Norah's coming," Mom said, as if there had never been any doubt.

"Is she mad?" I asked. "Did you speak to her?"

"Courtney," my mother snapped, "I don't have time for this. My expectation is that everyone will act like an adult."

What an absurd thing to expect. I decided that if I was smart at all—and my cello, sitting untouched in the corner despite my full knowledge that I should practice, suggested that I wasn't in the least smart—I would stay home.

"I don't want to go to this dinner," I told Lucas when he

emerged from the forty-minute shower he'd taken to wash away Buffalo to find me flopped across the sofa like an opera heroine.

"Then don't," Lucas said in that maddening male way.

"I have to." I removed my arm from over my eyes, but couldn't bring myself to sit up. "I feel that I have to at least *try* to get Raine and Norah to *act* like they get along since they're really only dealing with each other for me."

"You don't *have to* do anything," Lucas contradicted me. He padded out to the end of the couch and looked down at me. His mouth twitched slightly as he took in my splayed-out pose, but he didn't comment on it. Just as I didn't comment on his hair, which was standing up in spikes as if he'd actually been trying to pull it out in the shower.

"In a cosmic sense, no, of course I don't *have to*," I agreed. Foolish man.

"In every sense," he said.

"I can't let them attack each other. Raine being home is like a red flag for Norah. And Norah's always hated Matt Cheney, so having him along is like fuel to the fire." I shook my head. "She may never forgive me."

"I thought you already doubted that she'd forgive you for going to California in the first place," Lucas pointed out. "So if she's already not going to forgive you, who cares?"

Stupid male logic. I didn't dignify that with a response.

"And how come you didn't mention that Matt was coming, too?" he asked then, tilting his head slightly as he gazed at me.

I blinked at him.

"What? I told you that ages ago."

"No, you didn't."

"I told you. When Raine called? And told me she was coming, and let me work up to being excited about it—remember the life coach?"

"I remember the life coach." Lucas eyed me. "I remember the entire conversation. You know what I don't remember coming up at all? Matt Cheney."

"Well, I told you she said he was coming." I was all too able to hear that I sounded obstinate and annoyed.

As usual, this aggressively pissy tone served only to make Lucas laugh at me.

"You are so full of shit," he informed me, his eyes daring me to keep going.

As usual, I was forced to laugh myself, damn him. I struggled to sit up then.

"I thought I told you," I muttered, while he continued laughing.

"Yeah, so I hear." He studied me for a moment. "I'm not threatened by your ex-boyfriend, Courtney. But it seems like you might be."

"That's the most ridiculous thing I've ever heard!" I practically sputtered. "Why would I be threatened by Matt Cheney, of all people?"

"And I'm definitely interested in the fact you hid that he was coming to Philly." He shifted his weight, standing there in just his towel.

"I thought I told you," I said again.

"Makes me wonder what else you think you told me," he said quietly.

Which, of course, I couldn't answer.

"Ha-ha," I said. "Very funny."

"I'm getting dressed," he said with a hard look at me, and then he walked away.

Terrific, I thought, scowling at the ceiling again. *This is already going well.*

chapter sixteen

Walking into my mother's house a few days later was like walking into the past. From the sound of Matt's laughter back in the kitchen to Raine's unmistakable voice to Norah's more measured tones. I could hear all of them the moment Lucas and I walked in the door, and it catapulted me backward into another time.

"This is weird," I whispered.

Lucas looked at me as we stood there in my mother's brick foyer. His presence grounded me very much in the here and now. I concentrated on that.

"This is what you wanted," he pointed out. Unhelpfully, I thought, but then, he was probably still pissed about the whole Matt misunderstanding.

"I thought I told you," I said for about the seventeen zillionth time.

"So you keep saying." He just stood there with that cool look in his eyes. It made me crazy. And the truth was, I really did think I'd told him.

Or anyway, I didn't remember deciding *not* to tell him.

"Okay, then," I muttered, and headed for the kitchen. I could hear him follow me. I stopped at the threshold and peered inside, apprehensive.

It wasn't a Rockwell painting, but on the surface at least, everything was fine. Raine was cooing over little Eliot, while Norah looked on, a smile frozen on her mouth and her arms crossed over her torso. Phil was making awkward, mutually monosyllabic conversation with a surly-looking (though thankfully fully clothed) Matt Cheney over by the refrigerator. Mom bustled around at the stove, with an incongruous green apron tied over her shorts.

Everybody seemed tense, but as if they were trying. Exactly as they should look, in other words. It was nice to see everyone making so much of an effort. More of an effort than I could remember anyone making before, that was for sure.

Matt was the only one who looked up to see us standing there. His eyes met mine across the span of my mother's kitchen floor. It took me back years. Then his lips tightened slightly, and he looked away. I squared my shoulders, as if he'd already pushed me off balance.

"Hey guys, check it out," Matt drawled from his position of extreme leaning near the fridge. "It's the happy couple."

"Uh-huh," Lucas murmured in my ear. "You thought you told me."

I had time for only the smallest of glares before Lucas transformed himself into Happy, Easygoing Guy—the Lucas he presented to all of his clients, all of his future in-laws, and anyone else who he felt would benefit from perceiving him as a laid-back, relaxed sort of guy.

He hugged Norah and then Raine, kissed Mom on her cheek, and then went over and did the whole handshaking ritual with Phil and Matt. He was good at it, too. The fact that he could be depended upon to make any social event easier was just one of the many reasons I loved him. Even when I was annoyed with him. And why was I annoyed with him? Because he was annoyed with me. There it was, the sum total of my emotional maturity.

For my part, I exchanged a warm smile with my mother, a frostier one with Matt, and then inched over to watch my sisters interact with each other.

"I can't believe how much he looks like you!" Raine was cooing, smiling at Eliot, who shrugged away from her and started shouting my name when he saw me. I snatched him up in a hug when he reached me, just in time to hear Norah's reply:

"That's funny," she said coolly. "We think he looks like Phil."

"Hi, guys," I said brightly.

And so it began.

"It's actually really nice to be back home," Raine said a few hours later, stretching a bit against the back of her chair. "I'm so glad you invited me, Courtney. Although I forgot how humid it gets here in the summer!"

How anyone could forget the omnipresent Pennsylvania

humidity was a mystery to me. It defined summer in the Mid-Atlantic region, as far as I knew. In defiance of this, we had had dinner outside on Mom's patio, with the full heft of the Pennsylvania summer all around us.

It had been a pleasant enough evening so far. Everyone seemed to be very careful to keep inside their own lines. Raine talked about her life in San Francisco, and Norah pretended to be interested. *A photo essay featuring your sex organs?* she'd asked in her emotionless, professorial voice. *How second-wave feminist of you.* Norah then listed her academic achievements, while Raine acted riveted. *The figure of Prometheus in British literature during the Industrial Revolution?* she'd echoed. *Bet that's a full class.* If I had pointed out how alike they were in this, right down to their matching fake smiles, they would never have believed me. But I saw how obvious it was they were sisters. The same, despite their differences.

Lucas, Matt, and Phil, devoid of the usual safe male topics as none of them were particular sports fans, had managed to bridge the gap by having Phil discuss the physics of animated television shows, since both Lucas and Matt spent a lot of time watching the Cartoon Network.

I tried to ignore how unsettling I found it that Lucas and Matt had anything at all in common, even TV habits.

Eliot, bored hours before, ran around in circles on the back lawn with his favorite toy airplane.

"This is going better than I expected," I murmured to Mom as I helped her clear plates to make way for dessert.

"Only if you squint your eyes and don't really pay

attention," she retorted, but she was smiling. She headed back inside through the screen door.

Phil excused himself to go discuss aviation with his son, and I sat back down next to Lucas. Matt looked at me, then turned away. I pretended I didn't mind, and smiled at Lucas instead. He smiled back, but it made me uneasy.

Or maybe I was just psychic, because Norah sighed then, loud in the darkening evening.

"Oh, come on," she said impatiently.

"What?" Raine was laughing. She noticed she had all of our attention, and raised one bare shoulder. Her eyes twinkled at me. "I was just telling Norah that I thought it would make Dad happy to see us all in one place."

So much for our *better than expected* evening, I thought philosophically. I wondered why, exactly, Raine had to go there. On her first night back. Was it because she couldn't abide the dishonesty of small talk, as I'd heard her declare once? Or was it more along the lines of what Verena had claimed—that she was her own version of a control freak, and pushing Norah's buttons was her method of getting her way?

"If Dad was so interested in seeing all his little girls together," Norah said quietly, deliberately, as Raine must have known she would, "then maybe he might have stuck around to meet Courtney. Maybe he wouldn't have taken off for Hollywood."

"Nothing changes," Raine said then, leaning back in her chair as if she were relaxed. Though I could see she was nothing near relaxed. She cocked her head slightly to the side. "Dad was an *artist*, Norah."

She said the word as if it explained everything. As if, having said it, there was no need for explanations.

Norah turned to look at Raine. I thought she looked almost kind, which, of course, was terrifying.

"He was the father of two, with another one on the way," she replied evenly. "Whatever else he might have been, that should have been his first priority."

Raine shook her head. "You just can't understand what it's like to be an artist," she said. Almost as if that fact made her sad.

Norah actually smiled. Not nicely.

"And you can?" she asked. She let out a sharp little breath, through her nose, that was almost a laugh. "I'm sorry, did I miss something? I thought you were a waitress."

I felt myself tense at that. I also felt Matt turn and fix that cold stare on me, no doubt blaming me for this, the way he always had. *Great.*

"She works in a bar, Norah," I said hurriedly. "I told you that."

"My mistake," Norah said acidly. "Not a waitress, then. A bartender." Her tone made it clear how little she thought of that distinction.

Next to me, Lucas was looking back and forth between my sisters like they were playing a particularly fascinating game of tennis.

"That's right," Raine said. "Disparage me all you want. It doesn't change the fact that you're the only one in this family without a single artistic impulse." She blinked at Norah. "That must be terrible for you. It explains why you feel you have to be so controlling of the rest of us."

"Okay, guys," I threw in, trying to stop them. But the light of battle was in Norah's eyes, and she wasn't about to back down.

"Is that what you call it?" she asked Raine. She made little quote marks with her fingers. "'Artistic impulse'?" She pursed her lips. "Exactly what is so artistic about ruining your sister's wedding and then skulking away in the dead of night?"

"Hey," Matt said. Everyone looked at him then. Perhaps we were sharing the same flashbacks of the times he'd been even more involved in all the Cassel family fights. I had a particularly vivid recollection of him hauling Raine into the air by her waist, to keep her from diving across the kitchen table at Norah's neck. He and Raine had been about fifteen. "I don't think we need to get into this tonight."

"Of course *you* don't think so," Norah said icily. "But no one asked you, did they?"

"Very nice." Raine shook her head. "This is how you treat a guest?"

"Matt Cheney is no guest," Norah said with a snort. "At this point he's like a cousin. The kind who shows up for dinner and never leaves."

"This is all getting very intense," Lucas broke in at this point, while the other three all but snarled at one another. He sent his wide grin around the group like a beacon, inviting them to return it. "And I don't know anyone well enough to enjoy the personal insults."

That made Matt smile—albeit reluctantly. Norah and Raine eyed each other with wariness.

"This started because we were talking about Dad, and all of us being here," I said, quickly jumping into the sudden quiet. "And I do think it's great that we're all here, no matter what. I'm really happy that Lucas and my engagement party can bring us back together."

"I know it's not popular," Raine said, unwilling to let it go, "but I believe our father loved us very much. Even you, Norah." I felt an uncharacteristic twinge of annoyance.

Norah looked down for a moment. I thought she might let it go, but then I saw the light in her eyes when she lifted her head.

No such luck.

"Phil loves me, and he loves Eliot," Norah replied tartly. "Do you know how I know he does? Because he's *here*. He lives in the same house, having the same life. If he up and moved to the opposite coast, I might have to rethink."

"Why must you make every situation so tense?" Raine asked her, sounding exasperated. "Why can't we have one nice family dinner?"

"We've had a whole lot of nice family dinners," Norah said. Her eyebrows arched upward. "While you were gone."

Mom chose that moment to reappear at the back door, bearing cake. Not any single, solitary cake. In deference to our wildly divergent tastes, she'd created her old standby: three small, separate cakes on one platter. Chocolate with raspberry filling for Norah. Red velvet cake with cream cheese frosting for Raine. And the lightest, most delicious angel food cake for me. Cassel Cake, we'd always called it, because it was ours and the best part was, this way no one had to share.

"All my girls together," Mom said as she came and set the platter down on the picnic table. If she noticed the strained silence, she gave no sign. "Here's to a wonderful summer."

The next morning, I woke up on a mission.

My sisters wanted to sit and soak in their lifetime of antagonism. I wanted everyone to get along. Therefore, I was the one who had to do something about it. Forcing them to interact wasn't going to work, clearly. I had no choice but to appeal to their better natures.

I got to Norah's house a little before ten and settled myself on the steps. It was hard to get up so early, and all I'd done was rattle around my apartment. I wasn't sure how parents did it, day after day. Or, for that matter, business-people who had to be places by nine in the morning. I wasn't sure how Norah combined the parent part of herself with the professor. I was having a hard enough time just thinking the word *wife*.

All around me, the summer morning sang as it kicked into gear. Birds chirped above me in the old trees, and the air smelled like grass and flowers. It was already hot, and I was glad I'd worn the shorts I'd made by cutting up the jeans I'd loved at the conservatory, even if my legs were pale enough to blind unsuspecting pedestrians. I had fortification in the form of a huge café mocha from Starbucks, which comprised three of my favorite foods in one beverage: caffeine, sugar, and sweet, delicious chocolate.

The longer I sat still, the warmer it got. I wished I'd worn my flip-flops, because I was convinced I could feel my toes sweat in my favorite pair of off-white, low Chuck Taylors. I rummaged around in my ratty purse until I found a hair elastic, and bundled my hair up on the top of my head. Not necessarily the most attractive hairstyle, but my neck felt cooler immediately.

As I nursed my mocha, I stared at the spot down on the sidewalk below, where Lucas had proposed. I smiled a little bit, remembering the look on his face and the way I'd knelt down, too, letting the chill and wet seep into my jeans. I couldn't believe that had been six months ago now. I played with my ring, turning it over and over with my thumb. I was used to it now, though I still caught myself staring at it from time to time, caught anew by how pretty it was. I hadn't truly appreciated the genius of Lucas's choice of proposal spot until now, however. Every time I came to Norah's house—particularly on unpleasant missions like this one—I would remember one of the best moments of my life. He was crafty, that Lucas.

"Aunt Courtney!" Eliot cried in delight, spying me from down the block. Though what he actually said sounded more like *Corny*. He let go of Norah's hand and lurched toward me in that half-drunk baby walk of his. I jumped up to meet his headlong dash.

"How's my favorite nephew?" I asked, swooping him into my arms in a big hug. I pressed kisses into his soft, sticky cheeks, until he squealed with delight and I felt that much more connected to life—and Norah—because I loved him so much.

My sister said nothing, though her eyebrows practically

reached over her head and touched her bun. I knew she could tell I wasn't there by chance. She wasn't stupid: she knew I had an agenda.

Part of me felt guilty for using my nephew against her, but it was only a small part. I held the door for her and her stroller. I helped her feed Eliot lunch, and did the dishes when she took him upstairs and put him down for his nap. I knew she responded well to acts of service, and I wasn't above using whatever tools I could.

When she came back down and stood in the doorway, I was wiping my hands dry on one of the matching towels that hung in a perfect line on her oven door. I struggled to fold it back into its place, and failed, leaving it unsightly and out of order.

"To what do I owe this honor?" she asked, sounding almost amused.

"I want to talk about Raine," I said, because why not launch right into it? "I feel like I should tell you some things."

"What could you possibly tell me about *Lorraine* that I don't already know?" Norah asked, moving past me into the kitchen and refolding the towel with two quick jerks.

"She's not here for fun," I told her. "She wanted to come back to deal with everything that happened. She told me she wants to confront her demons."

"And she brought that Matt Cheney with her," Norah said after a moment, watching me closely. "That's a thoughtful engagement present for you. What I'm not grasping is why he's staying in your childhood bedroom. I thought he had family here."

I hadn't known until that moment where, exactly, in my mother's house Matt was staying, and imagining him ensconced in my pretty blue room with its flowery bedspread made me feel...strange. Maybe because I had spent so much time and energy imagining him there. I swallowed.

"He lived with his grandfather way back when," I said, clicking into informational mode for Norah, who had never seemed to care in her entire previous life about Matt Cheney's living arrangements. "But apparently he moved to Florida a few years ago. Matt's grandfather, I mean. Anyway, they weren't close."

Norah studied my face, looking for something. I quelled the urge to fidget. I told myself I felt calm and serene, and tried to exude it.

"Why are you making that face?" Norah asked.

I stopped exuding.

"I'm not making any face," I said. "I just wanted to tell you. So you could see where she was coming from, and maybe reach out. I mean, we're all sisters, right?"

"It's really nice of you to think of me," Norah said, her tone somewhere between sarcastic and irritated.

"Don't be like this. It doesn't have to be this huge, terrible thing. We should all try to—" I broke off, not sure what I was trying to say.

"Get along?" Norah finished for me. She cocked her head to one side. "What a great idea. Too bad Raine and I have never gotten along. But I'm sure we'll just set that aside now because you've decided it's time."

"Well, why not?" I asked.

"Grow up, Courtney," Norah said, but it came out like a sigh. "I'm not going to tiptoe around Raine because she's finally decided to come home. It's not my fault she put off facing the music for years."

"I'm serious." I warmed to the topic. "Why can't we all decide that it's time to get over the past? If we wanted to, we could draw a line and decide to be done with it."

"Yes, but there's a crucial distinction," Norah said, and now she sounded tired. "Raine is angry because she decided to be when she was about ten, and because she wants to have issues. She thinks it makes her more interesting. I, on the other hand, am angry because she singlehandedly ruined my wedding. Can you see the difference between the two?"

"I understand the difference, Norah, I really do."

"Good, because I'm beginning to think I'm going insane here," she said. "That, or everyone else is in an alternate dimension wherein Raine and my behavior is considered to be the same."

"But you can decide to stop being angry about that." I was pleading with her. "You can decide to let bygones be bygones."

"And once again, Raine gets a free pass," Norah said in a low voice. "Once again, Raine's actions have no consequences." She shrugged unhappily. "That's not how I live my life."

"I don't think it has to be about how you live your life," I ventured. "It could be about choosing to overlook some stuff—no one's saying it isn't valid stuff—for the sake of the greater good. This is the only family we have."

For a long moment, we looked at each other.

"I don't accept that the family you're dealt is the one you have to put up with," Norah said after a while. Her chin rose a little. "And I don't accept that I should ever have to deal with Raine, who, by the way, has yet to apologize."

"Come on, Norah..."

"And the worst part is," she continued, her chin high, "you don't even realize that she's going to do to you what she does to everyone, do you? Didn't you hear what she said to me at Mom's? She'll judge you, and your life, and everything you hold dear. Then she'll ruin something, just because she can."

"I believe that we can just...be sisters," I said. "I believe that we can do it, if we want to."

Norah looked at me for a while, and the anger left her face. She shook her head once, as if something had changed and I made her sad.

It was worse, somehow, than her anger.

"Maybe this isn't really about how I live my life," she said with a note of finality in her voice. "Maybe it's about how you live yours."

chapter seventeen

Later that afternoon, I sat in our living room and thought about what Norah had said. About how Raine—and, of course, Matt—would judge me and the life I'd made without them.

It was one thing to stand on a hill in San Francisco and wonder how my life might have been different if I'd chosen a different path. It was one thing to play *what if* games in my head and pin them all onto a sunswept city with mythical hills and trolley cars. I could understand the urge to be different. It was in my genes, it seemed, from my father to Raine. I had felt the same urge at the top of Twin Peaks.

But here in Philadelphia, things were different. Because this was my real life. This was where I'd made my choices, and this was where I lived them.

Norah had hit a nerve, and I suspected she knew it: I was afraid that Raine and Matt would pity me when they saw the way I lived.

I was afraid they would be right.

After all, I'd been terrified in San Francisco that Raine

already pitied my life, thought it small, from thousands of miles away. I was even more terrified now that she could see it for herself.

I looked around, making a list and checking it twice, so I could get to each item before Raine did. I decided to try hating all of it, in preparation. It was like a rehearsal.

I hated my apartment. It had a terrible layout, with the bedrooms one on top of the other and tiny to boot. It was cramped and small, and the only nice thing about it was the bay window in the living room, which hardly made up for the puny kitchen and drafty corners.

I hated our cats, who I had to physically disengage from the clothes I hung in my closet—all now sporting claw marks—because they thought it was fun to climb up anything that hung. And while on the topic, I found emptying the litter box disgusting in the extreme, and why did they think it was so much fun to scatter the litter all across the bathroom floor? It was a good thing we never really had guests.

I hated grubby, muggy Philadelphia. It was the City of Brotherly Love, but not, in the Cassel family, sisterly affection of any kind. Instead of glorious bay views we had the Delaware River on one side of Center City and the Schuykill on the other. Hardly the same thing. No Twin Peaks—the highest point in Philadelphia was Chestnut Hill.

I hated Norah for the fact she'd made me feel so ashamed of myself for looking up Raine in the first place. And because she was so vocal about how much everything hurt her feelings.

I hated Lucas, of course, because he was untattooed, unmysterious, and never smirked while leaning against things for support. And he was always so freaking calm. And because lately he'd been working so hard that sometimes I felt like a widow to his computer screen.

I hated my job, too. Because it was supposed to be artistic, but often felt like a slog of practicing and rehearsing. Because we had to play the same music so much, to please the audiences who never tired of *The Four Seasons*. I never tired of Vivaldi either, but sometimes I tired of playing it. Because it would never involve exposing myself or my genitalia for all the world to see. And because I felt guilty that the entire month of June and part of July had passed and I'd barely touched my cello at all.

Last but not least, I hated my cello. It lay in its case near my music stand, and I didn't have to open it to see it in my mind. I didn't have to touch it to feel it beneath my hands, in perfect detail. I hated the sounds I could coax from it, the low, mellow, rich notes that had haunted me since I'd first heard them, when I was still a kid and didn't know any better.

I hated that I'd been so obsessed with one stupid instrument that I'd dedicated my whole life to it.

I sat there for a long time, bringing as much hate as I could, until my mood was significantly darker and I felt ashamed of every choice I'd made since I was a kid.

Only then could I relax, because all that self-flagellation made me realize how much I liked my life. I could enjoy it despite all the things I could find to dislike about it. That had to mean something.

And only then did I feel I was ready to seek out Raine, for more sisterly abuse.

"You should think about calling first, Princess," Matt said.

He filled up the door of my mother's house. He was dressed in khaki shorts and a gray T-shirt, and I told myself that was all for the best, because my mother's sleepy suburban neighborhood was definitely not ready for an appearance of the dragon. Neither was I.

"In fact," he continued after a moment, "it seems like you have some trouble with the general concept."

I was glad I'd spent so long practicing the hate today, because it was easy to direct it at him.

"This is my mother's house," I snapped, glaring at him.

"That's true," Matt agreed.

And then he just stood there, looking at me.

It was not lost on me that we seemed to have a lot of moments in doorways. I still remembered that night he'd appeared at this very door six years ago; there was the whole overwhelming dragon tattoo door situation at his house in San Francisco; and then, of course, the conversation outside the doors at my hotel. Maybe it was some kind of sign.

Doors that I should just slam shut, I thought darkly. Preferably on his foot.

"I wanted to see if Raine was here," I said finally, pushing past him and walking into the house. "And I'm not sure I need to give you any explanations for showing up at my own mother's house."

I stopped near the door to the living room, and looked through it toward the little room that served as my father's shrine. I wasn't sure what the presence of the sitting room meant, given what I now knew about my mother. I would have to think about that later, when my own past wasn't literally breathing down my neck.

"Nobody's here," Matt said from behind me. "Raine went off somewhere before I got up this morning. Who knows what she's doing, or when she'll be back. And your mom is at work."

"So you get to just hang out here in my childhood home," I said, turning. I looked at him. "How fun for you."

"I had some people to call," Matt replied, his eyes on me.

His mouth curved a little bit as he said it, and I was immediately plagued with old, jealous visions: that glossy-haired brunette girl that he'd towed around with him for a while, she of the pouty lips and impossible, gravity-defying breasts. Or that horrible high school girlfriend he'd fought with for years: the obnoxious Kelly Ferrante with her flippy hair and mean eyes.

Then I remembered that I was twenty-eight years old, not eighteen, and who Matt Cheney chose to call was no business of mine.

"I didn't think you knew anyone around here anymore," I said after a moment or two during which I had to forcibly remind myself that I wasn't in high school any longer.

"You'd be surprised what turns up," Matt said. "Or who."

I walked away from him, down the hall toward the kitchen, and, once there, rummaged through the refrigerator for something to snack on. I felt more than heard Matt follow me, and turned around when I'd found some grapes.

"So what are you going to do while you're here?" I asked him. "Just look up old friends and hang around?"

"I don't exactly have a schedule," he said. "I think it's called a vacation, but I wouldn't know. I haven't had one in years."

Too busy with his onerous duties as a bouncer at Space, no doubt. I managed not to snort aloud.

"I'm surprised you came at all." I looked at him, trying to read his mind and failing miserably. "At least Raine has family stuff to do. It must be weird to be back here."

"It's just a town," he said.

One you ran away from, I wanted to say. I should have.

"Raine thought she knew what she was getting into," Matt murmured, leaning a hip against the kitchen door-jamb. "But I couldn't let her walk into the fire alone, you know?"

"What fire?" I scoffed at him. "This is her family!"

"Like you guys are easy on her?" Matt fired back. "Come on, Courtney. Raine's everybody's favorite scapegoat."

"I think Raine and Norah have some stuff to work out, sure," I said, frowning. "But I wouldn't call Raine a *scapegoat*. I mean, she actually did do what Norah's accusing her of doing. She actually did cause a huge commotion at Norah's—"

"Yeah, the wedding." Matt made a face. "Don't you think she's holding on to that a little tight?"

"It was her wedding." I could only stare at him, feeling

helpless. That it was a familiar feeling didn't make it any better. "She's only planning to have the one."

"It's just a day," Matt told me. "You wear a stupid dress and people say shit that they already believe, or they wouldn't be there in the first place. I don't understand what the big deal is."

It was the way he said it, too. Like he was trying to hurt me. As if I had personally created the entire concept of weddings and foisted them upon the world. The feeling this produced in the pit of my stomach also made me feel like I was back in high school again. Ninth grade, to be precise. Matt could so easily make me feel this way: young, stupid, and clueless.

Then again, this whole interaction felt as if it could be taking place about fifteen years ago, back before it had even crossed my mind that someday Matt might reciprocate my feelings. I would have come home from orchestra practice, or one of my tutors, to find Matt looming around in the kitchen, Raine off somewhere doing something mysterious, and my mother still at work in the law office. I would gaze at Matt adoringly, he would alternately ignore me or say strange things designed to confuse me, and then Raine would appear or call and he would forget I existed.

Just like old times.

"I guess this explains why you're not married," I said then, determined not to show him how unsteady I felt.

"Maybe I just haven't found the right girl." He smirked at me.

"I think you should give that Bronwen a chance," I told

him, smirking right back. "Some of the things I saw her do in yoga class were truly awe-inspiring."

"Yeah, well." Matt shrugged. "Bronwen is about seven different kinds of a mess."

He didn't elaborate. I wasn't sure it was required. Though I did enjoy imagining seven different messes, all of them Bronwen-shaped.

"Okay," I said, throwing the picked-clean grape vine into the trash beneath the sink. "I'm going to head back. Tell Raine I came by."

"I'll do that."

He didn't move when I walked toward the door he was blocking. I hated myself for it, but I stopped a few feet away and searched his face.

"What are you doing?" I asked, hearing my voice go sort of soft and hating that, too.

Matt looked at me. Something in his eyes flashed, then darkened.

I knew exactly what he was thinking.

And I stopped breathing.

He didn't move. I didn't dare.

But in my head, I remembered.

I remembered the first time he'd kissed me, in this very kitchen. I had been talking too much, nervous and fluttering around while he just watched me. When I'd turned back to look at him he'd reached out a hand, wrapped it around the nape of my neck, and settled his mouth against mine in one smooth movement.

I hadn't actually swooned. I'd only felt like I might.

I felt the same way all these years later.

I jerked my gaze away from his and concentrated for a moment on the baseboard near his foot. *Breathe*, I ordered myself.

"So we're not even going to talk about the conversation we had?" he asked after a long moment. "We're pretending it never happened?"

"What conversation?" I asked, trying to pretend I had no idea what he was talking about.

"Fine," he said. "Whatever, Courtney. Hide in there if you have to."

"I'm not hiding anywhere," I told him, feeling temper crackle through me. "I don't want to talk about it." And then something else spilled out of me, before I could think it through. "And do you know what would be great? If you would stop acting like you know me so well. You really don't."

"I never said I did," Matt replied, but it was clear to me that I'd lost points somehow. Or that he'd won them, which was worse.

"You left me," I said, because it couldn't be said enough.

"You keep throwing that in my face," he retorted.

"Because it's true, and it's like you can't seem to remember that part of it."

"I remember." His voice turned almost dangerous. "I remember everything."

We were so close.

And there was something about him. He was magnetic. It was like I couldn't keep from imagining what it would be like to lean over—to move closer—to *do* something with all these memories that threatened to swamp me.

As if he could read my mind, he closed the distance between us. His green eyes seared into mine. I stared back at him.

And then he bent his head.

So close that I could feel his breath. That I could almost taste him——

Which was when reality intruded. Painfully.

Lucas, I thought. His name screamed across my brain.

"God!" I heard myself swear. "No!"

I threw out a hand and slapped it against Matt's chest, holding him back but more than that, pushing myself away from him.

I couldn't believe what had happened. What had already happened, and what had almost happened.

I couldn't bear to look at him.

"I have to go," I whispered, and bolted.

"So let me get this straight," Verena said a few hours later, squinting at me through the smoke that dominated the sidewalk outside Scruffy's, a hole-in-the-wall bar that hosted an open mike night every Tuesday. "You actually went all the way out to your mother's house? And then all the way back? Without even seeing Raine? Why would you do that?"

We were waiting for it to be Verena's turn at the mike, and so were standing with a collection of people who looked as if they fit in with a bar called Scruffy's. These, supposedly, were Philadelphia's next generation of comics. Most were muttering to themselves and looking about as far from funny as it was possible to get.

"I thought the preemptive strike was the way to go," I said, leaning back against the brick wall, angling myself away from a short, bald guy who looked faintly homicidal. "It worked with Norah. Sort of."

"But that's like an hour round-trip!" Verena frowned, obviously calculating the distance in her head. "You completely refused to go to that bridal shop the other day because you claimed the fifteen-minute round-trip was too far, but you can make an *hour* round-trip—"

"Please let go of the travel details," I begged her. "Concentrate on everything I just told you." Not that I had told her the most important part of the day—the near miss kiss. I couldn't tell her—or anyone, even myself, really. Because I was still trying to come to terms with the fact it had happened. And what it meant about me.

"There's nothing to concentrate on," Verena said matter-of-factly, her brow smoothing as she looked at me. "It's all business as usual. Raine and Norah fight, Matt broods and snarls. It might as well be ten years ago."

"It definitely feels like it's ten years ago."

"The key difference being, of course, that it is *not* ten years ago," Verena said.

"Are you sure?" I asked, only half-kidding.

"You know, I don't get along with my brother all that well either," she said, smoothing her hair back, "so after years of war, we just don't talk about things that will start a fight. Problem solved."

"Part of me thinks that they must enjoy it," I said, "because why else would they do it every time they lay eyes on each other?"

"They clearly get something out of it," Verena said with a sniff. She smiled very fakely at another comic on the sidewalk, who I knew, from previous open mike experiences, Verena thought was dreadfully unfunny.

"And do you know how weird it was to be hanging out with Matt Cheney in my mother's house?" I asked when the fake smile had been returned, social conventions had been attended to, and we could get back to our conversation. "It could have been any afternoon from high school. Except I didn't have to run upstairs and practice."

"I'm sure it was all kinds of weird." Verena studied my expression. Her lips pursed slightly, and I was convinced she could somehow *see* what I refused to think about. "Luckily, one way to distinguish now from high school is the existence of your fiancé. Where was he while you were playing 'Auld Lang Syne' with Matt Cheney?"

"Thank you," I said sarcastically. "If it weren't for you, I might forget I was engaged at all."

"I wonder," she snapped right back. Her eyes narrowed. "And tell me you didn't let Matt Cheney get under your skin." She sighed when I didn't respond. "You didn't, did you?"

"I don't know," I admitted. "He's good at it. He had years and years of practice. It's like riding a bike for him."

"You're not still in love with him, Courtney." Verena's stare was hard, determined.

"Of course not," I said, annoyed, as if she'd phrased it as

a question. "It's really bizarre to be dealing with him again, that's all. But I'm definitely not still in love with him."

"And you know what?" She shook her head at me. "I'm not sure you ever were."

I gaped at her.

"What are you talking about? I loved him so much it *defined* me!" I was actually a little bit offended that she would say otherwise.

"That's not love," Verena said, and let out a snort. "Please."

"I think, of the two of us, I'm the one who knows how I felt about him," I told her. Through my teeth.

"I know how I felt about Luke Perry in *90210*," she retorted. "I can only guess how he felt about me."

"I don't think that you can compare my first love to your celebrity crush!" I snapped at her.

"Oh, come on," Verena said. "You had a crush on him. For your whole life. Then you got together, and then he left. That's not love. That's...a CW series. Seriously."

"It was a little more than that!" I argued hotly.

"For you, yes," she agreed. "But that doesn't make it love. Do you want to know how I know? How I'm so sure that I'm not even trying to be respectful of your feelings?"

I could only stare at her.

"Not really," I muttered.

She ignored me.

"Because you were never happy with him," she told me. "You were always worried, or off-balance, or upset about something. And then, occasionally, you'd be giddy. But mostly you just cried."

I dropped my gaze to the ground, because she was

right: I'd spent most of that summer in agony. Would he call me back, or would he disappear for the weekend without a word? Would he tell me what he was thinking when his eyes went all sad, or would he pretend nothing was wrong, shutting me out? Would he tease me in that affectionate way he had, or would he make me feel awkward and young with all his mocking comments? I never knew how he felt about me. I hadn't known, in fact, until he'd thrown it at me in San Francisco.

"I loved him," I told Verena. "I always did."

"Why are you arguing this?" she asked, her brows drawing together. "Please, *please* don't tell me this craziness is happening again. *Please* don't tell me you think Matt Fucking Cheney can even hold a candle to Lucas!"

"Of course I don't," I told her, kicking at the concrete sidewalk with the toe of my Converse sneaker. It was looking a whole lot more *off* than *white*. "Don't be ridiculous."

But she just stared at me.

There was a bustle at the door, and then a list of names was rattled off by the guy with a clipboard. As Verena's name was on it, I was saved from that stare, and gave her an enthusiastic thumbs-up instead of having to respond.

"We are not finished having this conversation," she informed me, and then stepped inside.

I remained outside in the thick summer evening. Verena forbade me to watch her act when it was, as she put it, in the vegetable-tossing stage. As she was still trying out new material, my job was to stand outside and tell her later if I could hear the crowd (such as it was, in Scruffy's) respond to her few minutes at the mike.

I stood there, with the traffic moving up and down the street in front of me, and let my confusion take full control of me.

How could I have nearly kissed him? Or—to be more precise—stood there so passively while he nearly kissed me? How could I still be attracted to him when he'd hurt me so badly?

Verena didn't think it had ever been love, but I knew better. Didn't I?

And how could any of this be happening, when I was engaged to marry Lucas?

Engaged, a little voice whispered inside me, *but not exactly thrilled about it. Not unleashing your inner Bridezilla and rolling with it. Avoiding trips to the bridal shop and freaking out about the very idea of setting a date. Not the most excited bride-to-be, are you?*

I felt like there were two of me, the way I'd felt ever since the day that Lucas had proposed. One of them was the ring-wearing, happy fiancée. Sometimes I accessed her on those venue-scouting missions with Mom. And she seemed to surface most when Lucas and I were alone. When I forgot about the things I hadn't told him—of which there were now more, and worse—and simply basked in him.

But there was still the old me in there, lurking around, and I was beginning to realize she was a serious problem. She didn't like the word *wife*, for one thing. She wasn't sure she wanted to become one. And she had twenty-eight years of mostly unrequited feelings for Matt Cheney to contend with.

Calling it a problem seemed to dramatically understate

the issue, I thought then, in a panic. Maybe there weren't two of me, even in a metaphoric sense. Could it be that I didn't really want to marry Lucas? Was that why Matt Cheney still had so much power over me?

I hated even thinking it.

"Hi," said the tiny, murderous-looking bald man directly beneath my elbow.

"Hi," I said, startled. I hoped he hadn't seen me jump. I couldn't have been further away in my own head.

"I believe in love," he told me, every line on his face tense, his brows tight together. He reached over and held onto my wrist, as if in punctuation. "Love is pain. Your friend didn't get that, but I do."

"Well," I said. Still very politely. Because what else was there to say? And also, he was still holding my arm. "Thanks for your support."

chapter eighteen

Raine didn't call me to let me know she'd received my message-via-Matt. Instead, she showed up at our door the next afternoon.

"Surprise!" she singsonged, sashaying past me when I opened the door. She was wearing a selection of lightweight, bright and patterned scarves—several tied together in a complicated series of knots taking the place of a shirt, one as a headband, and another that sort of fluttered behind her like a mauve train. I followed her into my living room, inhaling the incense-y scent that she left in her wake. I had the uncharitable thought that she had shown up like this as payback. Had I known she was coming, I might have washed the dishes in the sink or made sure the litterbox was clean. I might even have taken a shower. Before she arrived, doing so had seemed like an unnecessary break from the guilt trip I was giving myself all morning.

Raine looked around the living room. I remembered the way I'd looked for evidence of her in her living room in San Francisco, and looked around myself. Our apartment was a not-very-eclectic mix of IKEA, my mom's attic, and some of Lucas's mother's shabby chic castoffs for good measure. There were various concert playbills that I'd framed to keep track of some of the shows I'd performed in that I found most memorable. There was a print of a theatrical production of *Don Quixote* we felt we had to buy to adorn our brand-new apartment—the one we were finally sharing, in defiance of Norah's edict against premarital cohabitation.

And now Raine was here to judge what I'd become.

I was being silly, I told myself. Despite my hate-a-thon, she was only here to say hello. To hang out and have more sister time, the way we had in California.

I would have found this easier to believe if she hadn't had that strange, challenging look on her face.

"This is a really cute place," Raine said now. "I always forget these old East Coast apartments can have so many different nooks and crannies."

By this, I was almost positive, she meant that our place was small, with numerous dark corners. I tried to remind myself that I would not exactly be comfortable in Raine's rundown, collegiate-feeling community house out in California, so why should I expect her to be comfortable in my house here? It wasn't as if I thought we were the same person.

But, "We like it" was all I said.

I wished Lucas wasn't so busy, that he hadn't gotten that new client last week, which meant he was lost somewhere in his office, designing logic trees and mapping out code for a brand-new security job. And then I felt incredibly guilty that I thought I deserved to be rescued by Lucas when I repaid him by almost kissing Matt Cheney.

I was, I realized, a gigantic asshole.

"I'm sorry I missed you yesterday," Raine said, settling herself in the middle of the couch. Her scarves fluttered about her and then came to rest against her sides, undulating slightly as she breathed. She looked as boneless as one of the cats—both of whom had disappeared the moment Raine crossed the threshold.

"It was pointed out to me that I should have called first," I said, waving her apology away. "And it's really an easy train ride, anyway." I deliberately chose not to think of Verena as I said that, and her disbelief that I had traveled so far for so little reason.

"Matt said you seemed mad that he was there," Raine said. I felt the back of my neck tingle, and realized I recognized the edge in her voice. She usually used it on Norah. "I thought I told you he was coming. I thought you were okay with it. *He* thought everything was cool between you two."

Which, of course, meant that he and Raine had discussed it.

"Oh, well, sure," I stammered, because my mind was racing. What had he told her? Did she know? About what had happened six years ago? About what had happened yesterday? "I mean, of course it's—"

I broke off and forced myself to take a breath before continuing.

"I wasn't mad that he was there," I told her.

"I didn't think you would be," she said. "Matt can be

such a drama queen." She crooked a brow at me, daring me to disagree.

"Yeah," I agreed on cue, more because I wanted to agree with Raine than because I had ever given thought to Matt Cheney's drama queeniness.

I had the oddest sensation that Raine had confused me with Norah. *This is who Norah sees*, I thought. This prickly, challenging, upsetting person. But that didn't make any sense.

Raine looked over, and I watched her study my cello and music stand. They stood together in the bay window, with my music spread out across the window seat only the cats used, all of it arranged like a perfect picture. I had often taken that picture, in fact, when, like now, sunshine poured in the window and lit up my practice space. It looked like the perfect place to create music. I felt my hand twitch, as if reaching for a note.

"So do you really practice each day?" Raine asked. "Like when you were a kid?"

Naturally, this question made me look down at my hands, neither of which had touched the cello in weeks. Except for today, and that was to dust it. Some kind of professional I was this summer.

"Normally I do," I said, but then felt compelled to be honest. "During the season, definitely. I have to practice. They expect us to come to rehearsal with the piece already learned."

Raine shook her head as if I were a foreign, alien creature.

"I really don't know how you do it," she said, laughing slightly.

"Want me to give you a cello lesson?" It came to me out of nowhere, and I thought it was maybe the best idea I'd ever had. I could share the cello with Raine, and finally someone in my family would understand why it had taken over my whole life. I didn't know why it had never occurred to me before. Raine, obviously, was the most likely person to understand why it moved me so much— she was an artist, too.

"I couldn't," Raine said after a moment, looking from me to the cello and then back. She made a sad face. "I'm tone deaf."

"Oh." It kind of hurt that she hadn't jumped at the offer. Or even pretended to be interested. "You don't actually have to play anything hard. It would be fun!"

"Maybe some other time," Raine said. She sat forward. "I want to know about *you*, Courtney. Not your cello."

It was my turn to laugh. Raine gave me a quizzical look.

"They're kind of the same thing," I pointed out. "Two great tastes that taste great together. You can't have one without the other, you know?"

Raine clasped her hands together in front of her knees. Naturally, this made her scarves tremble.

"Do you still play your own music?" she asked.

"My own?" I echoed. I didn't know what she was talking about.

"You wrote a whole musical number for your senior year, I thought," Raine said. She frowned. "Am I making that up?"

I remembered that part of my senior project at the conservatory then, and laughed again.

"My God," I said. I shook my head. "I haven't thought about that piece in years. Which is a good thing. It was horrible."

"I remember being impressed," Raine said sternly, as if she'd caught me putting myself down.

"I'm sure it was fine for what it was," I said with a shrug.

"Courtney." She looked at me. "It was good."

Clearly, she thought I was being unnecessarily humble. I didn't know how to handle that, because I was speaking the simple truth. After all, I played good music all the time. I could tell the difference.

"I'm glad you thought so," I said, although what I really was, if I thought about it, was surprised she could even remember it. "But really, it was very amateurish. I'd be embarrassed if anyone at the Symphony got a hold of it."

Raine watched me. Closely enough that I began to feel vaguely uncomfortable. And, for some reason, overly aware of my naked feet on the smooth wood floor. I clenched my toes, then relaxed them.

"So you like it there," she said.

"Of course," I said warily. There was something in her tone that made me feel I shouldn't admit that. "It's an honor to be a part of an orchestra with such a great history. And I like the fact that I get to give back to the arts community here in Philly. It was what saved me when I was a kid."

I immediately wished I hadn't said that out loud, to someone who might not realize that I'd needed to be saved back when I was a kid. But she didn't seem to have any kind of emotional reaction. She just studied my face for a moment before speaking.

"Don't you get bored?" she asked.

"What do you mean?"

"Well, it's all the same old music, isn't it?" Raine asked. Her voice was sweet. The way it was when she told Norah that she was controlling. "Mozart, Bach, Beethoven. Doesn't it get old? All those dead white guys."

I stared at her for a long moment. The noontime sun was flooding in through the bay window, illuminating her breathtakingly pretty face and the mild curiosity written across it. I felt as if she'd punched me hard enough to steal my breath.

"The thing is," Lucas said from behind Raine, walking across the living room, "those dead white guys wrote some fucking amazing music. There's a reason we have whole radio stations dedicated to them centuries later. They were geniuses."

I hadn't even seen him back there, I'd been too focused on Raine.

"Plus," I said, because some part of me recognized that I didn't deserve his White Knight routine at the moment, "it's all about interpreting the music. Every time you play a note, it's different. The way you play it changes the interpretation. And of course, what the conductor wants changes things, too. Some conductors want to be more interpretive, some want to be traditional, it all depends."

I looked over at Lucas, who smiled at me. Which made me feel like the worst person who had ever lived. Then I looked back at Raine, who was nodding.

"That sounds great," she said, but I got the same feeling

I had back in Berkeley. That she wanted more for me than interpreting the work of long dead men. That she thought my doing so was disappointing, somehow, and meant that I wasn't living up to my potential. I looked down.

"I just poked my head out to say hello," Lucas said then, widening his stance as he stood there looking down at us. "I'm sorry I can't hang out, Raine, but I have way too much work to do. I had a couple of projects explode over the past few days."

"That's no problem," Raine said, rising to her feet. She seemed to move upward from her hips, without involving any other body part. It made her scarves writhe about her body like she was some kind of snake charmer.

Then she smiled at Lucas as she stood there.

"Everybody loves a working man," she drawled at him, and gave him a look I could only describe as saucy.

Lucas and I watched her as she swayed her way out of the room and then down the hall toward the bathroom. The bathroom door shut behind her, and Lucas turned slowly around to look at me.

"Are you okay?" he asked me, his voice soft. It was that softness, that caring, that I couldn't bear.

"What? Of course," I said. A tad aggressively. "I'm great."

"If you say so."

"Not everybody *gets* classical music," I told him with some heat. "It just doesn't speak to everybody. It's not a big deal."

"Okay," he said. He leaned over and kissed me. But I

couldn't look at him. For so many reasons. "I'll be in my office if you need me."

It was evening by the time I left Raine in the hubbub of 30th Street Station, where she planned to wander in and out of the shops for a while as she waited for her train back out to Mom's house. I took a Blue Line train to 13th and Market and then walked the rest of the way back home, feeling lower with every step I took. Raine and I had had a tense lunch, during which she had psychoanalyzed Norah to such a degree that it felt a good deal more like a character assassination. She had been dismissive of our mother and talked at length about how much she hated our hometown and everyone in it. And she'd done it all while watching me with that hard gleam in her eyes, like I was a part of the problem.

I would have been more upset about it, but I was too busy being preoccupied with what had happened in my living room. What she'd said. The fact was, it had never occurred to me, at age ten, to do anything other than play what I was taught. I'd loved the mellow beauty of the notes the cello sung; the way the melodies sounded threaded through with melancholy when played on a cello. I hadn't been capable of articulating that then, of course. I'd simply known that the cello spoke to me. I poured all my love and attention into the instrument, and it had never occurred to me to step back and critically assess the *kind* of music I played. I was just happy to be playing.

As time went on, I'd experimented here and there with

other forms of musical expression. I'd played for a while with a few friends at the conservatory in a kind of jazz group. I loved the cello-based rock of Rasputina, and I listened to Zoe Keating's mysterious and breathtaking solo cello albums as often as I listened to Yo-Yo Ma or Pablo Casals play Bach. I'd learned how to play the theme song to the TV show *Angel* because I thought it was so pretty and so mournful, and because whenever I played it in the middle of my practice sessions, it would bring Lucas out of his office and make us both laugh.

But the bulk of the music I played was, as Raine had pointed out, dead white men. Whatever I might try on the side, I always returned to the same basic repertoire. And after all these years of playing the same pieces again and again, I still loved them. I loved moving through musical eras, from the splendor of Baroque to the clarity of Classicism, and then into the imagination of Romanticism. Vivaldi to Mozart to Debussy. There were newer composers I suspected Raine had never heard of, like Samuel Barber or Béla Bartók. Living composers like Philip Glass. Making me and my cello a part of an ongoing musical conversation, one that never ended, but played again and again across the ages.

Was this failing, somehow, to live up to my potential? I turned this question over and over in my head as I turned onto our street. Classical music certainly wasn't the hippest or coolest thing in the world. It was about as traditional as it was possible to get. I didn't think of myself as traditional—I couldn't even bring myself to plan my own wedding.

Why was it, I wondered, that I felt so ordinary and unfulfilled whenever I was around Raine? Was this what Norah had warned me about? That she would judge my life and find it wanting? The trouble was, I wasn't sure whether or not Raine was judging me, but I sure was.

Was it so wrong that deep down, I'd wanted Raine to be impressed with what I'd become in her absence? That I'd wanted her to see me as more of an equal and less of a child?

The fact that she didn't seem to notice any change in me made me worry that I hadn't made any changes at all. It was as if I were still twenty-two as far as Raine was concerned. It made me think that maybe she was right, and I still was.

I let myself into the apartment and found Lucas stretched out on the couch, with a cat curled up under each arm. He was watching his favorite channel: the channel guide. He liked to know the sheer number of programs he could, at any moment, be watching.

I dropped my keys in the bowl near the phone, and then wandered over to collapse next to him. The little girl cat meowed a protest or a greeting; it sounded very much the same either way.

"Did you have fun?" Lucas asked.

"It was okay," I said, kicking off my shoes. I slumped back against the couch. Not used to having distance between us, it didn't occur to me to keep myself from confiding in him. "Did it ever occur to you that I might not be living up to my potential?"

Lucas sighed and clicked off the television. Startled, I turned to look at him.

"Did it ever occur to *you*," he asked, each word so slow and deliberate I got the feeling they'd been boiling in there, "that your sister Raine is jealous of you?"

I think my mouth actually fell open.

"And I have a radical idea," he said, temper kicking in his voice. "How about you tell her to fuck off instead of letting her play passive-aggressive games with your head?"

chapter nineteen

"What are you talking about?" I demanded, staring at Lucas as if he'd lost his mind.

"I'm talking about your sister," Lucas said in a very controlled, but still notably tense tone. "I heard her in here, making all her insinuations and talking about your career like having a chair on a major symphony orchestra is something you should be embarrassed about." He rolled his eyes. "Yet taking pictures of her own crotch and plastering them across a bar in San Francisco? That's art."

"There's something about Raine that's just *free*," I argued, feeling compelled to leap to the defense of those pictures for the second time. She was my *sister*, after all. He didn't understand the context. "She doesn't have to practice every day, she isn't compelled to do what anybody tells her, and she gets to live her life on her own terms."

Unlike Lucas and me, who worked all the time, and were forever answering to other people: Lucas to his clients, me to my fellow cellists, the orchestra, the conductor, the audiences—the list went on and on.

"And what does she do with all this glorious freedom?" Lucas asked. The sarcasm in his voice was scathing. "Oh, right, she tends bar. Not very well, as I remember. And she sticks a camera in her crotch and then is pretentious about it."

"Stop saying *crotch*!" I snapped at him. "Just because you and I might not understand Raine's art doesn't mean it's bad."

"In some places, they have a name for sticking cameras into your privates and sharing it with the world." His eyebrows rose. "And that word is 'porn.'"

"Those pictures were not *porn*."

"That's a good point," he retorted. "After all, porn is generally titillating."

I ran a hand over my face.

"You really want to have a debate about the artistic merit of Raine's photographs?" I asked after a moment. "Really, Lucas?"

He crossed his arms over his chest, probably because I'd invoked The Name in the middle of a fight. We'd discovered that we could always tell that it was a big deal when one of us called the other by Our Name, rather than an endearment.

"I can't understand why you let her talk to you like that," he said, and I could see the temper in his eyes. I saw it so rarely that I was a little taken back. "I don't understand anything that's happening in your family right now, if you want to know the truth."

"What's happening in my family is that we're all together

for the first time in six years," I said, annoyed that I had to remind him, "and I thought you knew how important this is to me."

Lucas sighed as if he thought I was being unreasonable, and leaned forward.

"Courtney," he said. Using The Name right back. "Of course I know how important this is to you. But why isn't it important to anyone else? Doesn't that bother you? Even a little bit?"

"Raine flew all the way across the country." I glared at him. "What else is she supposed to do?"

"Our engagement party is in ten days," Lucas said, as if that might have escaped my notice, with my mother calling daily about hors d'oeuvres. "You and your mother talk about it on the phone, but it never even comes up in conversation with your sisters. Don't you think that's weird?"

What I thought was that I felt entirely too emotional to be having this upsetting and hostile conversation about my family. And I also thought that I felt sucker punched. He had obviously been waiting around, dying to say these things to me.

Of all the things we should have been talking about, the Cassel family dynamics were not high on the list.

"I don't need all that fairy princess, it's-your-special-day, Bridezilla crap," I told him, because it was easier to concentrate on that part of it. "That's not who I am. I'm not the sort of person who needs to be the center of attention for the entire span of her engagement."

As he should know already, I thought.

"That's a good thing," Lucas bit out. "Because as far as

I can see, you're never going to be the center of attention at all. Raine supposedly flew all the way out here to see you and celebrate you, and so far the only thing anyone's talked about is ancient history."

"Again," I grated at him, "she's been away for years. Of course history is going to come up! It would be much weirder if we all ignored it, wouldn't it?"

"It's not just Raine," Lucas said, never looking away from me. "Even the day we got engaged couldn't be about us. Not even one meal. There were about fifteen minutes between congratulations and yet another big drama about Norah's wedding and her hurt feelings."

"Okay," I said impatiently, "I think there were some extenuating circumstances—"

"You know, I was sitting there the other night, listening to Norah and Raine throw down over who's the artist in the family," Lucas kept on, ignoring my protest.

"And now you want to have the argument, too?" I asked, completely confused. Why was he doing this? Did he know, somehow, about the almost-kiss? Was he using this round-about approach to fight about it?

"I knew you wouldn't say anything," Lucas said. I found I couldn't look away from him. "Because you never do."

"What was I supposed to say?" I shrugged. "They've been having that same fight for the past twenty-eight years. It's always better to just let them have it and try to contain the damage."

"You're missing the point," Lucas said. He looked almost sad, and frustrated, too. "There's exactly one artist in the Cassel family, Courtney. And it's you."

"I'm not that kind of artist," I demurred at once, shaking my head.

"No," Lucas agreed with an edge to his voice. "You're the professional, working kind. You actually make your living playing music. You don't wait tables on the side while making a whole lot of noise about how you have a *vision*. You just do your job, and you do it well. And yet, not one of your family members even mentioned that. They never do."

It began to dawn on me that he wasn't angry because he had found me out. He was genuinely angry on my behalf. He was trying to protect me.

I hadn't thought I was capable of feeling worse.

"I don't think they think of what I do as *art*," I said slowly.

"Of course they don't," Lucas replied, in a withering tone. "Because to do that, they would have to think about you in the first place."

"How can you say that?" I demanded, aware that tears were making tracks down my cheeks.

"I'm not trying to be cruel. I love you, and I hate this." He let out a frustrated noise.

"They're my *family*!" I told him, crying openly. I couldn't have said what, exactly, I was crying about.

"That doesn't mean they should get a free pass to treat you like you don't exist," Lucas threw back. He raked a hand through his thick auburn hair, making it spike up. Normally I found that adorable. "Your sister stood right in this living room and hit on me," he said, outraged. "Directly in front of you. What the hell was that? Who does something like that?"

"That's just Raine..." I started to say.

But I couldn't really defend that particular moment. *Everybody loves a working man* had been playing on a loop in my head all day. Until now I had been trying to pretend it hadn't happened.

"It's *fucked up*," Lucas said in a low, angry voice. "Your mom apparently checked out and has been leading a secret life for decades. Norah talks to you like you're a particularly dim-witted seven-year-old, incapable of making your own decisions. And Raine has made it perfectly clear that she doesn't care about you at all. I stood in the kitchen today and listened to her make you feel like shit about a career you've worked your ass off for every single day since you were a kid. It's obvious to me that they're all pathologically jealous of you, but I don't think that's ever even occurred to you."

"It hasn't occurred to me because it's ridiculous," I told him. "I had no idea how much you hated my family."

"Don't make this about me," Lucas said in a tight voice. "I love *you*. I care about your family, but I don't like how they treat you." He shook his head and looked around as if looking for inspiration, or evidence. "My mom keeps asking me how you're enjoying having both your sisters around, because she assumes that means they're out looking for wedding dresses with you, or helping you plan things. I haven't had the heart to tell her that they're far more interested in having the next round of their endless battle with each other."

"I'm sorry that your family is so much better than mine!" I yelled at him then, something cracking inside my chest. "Maybe if your father had run off while your mother was pregnant with you, you'd be a little more understanding now!"

There was a choked sort of silence then. If I could have, I would have reached out and plucked those words out of the air and shoved them back down inside where they belonged. But I could only breathe, and realize as I did so that each breath was ragged. And my lungs didn't seem to be doing their job at all.

"Is that was this is about?" Lucas asked softly, his eyes suddenly kind. Which was so much worse than what had come before.

I couldn't answer that. I wiped the tears from my cheeks.

"They might be dysfunctional, but they're all I have," I whispered toward the floor.

"Hey," Lucas said. I looked up.

"They are *not* all you have," he said. "You have me." He held out his hands as if he contained us both within his palms. "This is our family. Right here. This is what matters."

And to honor that, I had nearly kissed Matt Cheney. That was the kind of woman I was.

I felt my face crumple in, and then, without meaning to, I found myself sobbing. Lucas put his arms around me and held me tight against the heat of his hard chest.

"I'm sorry," I got out at some point, between sobs, and he just shushed me.

He held me like that for a long time, and when I woke up I was in our bed, and it was morning.

If I was very still, I could hear Lucas's voice through the wall. He was probably on the phone with a client, but all I could hear was the abstract music of his tenor voice. Faint and far, but it made me feel slightly better just to hear him nearby.

I was glad he was already up, because the truth was, I felt embarrassed. I stretched out on my stomach and felt a cat body tight in the V of my legs, making it impossible to roll over onto my back. So instead, I opened my eyes— noting they felt swollen and huge—and saw the other cat sitting on the very edge of the bed with her back to me. She was sitting very rigidly and staring with apparent rapt attention elsewhere, but her tail gave her away. It twitched and pointed accusingly at me, indicating in cat speak that while she couldn't be bothered to *look* at me, she was pissed about something. And it could be anything: it might be too hot, her food bowl might be at an unacceptable level, she might feel the litter box was not adequately maintained, she might just have a mood on.

She would have to get in line, I thought, and let my mind return to the night before.

I had poured everything I had into my cello. Everything I was, and became. All my love, hope, and dreams. Because the truth was, I'd had three parents and I'd had none, all at the same time. Lucas wasn't wrong about the level of interest my family had shown in my activities. I'd learned early on how to lug my cello on and off the train, even back when it was much taller than I was, because I was responsible for getting myself to my various tutors and schools on my own. I might have thought from time to time that my sisters and my mother could have shown a little more interest in what was going on with me, and I might have hated having to be the fatherless girl on those excruciating Dad Days at school, but none of that mattered when I was playing. I could fall into the music and let it take me somewhere far better, and more magical, than my forever sad, endlessly grief-stricken family.

We had been like soldiers in the same trench, I thought. That was how I'd described it once to Verena. We were all overwhelmed by the loss of Dad. Mom mourned, and taught us all how to mourn with her. We grew up with a ghost, and the difference between my sisters and me was that I was to blame for it.

Of course I knew that I, as a fetus, had nothing personally to do with a grown man's decision to leave his family. I knew this intellectually. But the truth was, Dad hadn't wanted a third child. He hadn't been happy working in pharmaceuticals at SmithKline. I had been the last straw. There was just no getting around the truth of that—and I knew that better than anyone; I'd been trying to get around the truth of it for twenty-eight years.

Somewhere inside, I knew that Lucas was right. I shouldn't accept how my family treated me when it upset me so much. But I also knew that he couldn't imagine how much that old guilt still motivated me. I was sure it was bound up in everything my sisters did or didn't do. I was convinced that sometimes they looked at me and wondered what might have happened if Mom had never gotten pregnant with me when she had.

Would Dad have stayed? Was he always going to leave

us or was I the straw that broke the camel's back? I couldn't be the only one who'd wondered about these things. I couldn't be the only one who'd figured that if looked at in a certain way, the Cassel family might have been better off if I'd never been born.

And when I looked at it that way, it seemed, the way it always had, not to matter so much that my family didn't treat me the way the Cleavers treated one another.

When I looked at it that way, I felt almost pathetically grateful any of them talked to me at all.

chapter twenty

I was confident I could have brooded about that for days, having already brooded about it on some level my whole life, but there was one part of what Lucas had said that I couldn't entirely push out of my mind: the dress.

Not the wedding dress. God.

My mind balked at the very idea of a wedding dress. I figured I would get to that eventually, after I dealt with choosing a wedding date, picking a wedding venue, and whatever else those terrifying magazines demanded brides do, tear-out sheets in hand, while becoming deeply serious about ring pillows and cake toppers. Items I currently could not have identified if my life depended upon it.

First things first. I needed something suitable to wear to our engagement party.

"You will not wear something *suitable* to your engagement party!" Verena gasped at me when I called her. I sensed that even mouthing the word *suitable* caused her physical harm. "You will wear something *stunning*!" She actually moaned. "How can we be friends? I don't understand."

"Fine," I replied, too exhausted to argue. "Want to go shopping this weekend?"

There was a small silence.

Then, "*Yes*," Verena breathed reverently. "I can't tell you how long I've been waiting to hear you utter those words."

It got out of control quickly. Verena wasn't satisfied with half-measures, so my vision of a quick circuit through Center City was promptly vetoed. Verena demanded the King of Prussia Mall, complete with some four hundred stores at our disposal.

"Why do we need four hundred stores?" I asked, because I was foolish. I had once lived with Verena, after all. I knew that "need" had nothing to do with it.

"We don't," she replied at once, with a derisive sniff. "We need only four: Macy's, Nordstrom's, Neiman Marcus, and Bloomingdale's." She considered. "And *maybe* Lord & Taylor, or, as I like to call it, Loud & Tacky. That would be our final, desperate attempt should all else fail, it goes without saying."

It snowballed from there, because the fact was, I was embarrassed that Lucas's mother had visions of my family life that he didn't have the heart to dispel. So I called both of my sisters and invited them to come shopping with Verena and me. I expected them both to decline the invitation, of course. I couldn't recall ever shopping with my sisters, and certainly not with both of them at the same time.

"I was going to head out there anyway this weekend,"

Norah told me when we spoke, sounding as surprised as I felt. "There wasn't anything festive in my closet, either."

So she was in. Which made me sure that Raine would find any possible reason under the sun to avoid the little outing. But I felt I had to offer anyway.

"Oh, I'd love to go," she drawled, sounding delighted at the very idea. "Sisterly bonding is actually a really critical part of a woman's development. I don't know if you know that, but it's super important, Courtney."

And that was how I found myself at the King of Prussia Mall, in King of Prussia, Pennsylvania, on a busy summer afternoon with both of my sisters.

"So far, so good," Verena muttered into my ear. Her eyebrows appeared to be permanently lodged up near her hairline, as she and I literally walked in between my two sisters—both of whom appeared to be on a mission to kill the other with a politeness so crisp it bordered on cold. Which, all things considered, I chose to take as a positive sign.

"I don't know what you mean by that," I muttered back, my eyes darting from one sister to the other. "This is obviously all going to go horribly wrong."

"Yes," Verena agreed. "But it hasn't *yet*." She sighed. "And that's really all we have to cling to here."

As a group, we headed for Macy's first, which Verena claimed was her favorite.

"Why?" Raine asked her. "Aren't all department stores the same?"

Verena glared at her. "Take that back," she demanded.

"I don't really shop that much," Raine said with a shrug.

"We are going to Macy's first," Verena said, her tone brooking no argument. "Follow me please, ladies."

As we set off on our march across the crowded mall, I watched Norah eye Raine up and down, from her very San Francisco-y sandals to her floor-length skirt, tank top, and no less than seventy-six strands of beads. Her gaze lingered on Raine's artfully tousled hair. Norah, meanwhile, looked beautifully pulled-together in a V-neck, black T-shirt and khaki shorts. The hot weather hadn't affected her slick, pulled-back ponytail in the slightest. She looked cool and imposing from her diamond-studded ears to her sensible black Merrells.

Verena had dressed for the occasion in a vintage yellow gown with a gigantic bow, and high-heeled stiletto sandals. Despite the fact that she was wearing footwear that would have crippled me to stand still in, she was setting the pace with her long strides.

Everyone seemed so...*extremely* themselves. I glanced at myself in a glossy storefront as we passed and noticed that I didn't look like much of anything. I was wearing the same comfortable cutoffs I always wore, and a white T-shirt. I'd piled my hair on top of my head with an elastic, and I had a light sweatshirt tied around my waist in case I got cold in the air-conditioning. I felt as if I could blend into any of the groups passing us without comment. No one would even notice. It was only when I was holding a cello that I burst out and became noticeable, I thought, consoling myself.

I paid more attention to the here and now when Raine peeled off into one of the small, expensive-looking boutiques along the way.

"Call me on my cell!" she cried, disappearing into the pounding techno music.

Norah, moments later, stopped walking outside Banana Republic.

"This is more my speed," she told me. "I'll catch up with you after I find what I need."

"Whatever," Verena said when Norah strode away. She linked her arm through mine. "It's better this way. I was having visions of them throwing down in the Marc Jacobs section."

I understood without having to ask that it would be unacceptable to ask who this Marc person was, so I just remained silent.

"I guess it's for the best that they wanted to do their own thing," I said as we stood on the Macy's escalator headed for the women's section. "I don't know what I want anyway, and having them stand around would just be a recipe for disaster."

The truth was, I couldn't help thinking about what Lucas had said. That they didn't care about me. That what they cared about was fighting with each other. No matter how hard I tried, I kept coming up against the unpleasant worry that he was right.

And I didn't want him to be right. Because that meant he must love me enough to know me, and my family, so well. Which was unbearable, because I was about three seconds away from collapsing in on myself from the guilt of what had happened with Matt. *Almost* happened with Matt.

The worst part was, I kept expecting Matt to do something crazy. Show up at my house. Call. I wasn't sure. I felt that at any moment he could burst forth and destroy the whole life I'd built. Or simply tell Lucas what I'd done and reveal that I'd destroyed it myself.

"What's going on?" Verena asked, peering at me. "You look like you're about to cry."

"No," I lied. "I'm not. I'm fine."

But she was frowning at me as we stepped from the escalator.

"I know that face, " she said, sucking in her breath. She looked horrified. And then she actually lifted up her hand and pointed at me. *"Matt Cheney!"* she cried, the way people might have cried *witch* in days of yore.

"What are you doing?" I tried to swat her hand down.

"You forget that I am the world's leading expert on how miserable you get about him," Verena hissed, still pointing. "I told you to stay away from him. Why don't you listen to me?"

"I'm listening to you!" I looked around wildly. "Everyone in the entire King of Prussia Mall is listening to you!"

"What about Lucas?" Verena demanded. "Did you stop for one second and think about him?"

"The day I went over to my mom's house, and Matt was there..." I couldn't bear to go on, but I didn't think I could stand the way she was looking at me, either. "There was this moment."

"A moment," she echoed. Disapproving Puritans in *The*

Scarlet Letter were less stern. She crossed her arms over her chest.

"It was like..." I blew out a breath. "He almost kissed me."

"Define *almost*," she snapped.

"We *almost* kissed," I snapped right back. "Almost, but then we didn't. We didn't actually touch."

"Did you slap him upside his head?" Verena asked angrily. "Maybe using the hand with the diamond ring?"

"I pushed him away," I said, sounding affronted, although I knew better. I had been saving myself more than stopping him.

"But you've been holding on to it ever since, haven't you," Verena said, her voice colder with every syllable. "I can't believe you. I can't believe you would throw away everything you have like this."

"I think you're overreacting."

"Really?" She shook her head. "I know where this ends already." She threw up her hands. Literally. "I can't watch you do this again, Courtney. I refuse."

And then she turned on her heel and walked away from me.

I made Verena's excuses to my sisters when they turned up. I claimed she'd had an allergy attack, which, given her feelings about Matt Cheney, wasn't far from the truth.

"Maybe she decided to go put on something more appropriate," Norah said with a sniff. "This is a suburban mall, not a burlesque show."

"Those of us who aren't happy looking like Soccer Mom Clones," Raine drawled, all kinds of patronizing, "express ourselves through our clothes."

Norah let her eyes travel from the top of Raine's head to her Birkenstocks.

"Let me guess," she murmured. "You're expressing your affinity for *Les Misérables*? Or is it the orthopedic shoes that define you?"

As Raine bared her teeth at Norah, I tuned them out and looked for something to wear. Without Verena, I worried I'd be lost, but it turned out I didn't have to worry. I knew the dress the moment I saw it, and I was even more sure the moment I slipped it on in the dressing room. It was a dark copper color, almost gold, that fit me like a column of fire and made my skin and hair come alive. Even with my hair twisted up on the back of my head in a scrunchie, I was struck dumb by my reflection.

I padded out of the dressing room in my bare feet to the larger, loungelike area, where my sisters sat waiting for me on the farthest possible opposite edges of the same couch. I could see no visible marks on either of them, so assumed they'd kept themselves to verbal sniping. Unlike some of their more memorable skirmishes.

I stopped thinking about their troubled history because I could see myself in the big mirror at the end of the room. I was all gold and flame.

Noticeable, as me. No cello involved.

I liked it. More than liked it.

Norah, a Banana Republic bag in hand because no store's inventory would dream of defying her when she needed something, nodded. She had a curious look on her face.

"You should wear that color more often," she said. "It does wonders for your skin. You look great."

"Thank you," I said. I instructed myself not to immediately wonder how my skin looked with every other hue in the color spectrum. I told myself—sternly—that she had not meant that the way it sounded.

Then I looked at Raine, who was eyeing me in a way I found familiar, though I couldn't quite place it.

"That's quite a dress," she said when she saw I was looking at her.

"It's good, right?" I asked.

"She looks wonderful," Norah said, glaring at Raine. "Doesn't she?"

But Raine was wearing the strangest expression then, and I had a picture-perfect memory of that yoga studio in Berkeley, and the look on Raine's face when she'd nodded hello to the odious Bronwen. It was that same look. The look I knew meant she didn't like Bronwen at all.

But that couldn't be right.

Bronwen was nasty and who knew what a long strange war she and Raine had been in. For all I knew, Bronwen was one of the housemates in that house in addition to being messy with Matt. That relationship was far more complicated than I could imagine, I was sure.

And anyway, I wasn't Bronwen. I was Raine's sister. Her favorite sister.

But that wasn't how she was looking at me.

"I'm so glad I got to see this," she told me, her voice soft and easy.

I found I couldn't believe it. She cocked her head to the side like she was some kind of sparrow.

"I had no idea how pretty you were."

"You have to drop whatever you're doing and come down here right now," Verena commanded me over the phone. "I'm regretting making this phone call even as I'm doing it."

It was noticeably loud and chaotic where she was, as I imagined it would be anywhere out and about in Philadelphia on a Friday night, and she was shouting over the background noise into her cell phone. In our apartment, by way of contrast, the AC was keeping everything cool, *Law & Order* was on television, Lucas was barricaded in his office, and everything was peaceful and good. Loud and chaotic was unappealing in the extreme.

"I thought we were in a fight," I said. "That was the impression I got when you disappeared in the King of Prussia Mall. Call me crazy."

"I decided, totally at the last minute, to come down to this new 'fusion' open mike night thing," Verena told me, much as if I hadn't spoken. "I read about it online this afternoon and I thought, what the hell? Why not try some fusion?"

"And then I definitely thought we were in a fight with the not talking for days," I continued. Because we could both have our own private conversation. "And I don't know what you mean by fusion, anyway."

"In this case, it means you get the stage for five min-utes and you can do whatever you want on it," she said, surprising me by responding directly to me. "I saw some kid with bongos, and no, I'm afraid I'm not kidding. It's seriously open mike. Spoken word followed by bongos fol-lowed by the comedy stylings of yours truly."

"So I guess we're not in a fight then." I waited. She was silent. "And now I'm confused again."

"We're not in a fight," she said finally, but I could hear her teeth grit as she said it. "You're my best friend no mat-ter what you do, Courtney. Even if it's masochistic, sui-cidal, and plain fucking stupid, that doesn't mean I don't love you."

"Um, thanks. I love you, too."

"I don't care if you love me right now," she snapped. "What I am *trying* to tell you is that when I signed up for my spot, guess who's name was already down for a 10:20 slot?"

"Someone famous?" I queried. "Ooh, was it someone *really* famous? Like David Letterman?"

I could actually feel the force of Verena's glare from across the span of Center City, Philadelphia.

"David Letterman?" she demanded. "Why would *David Letterman* be doing a five-minute open mike fusion event with an opening bongo act?"

"To keep his stand-up skills fresh?" I asked. My knowl-edge of stand-up comedy was limited to a romance novel I'd read once in junior high, that depressing Billy Crystal movie, and Verena's attempts, which usually involved her twisting things that she talked about anyway into "bits" that, unsurprisingly I felt, made people laugh.

"Um, no," Verena said after a moment. "David Letterman is not performing at The Lodge at 10:20 on a random Saturday night." She heaved a long-suffering sigh. "But, and may I someday forgive myself for this, Matt Cheney is."

chapter twenty-one

"Wait, where are you going?"

Lucas squinted up at me from the huge flat-screen monitor of one of his computers. He looked exhausted. But that was to be expected, as he'd been living in his office pretty much around the clock for going on weeks now.

And of course, everything was weird between us. Reason enough to hide in an office if you had one.

"Verena needs moral support," I told him, the lie out and sitting there in the middle of the office floor before I could do anything to stop it.

I hadn't planned to say that, I didn't think. I didn't know why I had. But once it had been said, I didn't see how I could take it back. If I now said, *Oh, and Matt Cheney is also performing, as a big coincidence*, he would know I was lying. That I had lied. That, more to the point, I thought there was something to lie about.

"Is she doing a new routine?" Lucas asked. "I liked her old one. I thought that whole part about the anorexic girls with pets who outweigh them was hilarious. She should keep that."

Now that I was actively lying, instead of simply not sharing information, I didn't know what to do. I shifted my weight from one foot to the other and hoped he wouldn't notice that I'd felt the need to put on a significant amount of mascara to go sit and support Verena.

"I like all her routines," I said, more to the space in the floor where my lie was still squatting than to him.

Lucas looked at me, and I could actually feel his attention sharpen, like he'd been distracted before but was just that moment realizing the full and obvious sketchiness of my behavior.

Then from behind him, the incoming e-mail alert beeped, and he blinked.

"Have fun," he said, his attention already shifting from me. "Laugh for me."

Because, of course, he trusted me.

A fact that caused shame to burn through me, though it didn't keep me from leaving.

When I arrived at the bar, in a mildly rundown section of West Philly, it was far more crowded than I'd expected it to be, given the neighborhood. Apparently, fusion was hip. I paid a small cover and then let my eyes adjust to the dim interior light inside. There was a comic onstage, bombing, if the high level of chatter from the rest of the place was anything to go by.

A closer look showed me that the comic onstage was, in fact, the very bald, very intense, and very short man who had offered me unsolicited moral support at the previous open mike event.

"Love," he ranted into the microphone, "is a sick old dog on a hot summer's day. *You know it's true, people!*"

The mike picked up some reverb when he screamed that last part, which definitely got him some attention. None of it positive. Verena had explained to me that sometimes, when the crowd was already lost, she antagonized them just to make sure they remembered her name. It was better than nothing, she felt.

Yet somehow, I didn't think that's what he was doing. Or anyway, not on purpose.

I applauded loudly for the small, angry man when he stormed off the stage, and never mind that I was largely on my own.

Knowing that the performers often hung out around the bar while they waited for their slot, and not wanting to run into Matt Cheney, at least not before I heard him play, I snuck around the side and found a small table almost behind a column. I could see the stage and the bar, but only someone looking for me would be able to spot me there. I felt sly. When the waitress came by, I ordered two beers and waited.

"Hey," Verena said about ten minutes later, slipping into the seat next to me. She looked stiff and cold—i.e., pissed at me—but she picked up the beer I'd ordered for her and took a pull. "How long have you been here?"

"Not long," I said. I frowned at her. "Is it weird that when

Lucas asked where I was going, I told him you needed moral support? And I didn't mention Matt Cheney at all?"

Verena blew out a breath. She flicked me a cold look from beneath the extravagant false eyelashes she was sporting for the evening.

"Do you really want me to answer that?" she asked testily.

"No." I sighed. "I already know what you think."

"I wish I knew what you were thinking," she retorted. "Lying to that sweet man of yours. And for what?" She waved her hand at the stage. "This nonsense? I almost wish you were fucking him in some motel room. At least that would be more honest."

"God, Verena," I muttered. My mind shied away from the word and the associated images. Not because I was a prude. But because thinking about fucking Matt Cheney could lead nowhere good.

"I said it would be more honest and I meant it," she snapped. "You wafting around like Ophelia is maddening. Let me remind you, Matt Cheney is not Hamlet. Not by a long shot."

"I get it," I said, meaning, *please shut up.* "You're the one who called me, remember?"

"Let me share with you what I hope happens here," she continued, unbothered by the fact I was scowling at her. "Didn't you say he was a bouncer now? I'm hoping he crashes and burns up there, so you can get that romantic idea of him right out of your head."

"It could happen," I agreed, but I doubted it.

I had always loved Matt's music. His scratchy voice and his acoustic guitar had been beyond beautiful to me. Even if he hadn't played in a long time, I imagined I would still feel that thrill inside that I associated with really, truly being moved by the music. I didn't think I'd enjoyed his music because I'd been so young and so in love with him, either. While those things might have affected other areas of my judgment, I was pretty sure they hadn't affected my hearing.

I had precious memories of that airless room up under the eaves in his grandfather's house. I would sit on the bed with my feet dangling free, and Matt would sit in his chair with his guitar and pluck melodies out of thin air. When I thought of his songs, I thought less of the finished ones he wrote and more of his intent look of concentration as he bent over the wooden neck of his guitar and messed around with small, haunting, little tunes. I'd felt suspended in the middle of something magical. It was hard, even all these years later, to shake the spell.

Verena said that wasn't love. I wasn't sure what else to call it.

"Let's totally sit here in silence," Verena said darkly. "We'll both think about the error of your ways."

By the time Matt came onstage I had almost forgotten why I was there. Okay, not really. But sitting in the dark, crowded room with Verena felt like a throwback to our days at the conservatory. Even the longing for Matt Cheney felt nostalgic. Sitting there, hidden in the audience, I felt there were no consequences to my actions. I was suspended in time, and I wanted the night to go on forever.

And then Matt walked across the stage, and it felt like time stopped altogether.

Knowing he didn't know I was there and couldn't see me past the stage lights, I let myself study him in a way I would be afraid to if he could see me do it.

He was still as absurdly, impossibly compelling as he'd ever been. That restless, thrumming energy moved through him like an electric current and made those dark green eyes hard to look away from. Up onstage, his gorgeous features morphed into something even better. The stage made everyone better-looking, especially if they could sing. This was simple fact.

As Matt pulled out a stool and sat on it, then strummed a few chords, the entire female population in the bar fell silent, the better to ogle him.

And it was about to get worse, I knew. They hadn't heard him sing yet.

"Hey," he said into the mike. It was odd to hear him over the speakers. Intimate and yet public. A voice I still wasn't used to hearing again, after so long. "I'm Matt Cheney."

There was a round of enthusiastic applause that had everything to do with the way his body was packed into those jeans and the glorious chest beneath his black T-shirt, and nothing at all to do with his name.

"This is a song about a girl," he said, his voice low and suggestive. He began to strum the guitar. "You know the girl I mean. She broke your heart a long time ago. And then she did it again, not so long ago." He looked almost rueful. He shifted his position on the bar stool. "And you know she'll probably break it again."

And then he began to sing.

The song flowed through the speakers like whiskey and

smoke. Matt sang of love and loneliness, of sacrificing everything and getting nothing in return, but holding on anyway. It was a quiet, heartbreaking song, and his voice caressed it, coaxing it into deeper meanings and possibilities.

"How can I believe you're here," he sang. *"When I don't know which of us I fear. You will always leave me in the end, and I will always want you back again."*

I felt the song deep down inside me, where I tried to tuck away those long, long years of loving him from afar as well as those few breathless months of actually being with him. The funny thing about a broken heart was that it wasn't like glass; there weren't pieces or shards to be swept up. A heart was an organ. When it broke, it tore open. Years later, only scar tissue remained to remind you of the wound that had once been there.

I felt my own scars throb.

Matt sang about sex and magic, promises and separations, and as I listened to him I felt a complicated mix of relief and nostalgia.

I couldn't believe that I'd nearly kissed him.

I couldn't believe that I hadn't.

I also couldn't believe that I couldn't seem to control the secret excitement that pulsed in me at the idea that he'd clearly written songs about me in my absence. I had always wanted to be that kind of woman. The sort for whom songs were written, hearts were broken, and lives were altered. Didn't everyone?

And more than that, I had always wanted Matt Cheney to believe I was that woman.

That was really the crux of it, right there.

The song ended as quietly as it began, and then the room erupted in applause. I was holding my breath, and so I let it go. I was a little bit shaky.

"So much for my plan," Verena murmured. "That was quite a song. I think I forgot that he was talented."

I had nothing to say in response. I could only watch him on the stage.

Up there, he could never disappoint. There were no unreturned telephone calls, broken promises, or impromptu relocations to distant states. Up on that stage, he was golden and glorious, and I felt an emotion swell inside of me and threaten to burst free.

"Thank you," Matt said huskily. "I'm Matt Cheney."

"I love you, Matt Cheney!" some girl screamed like he was a teen idol, and the audience laughed.

"Thank God I'm not going on directly after this," Verena said under her breath. "Look at him up there—he's like the crowd's wet dream. I'm surprised women aren't throwing their panties at him."

He made as if to stand up then, but stopped. He smirked slightly, and leaned back into the microphone.

"Thanks," he said again. He paused. "And thank you, Raine, wherever you are tonight, for fucking up my whole life. At least it made a good song."

And, just like that, my world fell apart.

I should have known.

I should have known years ago, long before Matt had ever touched me, when the two of them first met and spent every waking moment together. I should have known back when they were freshmen in high school and would giggle like much younger kids and bar themselves in Raine's room. I should have known when they were both in their twenties and living a strange sort of bohemian life in and around Philly, or when they took off to follow Phish around the country together, for almost a year.

I really should have known when, in the middle of my relationship with Matt and Norah's wedding reception, Matt and Raine took off together for California.

I should have known when I found them still living together, still wrapped up in each other, in San Francisco. I should have known when Raine looked at me like she hated me in that dressing room, and the only thing that had changed was that I'd nearly kissed Matt.

How could I have lived in denial for so long?

They were the most important people in the world to each other. Nothing had ever come between them. How had I managed to convince myself that I might be able to when everyone else who'd ever tried had failed? How had I believed that my puny attempts at loving Matt or thinking the best of Raine could change anything?

"Are you all right?" Verena asked. Her voice was so careful. It made me ache. "I didn't see that coming, either."

"I'm fine," I assured her. "Really."

"You look like you're about to cry," Verena said, leaning closer, and now her voice was impatient. "Courtney, you have to let go of this. Right now. What does it matter? You're marrying someone else. Someone who would never do this to you."

"Everyone already knew about this," I said, almost in wonder. "How could I be so stupid?"

"I don't know why you're doing this to yourself," Verena said. "And I want to stay here, but I have to go backstage."

"Go," I said immediately. I fixed my eyes on her, though I couldn't quite focus. "You were right all along, even back then, and now I see it. Shouldn't you be happy?"

Verena made a face.

"I always thought I would be," she whispered. She leaned over and kissed me on the top of my head, and then she set off for the backstage entrance.

I sat there and tried to remember how to breathe.

The fact was, I didn't know what to do. Cry? Scream? Curl up into the fetal position and rock back and forth like a baby? All of the above?

I had no right to any of those responses. Maybe six years ago, they might have been appropriate, but now? I was engaged to Lucas. Life had completely moved on. What should it matter to me that they'd lied about their relationship?

And yet, it did.

I didn't know how long I'd been sitting there, when there was some commotion over near the bar, and I knew without having to look more closely that it was Matt Cheney, in all of his glory.

How could he look exactly the same as he always did? How could he so nonchalantly shatter all the things I'd believed and bear no outward sign of it? I didn't understand. It seemed to me that if someone hurt you, there should be some kind of boomerang effect. They should get hit with it, too, so it wasn't just you. So they didn't get off scot-free while you marinated in the pain.

But he looked perfectly fine. In fact, as a trio of girls settled into a giggly circle around him, he looked more than fine. They, I knew, would offer to ease his broken heart, because he did "wounded" so well. They would flatter him and flirt with him. Waste their whole lives trying to love him. Judging from his satisfied little smirk, he would let them.

And I had believed that he had loved me.

I had wanted to believe that what we shared, no matter what anyone else said, was love. True love. I had wanted to believe that more than anything in the world.

But the truth was, he had always loved Raine more.

Always.

And the only person on this earth who hadn't known that was me.

chapter twenty-two

"You seem down," Lucas said, coming into the bedroom while I was dressing. "Was it Verena's act? Did someone actually throw a rotten tomato the way she always says they might?"

"I'm just tired," I said, pulling a T-shirt on over my head. As it settled on my shoulders, I looked across the room and saw my gorgeous new dress hanging outside the closet, waiting for our celebration. It shimmered copper and bright, the way I should be feeling. It made my stomach hurt.

"Are you sure that's all it is?" Lucas asked. His voice was quiet, but still seemed to resonate. I looked over at him, saw the solemn gray of his eyes, and looked away.

I had woken up the morning after Matt's performance to realize that it was, tragically, Saturday, which meant that I would have to deal with my entire family without having time to process what had happened the night before, as we were scheduled for our last all-family dinner before the engagement party the following weekend.

Which was fine, I told myself. *Perfectly fine.* After all,

what was there to process? My slight shift in perception? The fact that I finally saw the world the way it really was? No processing required. The truth was just the truth.

"I don't feel like going to Family Dinner," I said, answering Lucas. "That's all. They're a little too much work and I'm supposed to be on vacation."

We stood there, not looking at each other. I wanted to reach out to him more than I could remember wanting anything else. But I knew I didn't deserve that kind of comfort. It was my fault there was this space between us. I'd created it, nurtured it, and now it had devoured us. I would have to deal with it on my own. Just as I would have to face the truths I'd finally learned last night on my own, since Lucas had decided he had to work rather than attend Family Dinner. I thought he was avoiding me. I couldn't blame him for it.

"When you get home," he said after a moment, "I think we should talk."

The worst five words in the world. I felt my stomach sink.

"Why?" I asked with an approximation of a smile. "You're not enjoying all this distance and weirdness?"

If he enjoyed my attempt at levity, he didn't show it.

"When I get home," I said. Because I knew, sooner or later, we would have to talk. We would talk, I would confess, and then...I didn't want to think about *and then*. But it was inevitable.

I made my way out to my mom's house alone, thinking that it was probably for the best. I didn't want to explain the distance between Lucas and me to anyone—assuming they even noticed. My family's track record for seeing the blatantly obvious when it was sitting there before them was not good, to put it mildly.

I didn't know what would happen to Lucas and me when I finally came clean. I couldn't bear to think of the possibilities, but there was nothing I could do about it now, except think about everything he'd said to me about my family. I knew he was right. What I didn't know was what I was going to do about it. Everything that involved my family seemed to be such an emotional pit of snakes. Even an engagement party, it seemed, couldn't simply be what it was: an occasion for everyone to gather and make merry. Instead, it had to be an opportunity not only to air our dirty laundry but shove it in each other's faces. As every family gathering seemed to be. I was the only one who clung to the vain hope that it might be different.

I was pretty sure that was the textbook definition of insanity.

I trudged up the front steps to the house and let myself inside, rearing back when I all but ran into Matt Cheney as he jogged down the steps, kitted out in highly incongruous gym gear. The Matt I'd known had always viewed exercise with deep suspicion, and usually from a safe distance. But then, I reminded myself bitterly, the Matt I'd known was about as real as unicorns and leprechauns, so why shouldn't he wear gym clothes?

He came to a stop in front of me, and I could hardly stand to look at him. So I didn't—I looked at my feet and crossed my arms over my body as if to shield me.

"Where's your boy?" Matt asked in that lazy voice, so insinuating.

"Working," I said, still not looking at him.

"Uh-huh." There was something smug in his tone. It confused me, and I looked up. "Did you tell him?"

Once again, I was forced to confront the possibility that I was exactly as naïve and stupid as everyone seemed to think.

Because it had not even occurred to me to prepare for the fact that Matt thought he'd won something after that scene in the kitchen. And of course he thought so: we'd nearly kissed and now here I was, without my fiancé. Score one for his power over me. I could see him thinking it.

Which, in turn, made me realize something I'd missed last night while I was too busy hurting: this was all a game to him.

"You're pathetic," I hissed at him. "All these years later and you're acting like a surly teenager. This isn't a game!"

"Don't get mad at me just because you feel guilty for what happened between us," he threw at me.

"Nothing happened between us," I said, and something shook loose inside me, as if I'd voiced a truth I'd been afraid to face before. How true that statement was. How pathetically, tragically true. "When you think about it, nothing ever did."

As I said it, something dawned on me for the first time. I remembered telling Lucas long ago that Matt had been such a big deal for me because he was the only male in my world outside classical music. But it wasn't just that. Matt Cheney was the only man I'd ever known. He'd been the only man in my life, ever. Especially when I considered my issues with my father—my birthright of abandonment. Talk about inappropriate Daddy issues.

How had I never noticed it before?

Of course I'd sought his approval. Of course I'd adored him. He'd been the only male around. He had, literally, been everything to me. I'd imprinted it all on him: daddy, boyfriend, older brother, first love.

I felt almost dizzy, and shook my head to clear it.

I opened my mouth to reply, but we were interrupted by Norah and her family at the front door. Norah was holding a covered dish in one hand and Eliot's hand in the other, but her eyes still pinned me to the wall. She looked fierce and frozen, all at once.

"I hope we're not interrupting anything," she said tartly. She and Matt glared at each other. Then she turned it on me.

"Don't be ridiculous," I told her, dismissing Matt without even a glance. "What could there be to interrupt?"

I headed for the back of the house, Norah hot on my heels. I could hear Phil behind us, engaging Matt in awkward conversation.

"Courtney, what the hell are you doing?" Norah demanded in an angry hiss, grabbing me by the elbow as we entered the kitchen. I turned to face her, but not before I looked through the window and saw Mom and Raine outside, walking across the yard toward the back door.

Great. Soon it would be a full house, and the usual fireworks could begin.

"I'm not doing anything," I told Norah. I shook my arm free.

"I feel like I'm having a flashback," she continued as if I hadn't spoken. "A horrible flashback. You can't huddle in corners having intense conversations with Matt anymore, Courtney! You have to get over this ridiculous crush! It wasn't cute way back when, and it borders on the pathological now!"

It was too much.

"It was not a *crush*," I managed to grit out at her. She made a noise of disgust.

"I'd say it's gone well beyond—"

"Norah, listen to me." I hardly recognized my own voice. "He was my first boyfriend. That whole summer, the summer before they disappeared? We were together."

As I said it, Phil walked into the kitchen with Eliot, oblivious to the tension between us.

"Matt said to tell Bev he's going for a run," Phil announced. I could hear the front door slam, as punctuation. I couldn't say I was surprised. Wasn't that the story of my life? The men who were supposed to love me took off when things got tough. Either way, they left. My father. Matt. Lucas, probably, when I got home and he had a chance to hear what I'd been keeping from him. I felt sick.

Norah looked at Phil, then blinked at me as if she couldn't process what I'd told her. Her expression might have been funny, under other circumstances. I shrugged, feeling both angry and defensive.

"It wasn't a crush," I whispered.

Mom and Raine came into the house then, and the commotion of it all took over. Norah and Raine went into their Viciously Polite Routine. I switched into autopilot.

There were tasks to complete: the table to set out on the patio in the simmering heat, dishes to arrange and carry. The bustle of domestic chores. If I raced around enough, maybe I could outrun the churning inside my head.

We sat down to an early dinner, out on the patio. I found myself watching Raine. Looking for clues to the truth I hadn't known before. She and Matt had been on and off for years, clearly. Which were they now? Did she love him? Had she yearned after him the way I had? Or was she the one who called the shots, who appeared or disappeared at will?

Mom and Norah talked about area preschools. Phil picked up Eliot when he started to fuss, planted a kiss on Norah's forehead, and disappeared with him into the house. The late afternoon edged into dusk. After a while, the conversation ebbed, and I realized it was just the four of us at the table. My sisters, my mother, and me. And all the baggage we carried with us and crowded into our little family circle. All the ghosts and the lies and the betrayals. Ancient history cheek by jowl with the present day and I didn't know, any longer, what I saw when I looked around.

"Uh-oh," Raine said with a laugh. "Welcome to the ominous silence portion of the evening. Someone better hurry up and say something, or who knows what could happen?"

"I think we all know exactly what could happen," Norah retorted with a sniff.

I thought, very clearly: *Here we go.* And then: *I can't do another round of this.*

I turned and looked directly at Raine. "Why didn't

you tell me years ago that you and Matt were more than friends?"

Raine's face briefly took on that expression I'd last seen in the dressing room at the King of Prussia Mall. It was still an upsetting expression to view on your sister's face, I found. Then she made a great show of blinking in astonishment.

"Wow," she said. She let out a small laugh. "Really? That's what you want to talk about?" She shrugged and looked sad. For me. "I thought you were over that whole thing."

Mom looked sad as well, I thought. But then, she also thought I was the bunny boiler in this scenario. Norah frowned.

"It's probably difficult for Courtney to get over the fact that you ran off to California with her first boyfriend," Norah snapped at Raine. "And—shocker—I think you'll find most people would be similarly unable to get past that kind of thing."

I hadn't been expecting Norah's support, and neither, it seemed, had Raine. I let out the breath I'd been holding in a rush. Mom looked at me as comprehension dawned across her face. But if I'd thought the truth of my relationship with Matt would change things, I was mistaken.

"Kind of the way *most people* might be opposed to their younger sister getting together with their boyfriend?" Raine snapped at Norah. Her gaze was hard when she turned to me. "How could you get together with him, Courtney, when you spent your whole life watching him be with me?" She let out a small laugh. "Why would you want to?"

"Which brings me back to my original question," I said

quietly. "Why did you lie about your relationship with him?"

"Why did you?" she countered.

Raine and I stared at each other across the table. I was sure I could see actual dislike in her eyes. I didn't know what to do with that. But then, that was a feeling I was starting to get used to.

"Because she lies about everything," Norah said with a sigh. "It's what she does, Courtney."

Raine turned a withering look on Norah, but instead of saying anything, looked to Mom instead.

"See?" She shook her head. "She's the instigator, not me. She goes out of her way to make every single moment a character assassination."

"Are you *tattling* on me?" Norah's voice was amazed, and cuttingly sarcastic. "You're *telling Mom* on me?"

"That's enough out of both of you," Mom said then, but it was like ordering a wave not to break. Raine was already scowling at Norah.

"You're so desperate to claim the moral high ground, aren't you?" she sneered.

"That's because I *have* the moral high ground," Norah retorted with a sharp laugh. "I thought it was bad enough what you did to my wedding. But the fact you broke Courtney's heart as well? All in one fell swoop? What *aren't* you capable of?"

"And you wonder why I didn't come home for six years." I wasn't sure who Raine was speaking to. Her voice was low, and furious. "I don't know why it even surprises me anymore. This is what you do, Norah. You drive people away. No wonder Dad had to get the hell out of here!"

We all sort of froze at that one. I saw Norah's eyes practically shine red with temper, and she opened her mouth—

But Mom cut her off.

"Enough," she said, slapping her hands down on the table. Her palms cracked loud in the night. "The two of you and this constant bickering! Where does it end? I'm about to write the pair of you off altogether!"

It was an uncharacteristic flare-up on her part, one she punctuated by snatching up her plate and stalking toward the back door. It slammed behind her.

"And off she goes," Norah said. "Unbelievable."

She and Raine laughed a short sort of laugh together. I looked at each of them. I didn't know which part was more surprising—that they agreed on something so much that they could share a chuckle over it, or that they were *capable* of agreeing on something in the first place.

"The fact is," Norah said, turning to me, "you're the baby. You probably don't remember how destroyed she was when he left. She mourned him for whole decades, and believe me, I know, because I had to pick up the pieces."

"She never stopped dating that guy," I informed her. Because she wasn't the only one who knew things. "Leonard. They've been together for years."

My sisters looked at me as if I had announced that a spaceship had landed three feet to the left of us, in Mom's bushes, and aliens were emerging as we spoke.

"I saw them. She told me all about it."

"Courtney, give it a rest," Raine said then. "It's not funny."

It had never occurred to me that they would refuse to believe me. I didn't quite know what to do.

"So let me see if I'm following this," I said, and I could hear the temper crackling in my voice. "I'm gullible. I'm naïve and a bit stupid. I didn't know what was happening then, or, clearly, now. I'm not even allowed to have an opinion about the things our mother told me personally, because what I remember about our childhood is worthless. Am I missing something?"

"Settle down, Courtney," Norah ordered me, every inch the bossy older sister. "I understand that you're upset."

"I'm not upset," I contradicted her. "I just don't agree with you. Historically, you don't like that very much."

"Historically, everyone did the best they could for you." Norah even waved her hand a little bit, dismissively.

Because they knew best, was the unsaid undercurrent there. I couldn't see how to interpret that as anything but a confirmation of what I'd said three seconds before.

When was I going to matter? Lucas had asked the question, and I couldn't let myself think about Lucas at the moment, but I could let his outrage on my behalf motivate me.

"No, you didn't," I said. Fiercely.

Norah raised a quizzical brow at me, professor to unruly student. Raine was sipping at her wine, perfectly content, in the center of another maelstrom.

"No, who didn't?" she asked, almost lazily.

"No, everyone did not do the best for me they could," I snapped out. And then I just kept going. "What everyone did was abandon me. I'm not talking about Dad. If I hadn't had my cello, what would I have had? Certainly nothing from this family. Certainly nothing from either of you."

"I practically raised you myself!" Norah retorted. "Mom was nowhere to be found, and I was the one who picked up the slack around here."

"Mom was working, Norah," I snapped at her. "Not off wailing at Dad's grave, or eating bon-bons, or whatever you tell yourself. *Working.*"

"*I* never abandoned you!" she hurled at me.

"The two of you have only ever been interested in fighting with each other, and scoring points," I threw back at her. "You boss me around, and you,"—I turned to Raine—"try to make me feel bad about my life."

"You control how you feel," Raine replied, all kinds of San Francisco Zen. "You shouldn't let other people take your power."

And the worst part was, she was right. Hippie-dippy as that might sound, she was absolutely right. I'd let her bully me, passive-aggressively and outwardly, with all her talk of tiny lives and dead white composers. She couldn't have done it so well without my silence and inability to stand up for myself. I was complicit in how badly she'd made me feel. And I hated that.

"This might come as a shock to you," I told her, furious at all of it, her part as well as mine. "But it's actually *hard* to do what I do. It takes years of practice to even get into the orchestra, and constant practice to stay on it. It's not a *backup plan* or somehow disappointing to play dead white guys, it's prestigious. How can you not see that?"

"My God." Raine's eyes were lit up with something calculating as she gazed back at me, her voice wondering. "Is this about your Matt issues? I feel like I don't know you at all, Courtney."

"I feel like you don't, either," I agreed. "And no, this isn't about Matt. It's about the fact that you should think before you put down the career I've spent my entire life working toward."

"I had no idea you were so conceited," Raine said. As if it hurt her to be so wrong about me.

"Conceited?" I repeated. I couldn't believe she'd said it. Or that Norah wasn't jumping in there to defend me.

I looked from one sister to the other, and then back.

"Are you kidding me?" I asked. Rhetorically. "How am I conceited?"

"It's bad enough we've had to spend our whole lives bowing down to you and your cello," Raine continued, her eyes hard on mine. "Courtney has to practice. Courtney has to have extra classes and special tutors. Courtney has her seven hundredth recital. Courtney has to get all the attention, because she's such a prodigy. I had no idea you were still so enamored of yourself."

"I don't think that's fair," Norah interjected. As defenses went, I thought that was pretty lame.

"I'm surprised you have the nerve, to be honest." Raine was still looking at me, her chin jutting out. "After all we did for you."

"Like what, exactly, did you do for me?" I asked her

acidly. "Sleep with my boyfriend? Steal him? At least Norah did the grocery shopping."

"You know what?" Raine got to her feet. "I've had enough. I don't need this. I came back home to reconnect, but it seems like neither one of you is interested, and that's fine. I'm happy to go right back to my life, with my actual friends, where people appreciate me."

I thought of that wacky bar in Cow Hollow, and the woman who had gushed over Raine's photographs, and I thought that she probably preferred adoration to simple appreciation.

"Taking your ball and going home, again?" Norah asked. "Typical. I realize you expected everyone to welcome your prodigal self with open arms, Raine, but after everything you did the last time you were home, are you truly surprised it didn't end up that way?"

"I'm not surprised by anything," Raine said with a sniff. Then she looked over at me. "Except you, Courtney. I should have realized that you aren't *trapped* in a small little life. You've *chosen* it."

"You don't know a thing about my life," I told her, a sudden, hot river of fury roaring in my ears and making my voice shake.

"Don't try to justify selling out to me," she threw back at me. "I'm sorry that you're so divorced from your own artistic drive that you can't even see what you're doing anymore." She laid a hand across her heart. "I live my art, Courtney. I can't even comprehend what you do."

"This is all my fault," I said then, feeling slightly light-headed. "I had this fantasy about our family, about sisters.

But I don't have it anymore. I don't care if either one of you comes to my engagement party. Or my wedding."

"Very dramatic," Norah said into the humming sort of silence that followed that, her voice as impatient as ever, "but don't be silly. We can all pull ourselves together—"

"I don't care," I said again, and the craziest thing of all was that I meant it. I honestly didn't care what Raine or Norah did. At that moment, I could have cheerfully washed my hands of my entire dysfunctional family.

And then I wondered, *Why not do exactly that?*

"Of course you care," Norah was saying crossly.

"Norah."

Something in my tone must have surprised her, because she stopped talking. Raine was standing a few feet away, her eyes narrow as she watched me.

"I really don't," I told them both quietly. So there could be no mistake. "Lucas has enough family for the both of us."

But of course, I couldn't call Lucas, or run to him, because even though I wanted to, that would mean a conversation I wasn't ready to have. Maybe ever. Also, after my recent behavior, I didn't deserve him and I knew it. So when I got on the train, I called Verena.

"I'm not sure we're talking," she said instead of saying hello. "I may be staging a protest against all things Matt Cheney."

"I don't care what you're doing," I told her. "I need to go out and get very, very drunk. So drunk that I might wake up as someone else."

"That never really happens," she said with a sigh. "You always end up as you, only worse off. Believe me, I know."

"We'll see about that," I told her.

We met in Manayunk, a former manufacturing town turned emergent neighborhood to the northwest of Center City, where the bars were always crowded and Verena was always claiming she was *about* to get a loft space in which to celebrate her artistic vision. We set about warding off the approach of clean-cut yuppie sorts of men at a place called Tonic, as we sat near the bar and became a part of the crowd surging all around us.

I told Verena every detail of what had happened earlier at Family Dinner, and she expressed her outrage and disgust. In honor of my sisters and the fact they were currently and for all time dead to me, I decided that something called the Poison Apple Martini was my drink of choice. It called to mind fairy tales and evil stepsisters, and I felt it was appropriate. Verena chose to drink Cherry Bombs, because she was wearing red. And despite the fact I was knocking drinks back at an alarming rate, I didn't think I was drunk.

In the cab ride back into Center City, many hours and innumerable drinks later, I still didn't think I was drunk. I cursed out both of my sisters, at length, and confessed to the taxi driver that I suspected no member of my family had ever loved me *and I couldn't be asked to care*—because Verena was no longer listening to me, being far too busy sending X-rated text messages to various people in her phone book.

I waved a cheery good-bye to Verena outside my apartment building, and was taken aback to discover that someone had messed around with the outer door, making it almost impossible to open. It took me ages to turn the key in the lock. I made a mental note to speak to the landlord, and then staggered inside and up the stairs to our apartment.

I didn't think I was drunk when I threw open our front door, so hard that it rebounded off the wall and careened back into me. I thought it was strange that the hinges were so loose. I didn't think I was drunk when Lucas emerged from his office, rubbed his eyes, and stared at me.

"Look at the state you're in," he said, shaking his head. Or maybe he wasn't, in fact, shaking his head. "Do you know what time it is? I thought you were dead in a ditch!"

"I don't know what you're talking about," I said with great dignity. "Verena and I had a few drinks. So what? Stop trying to control me."

Or anyway, that's what I meant to say. I suspected what came out sounded a bit different.

"Go to bed, Courtney," Lucas said, and I could see that he was Not Happy With Me.

I thought he was behaving like a jealous, controlling freak, and told him so. At great length. Then I decided he was too crazy to deal with, so I headed toward our bedroom, stripped, and crawled into bed.

I *knew* I wasn't drunk. But I was exhausted beyond the telling of it.

It didn't cross my mind that I *might* have been drunk until several hours later, when I found myself naked and crouched on the cold tile floor of the bathroom, cheek against the toilet seat.

I really, really wanted to crawl back into my warm and soft bed, where I could drift off into much-needed sleep. And I would have, were it not for the odd seasickness I was experiencing.

It took me longer than it should have to figure out that no, the nausea and dizziness was not some strange flu that had come on while I dozed. Oh, no. It was my body's sin tax on debauchery.

I had been drunk—was in all likelihood still drunk—and now I had to pay.

I pulled Lucas's comfy robe down from the hook on the back of the bathroom door and pulled it around me for warmth, then cradled my head on my arms. Then, there was nothing to do but breathe and hope the horrible spinning went away.

I breathed in. I breathed out.

So far, so good.

It was amazing how the whole world could shrink down until it was no more than the space of our tiny green bathroom, with the ancient heat vent and the draft, and me with my head propped up in front of me.

I held myself perfectly still, and waited for sleep, only briefly waking up when Lucas appeared beside me, gathered me up, and carried me to bed.

chapter twenty-three

A few hours later, I woke up again and wished I were dead.

Mostly because I felt like I already was. It was immediately evident to me that I had been involved in a horrible, horrible accident.

I rubbed my hands over my face and tried to assess the damage. I appeared to be wearing a T-shirt. My hair was a rat's nest. I lifted my head off the pillow and felt the headache kick it up from a waltz to more of a Lindy Hop. Ouch.

I struggled into sitting position, and that was when I saw Lucas.

He was standing at the foot of the bed, dressed, his arms crossed, and a brooding sort of look on his face.

My heart kicked at me in my chest. There could be nothing good about Lucas brooding. By nature, Lucas was about laughter and discussion. Never brooding. That was the province of the Matt Cheneys of the world. Lucas had better things to do than brood.

"Hi," I said. Carefully. "I think I'm hung over," I

informed him, which was incredibly hard to do with a tongue that felt simultaneously swollen and dry, and that didn't even take into account the percussion section in my temples.

"I know you are," he told me.

I couldn't say I particularly enjoyed his tone.

"I guess I was pretty drunk last night," I continued when he fell silent, hoping that would spur him into speech.

"You could say that."

More silence.

Dread pooled in my belly and then spread out along my limbs. I tried to think back over the night, but it was so blurry. I remembered the look on his face when I'd come in. I also remembered talking.

God. I remembered talking *a lot.*

"I don't actually think you're controlling," I said then, cringing at the memory of my own drunk voice from last night. "I think that had more to do with my sisters."

Lucas continued to look at me for a long moment.

More brooding. I felt like squirming, except that would require moving, which I was afraid to do in my current state.

"And what about kissing Matt Cheney?" he asked. His voice was so calm. Pleasant. It took a moment for the words to sink in.

When they did, I actually felt the blood drain from my face.

"What?" I whispered. Pathetic.

"Funny," Lucas said. "That's what I said. And then you started rambling out a whole load of drunken nonsense—

my controlling you figured prominently—and then you passed out. *Then* you took a nap on the bathroom floor."

Every word sent a new wave of shame crashing over me. But there was something else wrapped up with it, if I was honest: relief. There was no need to worry about this conversation any longer. It was happening. All the horror and upset of the past month or so was about to be over. No doubt for good. I felt awful, but at least it couldn't get any worse. This was, literally, the worst thing I could imagine happening. And it was happening *right now*.

"I'm so sorry," I managed to say.

"Don't be sorry," Lucas said. He was holding himself still against the wall, but his eyes burned as he looked at me. "Tell me what happened."

So I did.

I told him about my secret hope that Matt Cheney would be with Raine in San Francisco, and my refusal to plan for it. I told him how confused I'd been when I'd seen Matt, and how worried I was that the confusion meant that things were bad between Lucas and me. I told him about Matt's appearance outside the hotel, and I told him what Matt had said. I left nothing out. I told him how I'd held on to that, and how, standing outside in Chestnut Hill later on, I'd deliberately decided to allow that secret space between us to grow. I'd encouraged it by not telling him what was going on.

I told him about heading out to see Raine, and how, in retrospect, I thought maybe I'd been hoping to force another confrontation with Matt. I told him about the near miss kiss in the kitchen doorway. I spared no detail. How close it had been. How far I'd gone and how I'd stopped it. I told him how terrible I'd felt when he'd gotten so angry with Raine on my behalf, and how I'd been incapable of admitting to him how little I deserved his consideration. I confessed that I'd lied to him about Verena's stand-up show. I told him I'd gone to see Matt, and I told him what I'd finally discovered. I told him every last detail of the conversation Matt and I had had in my mother's hallway, and then I told him all about Mom's confession, the fight with my sisters, and my subsequent need to drink myself silly.

"And the worst part is that I know I did this to myself," I said when I was finished. My throat was dry, and I'd twisted the sheets in my hands while talking. "I know I deserve whatever you're going to do. I just want you to know how sorry I am. For everything."

And then I bowed my head and waited.

I didn't know how people went about leaving one another openly, I reflected in those tense moments as I waited for his response. My father had taken off before I was born. Matt had done it in the dead of night. I didn't know how Lucas would do it. In the light of day? Would I be required to help?

It was a good thing I was so hung over. It allowed me to feel numb.

"Let me make sure I'm following this," Lucas said finally, in that same calm, almost pleasant voice. "You're expecting me to . . . what? Break up with you? Pack up and leave?"

I tried to swallow.

"If that's what you want."

"If that's what I want," he repeated. He looked down at the ground and laughed to himself, and then he pushed himself away from the wall and took a step forward, and he was furious. "What I *want* is to marry you and live happily ever after, Courtney. Do you know how you can tell? Because I *asked* you to marry me and live happily ever after. What part of that involves breaking up?"

"There are extenuating circumstances," I whispered. He was already using The Name. It was bad. "There are things I did." I couldn't say it again, not to his face. I couldn't bear it.

"Because you got thrown by your ex-boyfriend?" Temper moved across his face. "Did you think I somehow missed that at the time, Courtney? I hate to break it to you, but you're a terrible liar."

"Yeah, but I almost—"

"Did you kiss him?" Lucas demanded, cutting me off. "Don't tell me about how close your mouths were again, ever. Seriously. Just tell me if you actually kissed that guy."

I looked up. His eyes were narrow.

"No," I said. "I didn't kiss him."

Lucas held out his hands, palms up.

"Then maybe you should tell me what's really going on around here."

"I just told you." I stared at him. "At great length."

"You told me a lot of things, yes," Lucas agreed, irritably. "But what I can't help wondering is when you decided that your decision to keep things from me became *my* decision to break up with you."

"It seemed like the natural progression." I felt defensive, which I thought was strange, since this conversation wasn't going at all the way I'd feared it would.

"The natural progression of what? The way you beat yourself up?"

"Why would you want me?" The words felt pulled out of me. They hurt. "After what I did?"

He ran his hands through his hair, then met my gaze again.

"Do you want to marry me?" he asked.

"Yes. Of course, yes."

"Are you sure?" he asked, his voice much quieter. "Because that's not what it looks like. From over here, it looks like you'd rather undergo elective dental surgery than anything even resembling wedding planning. We've been engaged for half a year and we haven't even started talking about picking a date. And it looks like you bent over backwards to invent a reason that I'd have to break up with you. To the casual observer, this might look a lot like someone who doesn't want to get married. Am I right?"

"That's not what I—"

"You don't have to answer right away," he said, cutting me off. "I want you to be crystal clear about who I am, Courtney."

"I know who you are." I rubbed at my temples. "I know exactly who you are."

"I don't think you do." Lucas took a step closer to the bed, and though he held himself still, I could see that he was the most furious I'd ever seen him. "I'm not your father. And I'm not your jackass ex, either. I'm not going to leave you, and it pisses me off that you don't know this after all this time and that ring on your finger."

"Sometimes people leave," I told him, when I could finally find the words. "Sometimes they even have good reasons."

"Not me," he said. Flat and final. The phone in his office began to ring. "Why don't you think about that, for a change, instead of Matt Fucking Cheney."

He looked at me for another tense moment, and then he walked out of the room, presumably to go and answer his phone.

I realized that my symptoms had extended into nausea, and curled myself into the fetal position as I waited to see if it would tip over into something worse.

Welcome to your hangover, I told myself bitterly. *The only thing in the entire world worse than your problems.*

It took me a long time to drag myself out of bed, and I did so only to take up residence on the couch, where I cowered under the fleece throw, drank as much water as I could hold, and watched repeat episodes of *Law & Order: SVU* I'd recorded to our TiVo. Lucas had gone out to some business lunch or client meeting—I wasn't sure which, as his terse note did not elaborate beyond *gone out.*

The longer I lay there, the better I felt. Physically, that was. Unfortunately, I couldn't seem to turn off my brain. I couldn't get Lucas's words out of my head. And then they seemed to intertwine with everything that had been said at my mother's house the day before. Like a bow pulling out a note from something hushed into something that filled music halls, everything that had been said swelled inside my head until it blocked the rest out.

I thought about the realization I'd had while talking to Matt, that all my issues began and ended with my father. I had such complicated feelings about the idea of him. He was an imaginary construct for the most part, but one I'd grown used to over the years. All the myths of my father seemed to blend together in my head. He was a hero. He was a pig. He was a saint. He was the worst of sinners. He abandoned us. He loved us and missed us horribly. He never looked back.

What I felt more than anything was a sense of blurriness. There was no narrowing in on this man I'd never met. There was no understanding who he *really* was. He was gone, and the only things that remained were stories, and how those of us left behind fashioned ourselves based on these stories.

Norah was still so mad at him that all her stories cast him in a negative light. Raine was so desperately in love with the idea of him that she'd, in effect, modeled her life after his. Right up to the dramatic exit toward the West Coast. She needed everyone else to validate her vision of him. And me? I felt guilty.

Guilty for being born. For making him leave.

It was stunning, really, to sit there in my living room and see it all so clearly in front of me. I'd been self-effacing my whole life, and nature abhorred a vacuum. It was easier to concentrate on the in-your-face nature of Raine's dramas and exploits. Or Norah's academic achievements. Or my mother's absence, which I could see now in a different light, but had felt like an abandonment when I was small. Everyone else came first, and I'd helped make sure of it.

I thought about the way I'd accepted the role I'd been assigned—or the one I'd volunteered for—and assumed I deserved no better. It had taken Lucas's keen insight to make me see that. It had taken him to force me to look at how little I'd always thought of myself.

Something caught in my throat then.

It was horrifying, when I really considered it, that Lucas had to point out the depth, breadth, and fullness of my self-loathing. In defiance of what I'd achieved. In defiance of what, intellectually, I knew to be true about myself. None of that mattered when it came to my deep, emotional conviction that I was somehow responsible for making my father leave—that he had left, in fact, because of my inadequacies, and that this all led to the inexorable conclusion that I was unworthy somehow. Or so flawed that his leaving was the only rational response. I had accepted, long ago and without comment, that there was something heinously wrong with me.

How shocking that Lucas had seen all of this, pointed it out, and still I'd refused to look at it. He had seen how I let others treat me and, worse, how I treated myself.

And he loved me anyway.

That was the part that made my breath hitch.

He'd been trying to point that out to me this morning. That *I* was the one who didn't trust *him*. That I was the one who'd gone a little bit crazy, when he was the man who loved me. Had always loved me. Who didn't know the self-effacing, thirteen-year-old I became whenever the family stuff got intense.

Lucas knew a different Courtney. The grown-up. The professional. The woman who loved him, not the little girl who was afraid to. Lucas knew me as his partner. His equal. Someone who would stand by him, as he would stand by me. He would never see me as Norah's little sister, or Raine's worshipful follower. He only saw the best me, the me that I was with him.

I pulled myself off the couch, walked over to my music corner in the bright sunlight that fell through the bay window, pulled my cello from its case, tuned it quickly and efficiently, and then began to play.

I played from memory. I played all of my memories, one after the other, bad and good alike. My bow against the strings, my hand against the neck of the cello—that was all there was, and everything outside of that was the music.

I played loss and joy, discovery and anger. I played for the little girls who lost their father, and the adult women who lost him again and again, every time the story changed.

I played for my sisters, and I played against them, then I played them off each other. Brisk staccato for Norah, and dreamy darkness for Raine. Something majestic and sad for my mother. Something mournful and lost for the mystery of my father. My family was a lush collection of sounds with a starkness woven into the spaces between. I played them all.

I played dead white men and living women. I played

songs I'd never heard before and could never duplicate. I played and I played.

I played until my arms ached and my back protested and tears mingled with sweat along my jaw.

And then I pulled my bow from the strings and looked around me, as if I'd never seen the place before.

The apartment was still. The cats lay in an intricate ball on the couch, wound together on the throw. They eyed me without interest as I slowly got to my feet. One of them trilled a stray note at me.

But it was the man who stood behind them who captured my attention. I wasn't sure when he'd come in, I only knew I looked up at some point and he was there.

I crossed the room, realizing as I did so that I was breathing heavily, and I was still holding my bow in my hand.

Lucas watched me close the distance between us. His eyes were gray and far away, but I knew as he focused on me that he saw me with a clarity no one else ever had.

"I push you away," I announced. I hadn't known it until this moment, but I knew it was true. "I keep you at arm's length."

"Yes," he agreed, his eyebrows arching up slightly.

"I don't entirely trust you. I keep waiting for you to leave me."

"That, too." His mouth curved. "But not all the time, and I try not to take it personally."

I wanted to tell him, then, the things I hadn't known until today. The things I hadn't wanted to know, and had only ever accessed through my cello. The things I suspected he already knew.

I could have played it all for him, but I didn't know how to say it. I stood there with my heart pounding almost painfully against my ribs, and regretted, for the first time in my life, that I was more fluent in the language of music than I was in English.

"I'm sorry." It was the best I could do. "About everything."

"It's okay," he said, moving toward me.

"It's not," I whispered. I held out my hands. "I want to marry you more than anything in the world. I love you," I told him, and the inadequacy of the word frustrated me.

"I love you, too," he answered me, but quietly.

I thought about all the years and emotions and dreams I'd poured into my cello. And into dreams of who Matt Cheney could have been, if only he could have been someone different. I thought about all the energy and time and commitment. I loved my cello, and I had loved Matt once, too. But they were different kinds of love, and at the end of the day, far less rewarding.

"I don't think I'm any good at this," I confessed, emotion in my voice that threatened to close my throat. "You might have to help me. I never learned how to love something that could love me back."

That lay there between us. I thought I could almost see it there—ugly and true and swelling up to take over the room.

Lucas's face softened. He reached over and took my cheeks between his hands.

"We have a whole lifetime to figure that one out," he said. "You just need to keep your mouth out of extracurricular kissing range."

"I don't know what the hell I've been doing," I told him, feeling the tears start to come. "I don't know what that was all about. And you've been hiding away in your office, and I don't know what you've been doing either."

"I think I've been freaking out, too," Lucas said, smoothing a hand over my hair. He sounded a little bit dazed. "I bought you a ring and you said yes and now I wake up in the night with the compulsion to raise my income so we can do adult things like have savings. Buy a house. Talk about kids and act like a detergent ad. Like some 1950s head of the household, as if you don't have your own career..."

"You've been freaking out?" I asked, feeling tenderness course through me.

"Marriage is a big deal." He shrugged. "Forever is supposed to be a little bit overwhelming, isn't it? That's why it's forever."

I kissed him then, and Lucas kissed me back, and I sank into it. I wrapped my arms around him and he rested his forehead against mine, and we stood there together for a long, long time.

chapter twenty-four

The next morning, I was so thrilled to wake up knowing that things were right between Lucas and me that I had to lie there for a while, savoring it.

We'd spent the rest of the day talking, filling up that space I'd put between us. Making it so we overlapped again. So we were one, the way we were supposed to be. That took a lot of conversation, a lot of kissing, and the Chinese delivery place we kept on speed dial.

I might have savored it all day, but our buzzer went off in the kitchen, announcing someone's presence on our front step. Seconds later, both cats shot through the bedroom door and streaked across the room to burrow beneath the bed, as if pursued by the noise of the buzzer.

I frowned and looked at the clock, unable to imagine who would be stopping by at 9:30 in the morning. I swung out of bed and pulled on the nearest pair of pajama bottoms. Then I zipped up an old, green sweatshirt over my T-shirt. I was raking my hair back into a ponytail as I headed down the hallway, and turned the corner just as Lucas opened our front door.

Norah stood there, which was in itself amazing, because she didn't visit very often and when she did, her visits tended to be planned out months in advance. I was exaggerating. *Weeks* in advance. Norah wasn't much for the spontaneous drop-in visit. Or, I would have said, spontaneity of any kind.

And yet here she was on our doorstep, looking determined.

"Is something wrong?" I asked her as she stepped across the threshold and nodded at Lucas.

"No, of course not," she said. She looked at Lucas, and then at me, and then she took a visible breath. "Can we talk?" she asked me.

Lucas sent me an inquiring look, indicating that he'd be happy to run interference if I wasn't up to talking. But I shook my head. Something about yesterday's catharsis made me feel almost calm about Norah's appearance. Whatever she wanted to say, it couldn't possibly be any worse than the things I'd been saying to myself.

Lucas motioned that he'd be in his office, and he kissed me on the top of my head as he walked past me.

"I'll make some coffee," I told Norah.

I busied myself pulling mugs from the cabinet over the sink, and poured the divine-smelling macadamia nut coffee into each mug. Then I rooted around for the Splenda packets Norah preferred, and the sugar bowl for me. Norah followed me into the kitchen, looking around as if she'd never seen the apartment before. She looked at the pictures on the wall and the photographs in frames. Lucas and me in London. Me and Eliot in the lake at the beach.

I fixed my coffee with appropriate proportions of milk to sugar and offered her the same, only with fake sugar and less milk, and then we both moved into the living room. I sat on the chair as she settled herself on the couch, and then I watched her as she set her mug down on the coffee table in front of her. She put her purse on the ground. She ran her hands down her thighs, and then swallowed.

I was astounded to realize she was nervous. What could that mean? I wasn't sure I wanted to know.

"Are you sure everything's all right?" I asked tentatively.

"Phil and I had a big fight," she announced then, lacing her fingers together in front of her and putting them down on her lap, very precisely. Then she let out a short laugh. "Or, to be more precise, Phil ripped me a new one."

"I didn't think Phil did that," I said, startled. I thought of my brother-in-law as in his own world, at best. Prone to daydreaming about quantum physics and always available to offer incomprehensible (to me, anyway) explanations about things like electrons or the cosmos. I would have said he was incapable of ripping into anyone.

"It's funny," Norah said, looking down, her voice tight, "but everyone seems to think that he's a silent automaton who does my bidding. Which is insulting to both of us. He's the most independent person I've ever met, and I wouldn't actually be interested in someone I could order around, you know."

I attempted to process that. I had never seen Phil *not* do as Norah asked, but then, that didn't mean he was taking orders. It was entirely possible he *chose* to do it. A crucial distinction, that. Lucas often chose to do what I wanted, too, but I knew perfectly well that if he didn't want to do it, he wouldn't. The joys of an equal relationship.

"I didn't mean to insult you," I said.

"I know you didn't mean to insult me." She let out a breath. "I didn't come here to talk about my relationship with Phil. Which is fine."

"Good." Then why had she brought it up? I sipped my coffee and waited.

"Phil observes a whole lot more than people give him credit for," Norah continued after a moment. I got the impression she was choosing her words very carefully. Or that she'd practiced. I had a sudden, amusing vision of Norah and Phil practicing family discussions the way Lucas and I did. Why not?

I returned my attention to what she was saying.

"And he suggested to me that I've been letting my . . . *need* to somehow even the score with Raine blind me to what's happening with you."

"With me?" I echoed, surprised, pushing the vision of Norah practicing from my mind. "What do you mean?"

"I told him he was crazy," Norah said, her eyes meeting mine again. "Of course Courtney knows how much I love her, and how proud I am of her, I told him. *Of course* she doesn't think I have some jealous obsession with her cello and how talented she is, because *of course* she knows that it was always Raine who was angry about that. And he told me that I was letting my temper blind me to the fact that you, in fact, don't know those things."

I stared at her, wordless. Her lips tightened. She looked at me, and then she looked over at the cello in the corner.

"Phil and I go to at least two of your concerts each season," she said. "And the piece you played at our wedding was so beautiful it brought me to tears." She swung her head back toward me. "I don't think you're conceited, Courtney. I think you're amazing. I can't carry a tune, and I've never gotten over the fact I can't read music. I probably am jealous of you, too, but not in a bad way. I think it's fantastic that you do what you do. I brag about you all the time."

"Norah," I began, but she shushed me with an impatient sound.

"I know how I am," she said when I fell silent, her voice low but firm. "My life runs the way I want it to, and I'm proud of that." She took a breath. "But I hate the fact that you might have confused my control issues for something worse. I wouldn't try to micromanage you if I didn't love you, Courtney. I feel terrible that you don't know that."

"I do know it." My hands felt useless there in front of me, and my voice sounded harsh in the stillness of the room. "Of course I know it."

We looked at each other for a moment, then away. I thought the room felt smaller than it should.

"I hate that Raine is here," Norah said then. "I hate what she does." She met my gaze. "But it's been pointed out to me that I don't get to decide how you feel about her, or what you want to do about her. That none of what's happened since you decided to find her has anything to do with me." She shrugged. "And I'm struggling to accept that."

"Norah..." But I didn't know what I wanted to say.

"Nothing she said to you at Mom's has anything to do

with you," Norah said fiercely. "Of course it can be difficult to have a sister who's as talented as you are. It tends
to make you look a little hard at your own lack of talent,
I find. And for Raine, who needs to think of herself as
incredibly talented—if tragically undiscovered—it must
be heartbreaking to be in the same room as you."

I wondered how I felt about that. It was so hard to let go
of my idea of Raine. I pictured her as so unfettered, bright
and shining far above the kinds of lives other people lived.
The other Raine, the one who looked at me like I was a
rival and said horrible things to me, I had trouble accept-
ing. I kept thinking the second Raine wasn't real, that I
was misunderstanding her, that she was the first Raine
but lost somehow in translation.

"Well," Norah said then, into a silence I realized with a
start had gone long, "I hope you were speaking in the heat
of the moment when you said you didn't care if I was at
your engagement party. Because I want to be there, Courtney. I really do."

She braced herself, preparing for a hit.

Because she expected me to hit back at her.

Because that was her role. She was the bad guy. The
responsible one. The one who jumped into every uncomfortable situation first. Hadn't I spent years exasperated
with her, thinking of her as a pain in the ass? Knowing
she loved me but annoyed that it came with strings?

"I would love you to be there," I said, holding her gaze.
"I always wanted that. I just wanted her there, too, for
some reason." I took a breath. "And I didn't stop to think
about how that must have felt for you. I'm sorry."

"I appreciate that," she said softly.

I remembered standing in her house, and the look on her face. *Maybe this is about how you live your life*, she'd said.

"I don't think you're crazy," I said now. "Raine treated you badly. I don't know why I never jump to your defense the way you jump to mine. I think I should apologize for that, too."

"Go ahead," Norah invited me, with a small grin. "I'm always available for apologies."

"I think I'm having trouble letting go of who I wanted people to be," I said. "It turns out I have a lot invested in the roles we all play."

I glanced over at my cello, feeling the usual twinge of guilt and the accompanying twitch of my fingers. It felt different, today, however. The cello was just an instrument. I was the one who played it. Whatever love I put into it, that's what came out of it, but that wasn't all the love in the world. It was just music. I had more in my life than just a wooden instrument and a bow. I knew that today in a way I never had before.

"We're all invested in those roles," Norah said. "It's called being related to each other."

"I had some fantasy about the whole family..." I dismissed it, wrinkling my nose. "It was stupid. I guess I really am naïve."

"It was unlikely," Norah corrected me wryly. She smiled. "But not stupid, Courtney. Everybody has a fantasy about family." Her grin deepened. "That's why I made my own."

Everything felt better, and we both sipped our coffee, but she looked as awkward as I assumed I must.

"I wasn't lying about Mom," I said after a moment.

"I know." She made a face. "I told you, we're all invested in the roles we're supposed to play. How could Mom have a life? What would that say about my life? Welcome to my denial."

I considered her for a moment. "You're harder on yourself than you are on anyone else, and that's saying something."

"Well," she said. "I should come over here more often." Her face softened, and she looked away as if she didn't want me to see it. "I love you very much," she said.

"I love you too," I said in the same serious tone.

She nodded once, and then surprised me by laughing.

"And maybe someday," she said, a wicked light in her eye, "saying that won't feel medicinal and strange. Wouldn't that be nice?"

"Nice, sure." I grinned. "But not us."

"Okay, then." Her face resumed its usual expression. "Next stop, the engagement party, which will be absolutely flawless or I swear to you, I will kill that girl with my bare hands."

"Forget about Raine," I said with an ease I wanted very much to feel. "Who knows if she's even planning to come? I don't think she'll be a problem."

Famous last words.

chapter twenty-five

The day of our engagement party was hot and the sky was clear blue. It was a perfect July day in every way. Lucas and I spent the morning visiting with his family, most of whom had driven down for the party, and who were all staying in the same hotel in Center City. Around three o'clock, we left his significantly less dysfunctional family—or so it appeared to me, since they weren't mine—went home, and changed into our party clothes, admired each other, and then headed out to the suburbs for the party.

Out at the country club, we set up shop on the deck behind the clubhouse that overlooked the pretty lake where I'd learned to swim a million years before. Lucas and I had arrived early so we could be there to greet everyone and to attempt to convince my mother that she could lighten up a little bit, as she was accessing truly epic control freak levels.

"It's fine, Mom," I tried to soothe her. "The party is going to happen one way or another now, and it's going to be what it is." I felt very Zen as I said this. "We have to relax, that's all."

My mother was not, if her facial expression was anything to go by, particularly impressed with this approach.

"I have entirely too many people coming tonight to
relax," she told me in her driest tone. "I'm the hostess, not
the Guest of Honor."

Leonard, I noticed, was celebrating the outing of his
relationship by staying far out of her way at the bar. No
fool, Lucas headed over to join him.

As he walked away, Mom went on to catalogue the
numerous things that, in her opinion, had already gone
horribly wrong, most of them involving the apparently
surly waitstaff, about whom she planned to write more
than one strongly worded letter. Then, suddenly, she noticed the one thing that had *really* gone wrong.

"The favors!" she said.

"You didn't really make favors." I frowned at her. "Remember how we agreed that favors were unnecessary, over-the-
top, and a little bit creepy?"

"I remember you thought so," Mom said. "But then you
also find the entire concept of planning a wedding creepy,
so you'll forgive me if I didn't take your advice."

"What did you do?" I asked. "Engraved champagne
flutes? M&Ms with our initials? What?"

"None of the above," she retorted. "Lucas's mother sent
me one of his baby pictures, and I put it next to one of
yours and made prints. Simple and cute."

"I'll go get them," I said, because I was touched in ways
I didn't want to explore that she had gone to the trouble.
It was so sentimental and sweet—words I didn't associate
with my family.

"Don't be ridiculous," Mom said. "You can't leave your own party." She looked around the room. "Where's Norah?"

"Norah is not responsible for every last thing," I said, perhaps more sternly than was necessary. I cleared my throat. "I'll go. Really. Where are they?"

"I'll go," Mom said, frowning. "I can't remember if I left them in the kitchen or the bedroom."

"You're the hostess," I reminded her. "You have to stay. I'm the Guest of Honor—I can be a few minutes late. It's called an entrance."

And that was how I volunteered to drive the ten minutes back to the house and fetch them.

"I can go," Lucas said as he walked me out across the parking lot to the door of my mother's car, still holding his drink in complete defiance of the law. "I really don't mind."

"Your mother and aunts will be here any minute," I told him. "You need to stay."

"Hurry back," Lucas said, kissing me. "We have an engagement to celebrate."

I drove the familiar streets of my hometown, remembering all the other summers I'd done the same. Driving around the pretty little town made me nostalgic and restless all at the same time. It was as if ghosts of my former selves were hanging from the trees or just out of sight on every corner. It seemed funny to me that growing up involved so much shedding of selves. And when you least expected it, you tripped over your own ghosts again, because there always seemed to be something else to learn.

I parked the car out front and let myself into the house. It was quiet and dark in the front of the house, and there was a cardboard box next to the door. I peeked inside and saw the stack of prints. Lucas and I as babies. It made me smile. Mom must have forgotten the box on her way to the car.

I straightened, and then, maybe not surprisingly after the last few days, I found myself walking through the living room, into the sitting room. I stood there in the middle of the small room and looked around at all the pictures.

I found my old favorite photo of him quickly, but didn't pick it up. Instead, I held up a picture from a trip they'd taken to the Jersey Shore together. My mother had captured my father tanned and relaxed-looking, smiling in the sunshine, with the Atlantic bright and blue behind him. His dark hair curled slightly, and he looked completely at ease. Happy.

I might never really understand who he had been, but this was how I wanted to remember him. Young and happy. With any life he chose in front of him.

I moved the photo to the front of the table. I looked at it for another moment, and then I turned to go—

And nearly suffered a cardiac arrest because Raine was standing in the archway.

I actually jumped enough to put air between my feet and the ground.

"What are you *doing*?" I demanded.

"What are *you* doing?" she asked in reply. She pursed her lips slightly. "I thought there was an intruder."

I looked at her, decidedly underdressed in her ratty cutoff shorts, a tank top, and bare feet.

"So I guess you're not coming to the party," I said without inflection.

She raised her eyebrows in feigned surprise.

"I thought I wasn't invited," she said. Her tone very light, as if she had no opinion about that.

"It's up to you," I said after a moment.

Raine looked at me as if she was attempting to figure me out, and failing. Then she shook her head.

"Explain to me how we got here," she invited me. "You were so excited to see me when you came to San Francisco. Next thing I know you're calling me a liar and telling me you don't care if I come to your engagement party. I'm feeling extremely alienated from you, Courtney, and the animosity I'm sensing is really very painful."

I opened my mouth to argue, or defend myself, but then stopped. That was my knee-jerk response, and there was no time for knee jerking. There was a party being held in my honor across town, and I was about to be late for it.

Raine probably knew this, as she probably knew what time it was. And yet she wanted to stand here in the room dedicated to the father we were never going to know— who, I could see now, had a lot to do with our common interest in Matt Cheney—and discuss our relationship.

Norah would claim this was another attempt on Raine's part to be manipulative. Lucas would undoubtedly agree.

I realized that I actually agreed, too.

Because this was part of what she did. Create these dramatic scenes, demand this kind of attention. I remembered her on the floor of the front hall with armfuls of photographs, wailing. I thought about her current photographs on the wall of that bar across the country. She liked to make a scene. She forced scenes if she had to. With pictures or comments or strange looks or insinuating herself between you and whoever you loved.

"Is this the silent treatment?" she asked, her stare turning challenging. "Are you really just going to ignore me?"

"I don't think anyone could ignore you, Raine," I told her, quite honestly.

"I see Norah's gotten to you," she said, shaking her head as if the very idea caused her pain. "I'm not surprised."

"Nobody's 'gotten' to me," I assured her. "I just have a party to get to."

"Well, you should go then," she said, waving her arm with great, dramatic flourish. "A party is definitely more important than your sister."

"I'm going to go, because it's my engagement party," I told her very distinctly, "and because Lucas is my family now."

"I can't tell you what you should do," Raine said, in a tone that stated her actual opinion very clearly.

"I think you should come," I continued. Because what she was saying didn't change the fact that on some cosmic level, that was true. I had always wanted her there. Maybe not the version of her I was seeing at the moment, but that was something I would have to deal with some other day.

"I don't feel like anyone wants me in this family," she said with a brave sort of shrug. "Why would I inflict myself on all of you?"

I almost stepped around her and headed for the door then, but something stopped me from simply walking away. Maybe it was the fact that I knew things about love that she couldn't, because I was lucky enough to have Lucas and whatever twisted thing she had with Matt couldn't compare. Maybe it was the new, happy vision of my father in my mind. Maybe that was just wishful thinking.

"I came all the way to San Francisco to find you," I reminded her. "And Norah, who has every reason in the world to never speak to you again—as she swore she wouldn't six years ago—sucked it up and dealt with you being here."

"Norah attacked me repeatedly," Raine snapped.

"She could have holed up in her house and waited for you to leave," I snapped right back. "She chose to try to coexist, and that can't have been easy for her. You've never even bothered to apologize to her."

"I'll be sure to congratulate her the next time I see her," Raine said sarcastically. "What a triumph of spirit that must have been for her."

I ordered myself not to boil over at that one.

"My point," I gritted out, "is that you can't claim no one wants you in this family. Every one of us has tried to reach out to you in one way or another."

She let out a sort of laugh.

"What kind of reaching out are you talking about?" she asked. "The kind that involves Matt?"

I looked at her. One moment stretched into another.

"You can either come to the party today and *act* like a member of this family," I told her finally, "or you can do whatever it is you're doing and wallow in self-pity." I took a breath. "I'm hoping you'll come, but then, I'm naïve, gullible, whatever. You have to decide."

She studied my face for a moment, as if she didn't quite recognize me.

"It's up to you," I said quietly, and then I really did step around her, scoop up the box of favors, and head for the door.

I didn't look back, but I could swear I felt her watch me leave.

I raced back across town toward the country club, annoyed that Raine had taken so much of my time. Naturally, when I arrived back on the club grounds, the main parking area near the clubhouse was full. It was thanks to my party guests, as well as the usual summertime club members looking for a game of tennis or golf, and I had to park about as far away from my own party as it was possible to get. I pulled my strappy sandals off my feet for the walk back, because I thought they might cripple me if I tried to hustle in them.

Barefoot, carrying the box of favors on my hip, I took the shorter route back through the grove of trees that served as the barbecue area, and then headed down the walkway that skirted the small beach on the lakefront. The swimming floats were back in the water, bobbing against their moorings. Children played loud, energetic games in and out of the water, while parents chatted in canvas chairs or on blankets on the sand. I had fond memories of this club from my very early childhood, when I'd been one of the kids running in and out of the lake and building complicated sand structures I'd only fantasized were castles. But then I'd started playing the cello, and that had consumed my summer free time. I paused for a moment, looking at the dappled water in the late afternoon light, and allowed myself, once and for all, to accept the fact that I didn't regret that choice.

I would never know what sort of person I might have been if I'd never picked up the cello. If I'd spent my summers playing at this lake, my teenage years finding other ways to amuse myself. The idea of that other person was so foreign to me that I couldn't even imagine her. And I found that comforting. Because if I could envision another life, another me, it seemed to me that that life might be unreasonably tempting. My father was an excellent cautionary tale in that respect.

I was approaching the clubhouse from behind, so I could see my own party as I approached it, out on the deck in the evening air. There were already a number of people milling around with cocktails, contributing a happy sort of buzz to the late afternoon air. I picked up my pace.

I was just about to the edge of the lawn that led from the lake to the deck, when there was movement in my peripheral vision.

"Courtney."

I recognized the voice even as I turned, and saw Matt Cheney standing in the shadow of an oak tree.

My heart thumped a little bit in surprise, and I wondered if the two of them had planned to leap out at me tonight or if that was just a coincidence.

"I have to talk to you," Matt said, his voice low and urgent.

"It might have escaped your notice," I told him, not even pretending to keep the irritation out of my own voice, "but I have a party to go to. I'm actually one of the guests of honor, so if you'll excuse me...?"

"You don't understand," Matt said, taking a step closer.

"What don't I understand?" I asked, impatient.

"I love you," he said, as if the words were torn from him. "I never should have left you. Please. Give me another chance."

I assumed he hadn't actually said that, as it was the sort of declaration I'd once fantasized about, at great length and in significant detail.

Moments passed.

It only dawned on me that he'd really said that to me, that I hadn't slipped into an old fantasy steps away from my engagement party, when those green eyes of his flashed with temper.

"Do I have to beg?" he demanded. "Because I will, if that's what you want."

"You have got to be kidding me," I said, but it was more of a breath.

He stepped closer, so I could really look at him and see

the stubble on his face that suggested he'd had a rough few days. He looked tormented and racked with emotion, not looks I associated with him. He reached over and put a hand on my arm.

"I love you," he said again fiercely, and this time, I knew I wasn't dreaming it.

This time, I knew he meant it.

chapter twenty-six

"We can do what we should have done years ago," Matt said intently. "We're right here, in the exact same place where everything went wrong, Courtney. We can change it."

I was shaking my head before he was finished speaking.

"I can't believe you would come here and say these things to me." I took a step away from him. "Maybe you forgot that I'm having an engagement party?"

"There are so many things you don't understand." He looked away then, as if those things troubled him. He was so good at looking lost and troubled.

"I don't understand them because you took off *with my sister,*" I snapped at him. "If you wanted me to understand, maybe you shouldn't have abandoned me!"

I hadn't meant to use that word *abandon,* and hearing it come out of my mouth sent a chill through me. I had suspected that my feelings for Matt had a lot to do with my feelings about my father, but suddenly, I understood exactly how much.

"I don't know how to explain things with Raine," Matt

said. "But I didn't lie to you. Not really. Not about what matters."

"I don't think she would agree with that," I said, thinking of the way she'd changed after Matt and I had nearly kissed. He must have told her. She must have thought it was starting up again. How sad for everyone involved.

"You could have come with us when we left," Matt continued, his voice going scratchy. "But that never even crossed your mind. You never even considered it."

"You didn't give me a chance!" I retorted, outraged. "By the time I knew what was going on, you were halfway to California!"

"You made choices, too." He shook his head. "When it came down to it, you only *thought* you wanted to be with me. You could never decide what you loved more—me or your cello."

"You are not actually standing here and suggesting that you left me because you were jealous of an inanimate object," I hissed at him, shifting the box from my hip. "Please tell me I didn't hear that right."

"You didn't want to come with us," Matt said stubbornly. "You think you were left, but I know you decided to stay."

I looked away for a moment, toward the lush grass that led to the tennis courts. The shadows were beginning to stretch, and the sky was beginning to cool above me. My head was a jumble of incoherent thoughts and memories. But mostly what I thought of was that long walk I'd taken in San Francisco, and how long I'd stood at the crest of Twin Peaks and stared down at the city that should have been my home.

San Francisco had hit me like a love song, deep in my soul. I craved the crisp blue afternoons and cold mornings. The salt in the air, the pastel houses, the glorious red bridge. It was an incomparable city, and part of me would always wish I had gone there.

But that wasn't the same thing as wishing I had gone with Matt.

"See?" Matt said then, as if he sensed weakness. He let out a frustrated sort of noise. "Have you forgotten who you were back then?" he demanded. "You were going to change the world." He reached out a hand, but this time didn't touch me. "I've always loved you, Courtney. Have you forgotten that? Have you forgotten how much you loved me, too?"

"Have you forgotten that I'm in love with someone else?" I threw back at him. "That I'm engaged to him, and he's right over there on that deck?"

"You can't compare that guy to me," Matt said dismissively. "He's not even a musician. How can he ever really understand you?"

Oddly enough, that had never occurred to me before. I remembered, suddenly, how intensely I had dreamed of collaborating with Matt. I'd been convinced that the things we couldn't seem to talk about with words could somehow be smoothed over if only we could communicate with music. I'd ached sometimes, thinking of how beautiful our music could be. But we had never even played together.

Lucas, on the other hand, sometimes hung out on the couch while I practiced. Sometimes he would read a book. Sometimes he would just lie there and let the music swell all around him. He didn't sing, or tap out a rhythm, or in any way contribute to the music-making. And yet, somehow, I always thought of him as such a huge part of my music.

I thought about what Matt had just said, that I'd loved my cello more than him. He was right. I had only just figured out how to risk loving someone who could love me in return, someone who wouldn't leave me.

"I'm not going to defend Lucas to you," I told Matt then. Because I didn't have to.

"I know you're pissed about the Raine thing," Matt said in that same intense way, "and I'm not saying Lucas isn't a nice guy, but you can't really believe this is the right life for you. What happened to all your passion? Don't you remember what it was like when the world was huge and we could do anything we wanted?"

And the thing was, I did remember.

Ever since I'd gone to California, I'd worried that there was a life out there that I should have been living. That I'd missed the boat, or chosen the wrong path. Matt and Raine seemed to believe that I was kidding myself, and I could understand where they were coming from.

Because they didn't know what it was like to practice as hard as I did, every day. To them it sounded unbearable, like some kind of daily grind. They believed in uncertainty and creation at all costs. I could understand the lure of their kind of life. The part of me that had been a fine arts student yearned for that life.

But the professional musician in me knew things that they couldn't understand.

I knew that the world was never bigger, or more unlimited, than when I played a perfect note. Or when the melody kicked in and the orchestra swelled into song and all of us, together, became something greater than a collection of individual musicians: the music itself.

I had spent my life training so that I could be part of those perfect moments. They were called *movements* for a reason. When I was flying completely free, lost in the orchestra around me, entirely consumed in some of the most glorious music ever written. In order to be a part of that beauty, I had to commit to the daily practice, the discipline. It wasn't the life for everyone. But it was my life.

More important, it was how I felt every time I looked at Lucas.

"What are you thinking?" Matt demanded.

I focused on him, while somewhere in my mind, I heard concertos for strings, Bach suites in different keys.

"Come on," he said. "We can make a whole new life. You know we're great together."

"You were my first love," I told him. "I loved you for so long, and I loved you for a long time after you left, too."

"I know," he said. "You know I feel the same."

"But I'm not that girl anymore," I said now. "Somewhere inside, there's a part of me that wonders what might have happened to that girl if she'd gone with you to San Francisco—"

"You don't have to wonder!" he exclaimed. "You can do it!"

"I don't want to."

I said it quietly, but it was out there between us as if I'd shouted.

And something happened in me when I said it.

It was powerful to own your life, to choose it, to banish doubt and know you meant it with every fiber of your being. I knew that before this moment, I hadn't fully faced what had happened six years before. There had been so many *what ifs*. Matt had been the stand-in for so many of my hopes and fears, but the truth was, he was just a guy.

I hadn't wanted to go to California. I wanted the life I'd chosen, the life I'd worked so hard for.

I still wanted it.

I loved Lucas in ways I didn't have the words to express. Not to the exclusion of the world around us, the way it had been with Matt. But in a way that included the world, and made us a part of it. Like we were one glorious part of the larger orchestra of life all around us, and freer for it.

"I don't believe you," Matt said. But I could tell that he did believe me. He just didn't want to.

"I have a party to get to," I told him, not unkindly. "They can't really start without me."

That was when I noticed that there was another figure standing nearby, within hearing range.

I drank in the sight of Lucas in his khakis and his pressed white shirt. My modern-day Viking. He smiled when I looked his way, and pointed his chin toward the deck behind him.

"The natives are getting restless," he said.

Matt said my name again, but it was time for me to go. I smiled at him the way I'd wished he'd smiled at me in this very spot a long time ago, and then I turned and crossed the grass to Lucas.

"How long have you been standing here?" I asked him.

"A while." His eyes danced. He reached over and took the box of favors from me.

"Did you hear everything?"

"Pretty much."

I studied his face as I stopped before him.

"You don't seem upset."

"Courtney." He grinned as he said The Name. "Put on your shoes. You look gorgeous and we have guests to entertain."

I slipped the shoes back on and glanced back to see that Matt was no longer standing there by the tree. I hadn't heard him walk away. I felt a twinge of sadness, for all the could-have-beens that never were, but then I looked back at Lucas and found him smiling down at me.

Cellos wept. Melodies soared.

"You really don't mind the things he said?" I asked.

Lucas shook his head, very slowly. So there could be no mistake.

"I have nothing but confidence in you," he said. "And us. I told you I wasn't threatened by that guy."

"Not even when he showed up at our engagement party?" I asked, but I was smiling back at him. "That's taking confidence pretty far, I think."

"Which is why I'm not waiting for you up on the deck," Lucas replied immediately. "I thought I could exhibit my complete confidence from a little bit closer."

"Good thinking," I murmured.

"Are you ready?" he asked as he offered me his free hand.

I looked past him toward the deck. I saw my mother, resplendent in her bright dress, with Leonard at her side. I saw Norah and Phil, standing close together in a corner, talking to Verena. And also, standing in a circle of neighbors, I saw the short, glossy hair and cute little figure that could only belong to Raine.

It made me feel good to see them all, even though I knew nothing had been solved. I thought of my mother's Cassel Cake, her acknowledgment that no one dessert could possibly please all three of us. We were sisters. We knew one another best, and least. We would always want different cakes. We'd probably always fight about it.

The important thing was, we were all here.

God help me at the wedding.

I had gotten my wish. And yet what I really wanted had been with me all along.

The life I was supposed to live was right in front of me. Just waiting for me to appreciate it.

"I'm ready," I told Lucas.

I took his hand, held on to him tight, and then we walked into our life, together.

about the author

There are a lot of things I could say about my sister.

If *you* said these things, we would be in a fight.

And so it goes, the mystery of sisterhood.

I didn't set out to write a book about sisters. I started writing this book because I was interested in love.

First love, to be specific, and its relationship to true love. Because it seemed to me that they weren't the same thing, at least not for me or for most of the people I knew, and I wanted to explore the gap between the two. *First love versus true love* was what I thought in my head as I thought about this book.

But almost at once, I was confronted by another kind of love, and it turned out I was even more interested in writing about that. That, of course, was family love.

Ah, family. The love you're stuck with. The love that defines you, constructs you for better or worse, and teaches you everything you know about how to be a person—which if you are lucky you will use as a base from which to grow, and if you are not, you will have to unlearn while acting crazy throughout your twenties. (Or so I've heard.)

Altogether, these different kinds of love turned into the story of sisters lost and sisters found. It's the story of a woman who finally figures out the truth about her family—and the difference between the love you're born into and the love you choose.

You can find me at www.megancrane.com. Or www .welcometothe5spot.blogspot.com. Or just e-mail me at megan@megancrane.com and tell me all the things you think about your own sister that you'd beat someone else up for suggesting. I promise I won't tell!

Thanks for reading,

Megan

5 Names Your Sister Calls You When She Thinks You Can't Hear Her

(Or Worse, When She's Certain You Can):

1. **Bossy.** Hey, is it your fault she's such a space cadet? What would she do if you weren't around to handle *everything*? Oh right—nothing. Which is why you have to do everything in the first place.

2. **Snobby.** It's not that you're *actually* snobby, which implies a sort of general condescension toward others. No, it's that you *specifically disapprove* of *her* life choices, and you're happy to let her know it, too.

3. **Crazy.** Of course she thinks you're crazy. She also thinks that loser is decent boyfriend material, and who is she kidding with those clothes? They'd be more appropriate for an oversexed teenage pop idol, not that she asked you. Luckily, you're happy to share your opinion.

4. **Selfish.** That's true, you did exhibit absolutely no interest in the last three things she wanted you to do. Because those things were *all about her*, like everything else. And she has the gall to call *you* selfish? If she's even aware that other people *exist*, you'd die of shock!

5. **Just Like Mom.** As if. If anyone is Mom Junior, it's her. From her judgmental stare to her complete inability to exit a bathroom in under twenty-five minutes no matter what the issue. The two of them are practically peas in a pod, and as far as you can tell, you were delivered by the milkman.